"Hal," the President said, "what do I do?"

"I wish I could help you, sir, but I honestly don't know. My best people are on it."

"I've got people on one side of me telling me to declare martial law," the Man said. "There's a group of people in the Joint Chiefs of Staff who have already drawn up a contingency plan, but my instincts tell me that's the wrong approach. I need your honest opinion."

"I think you should level with the people, sir," Brognola replied. "You should go on television and tell them we have a dangerous situation to deal with. They should be vigilant, but not fearful."

The President pondered the advice. "That might work for a short time," he said. "But if we have a wave of shootings tomorrow, people are going to riot. And if that happens, I'll have no option but to declare martial law."

Don Pendleton's Mack Bolan®

Kill Shot

A GOLD EAGLE BOOK FROM

WORLDWIDE®

TORONTO • NEW YORK • LONDON
AMSTERDAM • PARIS • SYDNEY • HAMBURG
STOCKHOLM • ATHENS • TOKYO • MILAN
MADRID • WARSAW • BUDAPEST • AUCKLAND

Recycling programs
for this product may
not exist in your area.

First edition June 2011

ISBN-13: 978-0-373-61545-2

Special thanks and acknowledgment to
Darwin Holmstrom for his contribution to this work

KILL SHOT

I've seen enough cruelty and brutality to understand the difference between garden-variety guilt and genuine evil. Some people claim that there's no such thing as genuine evil, but they haven't seen what I've seen. I know that pure evil exists because I've stared it down countless times. And as long as it continues to appear, I will continue to face it unflinchingly.
—Mack Bolan

All things may corrupt when minds are prone to evil.
—Ovid
43 BC–AD#17

CHAPTER ONE

Boston, Massachusetts

Tom Gardner pushed the two-wheeled truck cart out into the bright sunlight that bathed the loading dock. He let his eyes adjust to the sun, then continued toward the orange Cantus Uniform and Linen Service van he'd backed up to the concrete ramp. After pushing the cart a few steps, he gave up on his aging eyes ever adjusting to the bright light after emerging from the gloomy interior of the diesel repair shop. He stopped to put on a pair of sunglasses. Even though the clock had yet to strike twelve, Gardner had already had a long day. He'd gotten an early start, making the first stop on his route before 5:00 a.m., and he only had two stops left.

Once he had the sunglasses in place, Gardner looked around at the bright blue sky rising above the tops of the warehouses, workshops and processing plants that comprised the Boston Marine Industrial Park. It was a sweet route; rather than driving all over the state, most of his stops were clustered around Logan International Airport and the Charles River Basin, meaning he could hit twice as many stops in half as much time as most Cantus drivers, which in turn meant that he earned twice as much money as most other drivers since they worked on commission. The choice route was a perk he'd earned for spending twenty-nine years on the job. The drivers with the most seniority got the best routes, and Gardner had the best of the best. It was hard work, and lugging uniforms and linens in and out of the truck year in, year out had taken a toll on his knees, but they only had to hold out another six months and he could retire.

Gardner glanced at his watch, which was synchronized with the atomic clock used to measure International Atomic Time. A precise man, Gardner knew that the international system of units defined a second as 9,192,631,770 cycles of radiation, and when his watch showed that it was exactly noon eastern time, it was exactly noon eastern time. His watch showed that it was seven seconds away from noon, meaning that he'd arrive at his delivery van at two seconds past noon. Gardner left no detail to chance.

He began the countdown in his head. As always, his timing was perfect. Barring unforeseen traffic jams, he'd finish his route at 1:15 p.m., be home eating lunch by 1:50 p.m. and be napping in front of his television by 2:30 p.m.

He looked at his watch to see the digital display flicker from 11:59.59 to 12:00.00. At that moment he felt a massive blow to the back of his head, and then all consciousness ceased. He didn't feel the bullet penetrate the back of his skull, drive through his reptilian brain stem, then exit out through his face in a geyser of blood, bone fragments and brain matter. He didn't hear the report, and he didn't feel a thing as his body was pitched forward over the two-wheeled truck cart and hurled to the concrete floor of the loading platform. For all his careful planning, Gardner's retirement had come early.

Manhattan, New York

STEVE GANSEN COULDN'T WIPE the stupid grin off of his face. He'd gambled everything, his entire career as a stockbroker, making a massive investment in what appeared to be a dying industry: book publishing. It had cost him his credibility, the respect of his peers and nearly his job—and his marriage—but today it had paid off. Big.

Not that Gansen was surprised that his apparent long-shot bet had come through. He'd studied a decade's worth of the company's quarterly business reports and he knew it was undervalued precisely because publishing was a dying industry. It was dying, but not quite dead yet, and Gansen knew that there were still a few dollars left to be made in the archaic technology of books. Now he clutched the *Wall Street Journal* in a white-knuckled death grip, rereading the lead story about a giant German publishing operation purchasing the publishing house in which he'd invested, quadrupling his investment, as well as the investments of those clients with the testicular fortitude to stay with him throughout this endeavor.

Gansen now had approximately fifty percent of the

client base he'd had going into this investment. Now those fifty percent were much richer for having believed in him.

He glanced up over his paper to see the clock face on the wall of the bank on the opposite side of the small park. It was just about noon. He noticed what appeared to be a person on top of the roof, just above the clock. The person appeared to be crouched down along the edge of the roof, pointing what appeared to be a black broom handle in Gansen's direction. The clock chimed the first recorded bell tone to indicate that it was exactly noon and Gansen saw a small burst of flame spread out from the end of the broom handle. What he didn't see was the .30-caliber bullet being propelled his direction at nearly three thousand feet per second. He felt a blow when the bullet entered the top of his head, but when it penetrated his skull, he felt nothing. And he never would feel anything again.

Baltimore, Maryland

SPENCER LOUCKS NURSED his ancient green Jeep Cherokee up to the gas pump. Like everything else in his life, his Jeep—Teal Steel, as he liked to call it—was falling apart. He'd always skated through life, counting on his sense of humor to grease the skids when the going got rough, but things had gone so wrong that even that wasn't enough anymore. First he'd lost his job. Next, a bout of post-breakup sex with his psychotic ex-girlfriend had led to a situation that Loucks had carefully avoided his entire life: fatherhood.

The kid was the one thing that kept Loucks going. He glanced into Teal Steel's backseat to make sure the little guy was secure in his car seat. The kid lived with his mother, technically, but she wasn't really equipped to handle a child so the boy spent most of his time with his dad. She'd been—there was really no way to sugarcoat it—a crack whore. She'd ended up in prison where she served five years for committing multiple felonies. In prison, she'd finally shed her various drug addictions, but she'd picked up an attitude. Now she reacted to every situation as if she was being attacked with a shank in the prison lunchroom.

She'd also found Jesus in prison, and she considered it her mission in life to ensure that everyone else on Earth shared that experience. Unfortunately, the confrontational way with which she dealt with every person she encountered led to her making few converts. Not that she didn't try; most of the time she left the boy with Loucks because she was busy out working with her church group.

The one thing she had going for herself was a superb body, which was what had attracted Loucks to her in the first place. Now, because of that hot body, Loucks was hopelessly intertwined with a psycho baby mama who would be part of his life for the rest of his life. At least he had the boy. He carried the little guy into the gas station, where he prepaid the attendant five bucks for gas. Five bucks would be barely enough for him to return the boy to his home, the way Teal Steel sucked gas, but it was all he had left after buying diapers and groceries.

Loucks set the nozzle in Jeep's filler spout and locked in the lever. He looked in at the boy, once again sleeping in his car seat, and waited for the lever to click off when the pump hit five dollars. He didn't have to wait long before he heard the "click." He looked at the pump. The pump had shut off at $4.88. Christ. Twelve cents worth of gas was barely a dribble, but given his current financial situation, Loucks needed every penny's worth that he could get. He looked at the baby in the backseat of the Jeep, then at the man working in the gas station's partitioned operator's booth inside the station. His over-developed sense of justice made him want to go and get his twelve cents worth of fuel, but the guy running the station probably didn't even speak English. Loucks was torn.

He leaned against the Jeep, contemplating not just the situation at hand, but all the bad decisions he'd made that led him to this point in his life. He was forty years old, and he could barely afford to be screwed out of twelve cents worth of gas. He was so lost in thought that he didn't notice the bright yellow sports car that pulled up beside him. At that moment he vaguely heard a crack in the distance, but before he could register the sound, his brain ceased functioning because of the .30-caliber bullet that pierced his head, splashing gore across the green expanse of the Jeep's roof.

MACK BOLAN TURNED THE Ferrari 599 GTO into the gas station, driving up the approach at a slight angle to avoid scraping the undercarriage of the low-slung Italian sports car on the pavement. It was, after all, a borrowed ride, a loaner from Hal Brognola, a top official at the Department of Justice and also the man in charge of the supersecret forces operating out of Stony Man Farm. As such, Brognola was the closest thing to a boss that the Executioner had, but he was also one of the soldier's oldest friends. When the rare opportunity for a vacation had arisen, Bolan had asked the big Fed if he could borrow a set of wheels. He'd expected a well-worn government fleet vehicle just about ready to make the transition to taxicab duty, at best a Crown Victoria with steel wheels and dog-dish hubcaps, at worst some toady little crap wagon.

Instead, Brognola had surprised him with the keys to the Ferrari, luxurious sports coupe with a potent V-12 engine lurking beneath its long, sleek hood. The car, painted a shade of yellow so bright staring at it too long might cause permanent burns on the corneas of a viewer's eyes, had been confiscated as part of the estate of a drug kingpin that Bolan had brought down. It was a rare treat for the Executioner to be able to enjoy the fruits of his labors.

And he was enjoying the Ferrari very much, as well as the long weekend itself, spent in Nags Head, North Carolina. But even more than the Ferrari, he'd enjoyed the company of the long, lithesome blonde seated in the car beside him.

Patricia Jensen, the stunning woman riding shotgun in the Ferrari, was an old friend. In truth, she was more than a friend; Bolan supposed she was what the hipsters called a friend with benefits. He'd met her years ago, while working on a case in Washington, D.C. He'd been shot in the thigh, and she was the doctor who stitched him up. Bolan knew she would gladly be more than a friend with benefits if he asked her, but the soldier had long since accepted the fact that his life didn't allow for long-term attachments. People who got too close to him ended up dead.

Bolan inserted his credit card into the pump and began filling the tank with the high-octane gasoline that the finicky Italian thoroughbred demanded. While the fuel filled the tank, he thought about the woman sitting inside the car. He's known her for nearly twenty years, and she seemed even more beautiful now than when he'd met her. Back then she was fresh out of medical school, finishing her internship. When he first met her, she'd had big hair, as did most other young women at the time. Now her hair was cut in a stylish bob, which made her gray eyes look even more startling than they had when framed by the big MTV hair she'd worn when they'd first met. She maybe had a few lines on her face that she hadn't had back then, but they just gave her face more character. The rest of her hadn't seemed to have changed much at all.

Something made Bolan break off his meditation on Jensen's charms. He couldn't place it, but for some reason he sensed danger. He had no reason to expect danger in a gas station just off the Baltimore-Washington Parkway, but the soldier hadn't survived countless battles by ignoring his intuition. He'd scanned the surroundings for potential danger when he drove into the gas station, as he always did whenever he entered a place, an action that was as unconscious as breathing for him, and he'd noted nothing out of place. The only other people at the station were the clerk and a sad sack-looking man filling gas in a rusty old Jeep, neither of whom seemed to present an obvious threat. Bolan noted that the sad sack had a toddler in a car seat in the back of the Jeep, making him an even more unlikely source of danger.

But something was wrong; Bolan could feel it. He started scoping out the surrounding buildings, his hand automatically resting on the Beretta 93-R in the shoulder harness beneath his charcoal sport jacket. There wasn't much for buildings in the surrounding area. The freeway bordered the station to the west and another gas station sat across the road to the north, but that station was out of business and completely deserted. A fast-food burger joint shared a parking lot with the station, and behind that was a storage rental facility. The only thing even slightly out of the ordinary was an SUV parked along the road to the east of the station, next to a large empty lot. Bolan couldn't tell if the SUV, an older Chevy Tahoe SS, was empty or not because of the dark tinted windows, but something seemed out of place.

Bolan tapped on the Ferrari's passenger window to get Jensen to roll down the window and hand him his binoculars so he could get a better look at the Tahoe, but before she could get the window down, Bolan heard a muffled *crack* and saw the head of the man driving the green Jeep burst open. The angle with which the bullet hit the man's head told Bolan that it had to have come from the vicinity of the Tahoe.

The soldier threw open the Ferrari's passenger door and he pulled Jensen from the vehicle. "Get down!" he told her, pulling her down behind the front fender, where the engine block would provide better protection between her and the Tahoe than would the thin aluminum bodywork that cloaked the car's chassis. Once she was safely behind the fender, Bolan pulled his .50-caliber Desert Eagle from the holster on his hip and leveled it at the Tahoe, but the vehicle had already taken off, all four tires laying down dark stripes on the pavement. The vehicle was conceivably within range of the powerful handgun, but Bolan couldn't be certain that the vehicle belonged to the shooter so he held his fire.

When he was certain the threat had passed and no further shots were coming, he went to check on the victim, though he knew he would find a corpse. No one could have survived a direct head shot like that, especially when it came from what must have been a high-powered rifle. The man was dead, as Bolan had expected. The child in the back smiled at Bolan.

"Patricia," Bolan shouted, "take care of the kid."

Jensen went to remove the child from the hot cab. Before she'd even begun to unbuckle the complex car-seat safety harness, Bolan had jumped into the Ferrari's driver's seat and punched the starter button.

The 670-horsepower 12-cylinder engine roared to life. Ferrari had built the GTO version of the 599 in extremely small quantities to homologate a production race car, and although it bore superficial similarities to the ordinary 599, the GTO was really a barely civilized race car. Bolan accelerated hard out of the gas station, no longer worried about scraping the undercarriage. Unlike the Tahoe, the Ferrari didn't leave any rubber, thanks to its Formula One–inspired traction control system. Instead, it accelerated like a Saturn V rocket blasting off for the moon.

The Tahoe had about a minute lead on Bolan. In SS trim the Tahoe was no slouch, its V-8 engine cranking out 345 horsepower, but it was still a three-ton truck with the aerodynamics of an oversized cinder block, while Bolan's Ferrari, with a top speed of almost 210 mph, was the fastest street-legal vehicle ever built. By the time he was half a mile away from the gas station his speedometer read 170 mph and he'd caught sight of the Tahoe. Ten seconds later he'd closed up the gap enough to read the license-plate numbers, or at least he could have read the license plate numbers if the Tahoe had license plates. A plastic placeholder proclaiming the name of a local used-car dealership occupied the space in the rear bumper reserved for license plates. Bolan noted the name of the dealership but seriously doubted that information would be of use. Most likely the vehicle was stolen and the thief had just tossed the license plates and screwed a random placeholder onto the bumper to avoid suspicion.

There was nothing random about what Bolan saw just above the license plate: a metal panel moving aside to reveal a three-inch hole. Bolan saw a faint flash of light from behind the hole and a bullet pierced his windshield, embedding in the headrest of the Ferrari's driver's seat, just millimeters from the soldier's right ear. A spiderweb of cracks crept out from the hole in the windshield. The speed at which Bolan drove most likely produced enough of a slipstream around the car to move the bullet slightly off its intended path, or else it could have been a kill shot.

The soldier didn't give the shooter enough time to line up a second shot. He squeezed the paddle shifter on the steering wheel twice, dropping the car into Fourth gear, steered into the left lane and floored the accelerator. The Ferrari took off like it had been shot from a cannon, and before the shooter's weapon had time to cycle another round he was up beside the Tahoe's rear bumper, leveling his Desert Eagle at the driver's window. The soldier's first round shattered the weakened windshield of his own vehicle and thousands of tiny chunks of safety glass exploded across the Ferrari's hood, most of which were then blown back into the cabin by the air blast. The second shot penetrated the driver's window of the Tahoe. Bolan had aimed for a spot just behind the driver's head, knowing that the spalling that the bullet would experience when hitting the glass at that angle would deflect its course.

His estimate appeared to be correct because the Tahoe suddenly veered hard right and plunged nose-first into the ditch alongside the road. The vehicle was still traveling at well over 100 mph and the right front of the hood caught the edge of the embankment opposite the road, flipping the truck in a barrel roll. The Tahoe cartwheeled across a weed-covered lot until it hit what looked like a rusted old storage tank of some sort, wrapping itself around the tank is if the two were part of some modern-art sculpture.

Bolan braked hard and came to a quick stop. He ran across the lot to try to find survivors to interrogate, but knew the odds were against him when he saw the flames rising up from the vehicle. The Tahoe had careened several hundred yards before hitting the tank, and by the time Bolan had crossed half that distance, the small flickers of flame had turned into a raging inferno. When he was within thirty yards, the Tahoe's gas tank exploded, sending a wave of heat over the soldier, nearly knocking him off his feet.

Bolan got as close as he could to the burning vehicle, but it was far too late to extract any survivors. Flames rose one hundred feet in the air above the remains of the truck. The wreck might still hold some clues, but they would have to be ferreted out by a team of forensic specialists. The soldier watched the flames consume the vehicle, wondering what he had just stumbled across. Was it a hit of some sort? Bolan knew very little about the victim, but from what he had seen, the man seemed an unlikely target for organized crime. The guy had the air of desperation about him, to be sure, but it didn't strike Bolan as the sort of desperation of a drug addict or gambler who might owe money to the Mafia. The guy looked like he'd fallen on hard times, but he looked healthy, without the pallor and gauntness of a meth addict. And his baby looked healthier and cleaner than had any child of drug-addicted parents that Bolan had ever encountered. Gambling debts might be more likely, but again, the man didn't look like he even had the resources to gamble at any level high enough to incur the wrath of the Mob.

But what made even less sense, and what Bolan found more worrisome, was that the victim might have been chosen at random. That made the least sense. Why would someone expend the effort to create a vehicle that was in effect an elaborate mobile sniper hide just to assassinate some random citizen? The only possible answers to that question were all chilling to consider.

CHAPTER TWO

Stony Man Farm, Virginia

At the exact moment the clock struck noon eastern time, snipers had hit targets in every major metropolitan area from Bangor, Maine to Key West, Florida. In all, fifty-six innocent Americans had lost their lives. Exactly one hour later, when the clock struck noon central time, snipers had taken out another seventy-five people in cities from Bismarck, North Dakota, to Mobile, Alabama. By the time Mack Bolan arrived at Stony Man Farm, headquarters of an intelligence organization that operated so far under the radar that only the President of the United States and a few select people knew of its existence, snipers had hit targets in cities within the mountain time zone, killing another forty-nine people, again striking exactly at noon.

Bolan arrived at Stony Man in the battered Ferrari at exactly 2:49 p.m. eastern time. The soldier knew that they had just eleven minutes before more innocent civilians were slaughtered up and down the West Coast. Eleven minutes, and there wasn't a damned thing Bolan could do about it. He'd been in constant contact with Hal Brognola and the crew at Stony Man Farm since just after the Tahoe had burst into flames. He'd returned to the Farm as quickly as possible, but the panic that had ensued after the shootings had ground traffic to a halt. Even though Bolan had been at the wheel of one of the fastest cars on the planet, it still couldn't fly, and flight would have been the only way to circumvent the miles and miles of snarled traffic that Bolan had been forced to negotiate.

Normally the state of the borrowed Ferrari would have required a bit of explanation, but Brognola and the crew at Stony Man had far more important matters to attend. Like trying to prevent another wave of killings on the West Coast when clocks in the pacific time zone struck noon. Bolan entered the War Room.

"What security measures have we got in place on the West Coast?" Bolan asked without preamble. There wasn't time for him to get out there himself before the clock struck twelve, but Bolan hoped that Brognola and the crew had done everything possible to prevent a slaughter on the West Coast.

"We've activated every former blacksuit we could contact," the big Fed said. Blacksuits were operatives who'd been trained for duty at Stony Man Farm. Mostly blacksuit candidates came from the ranks of law-enforcement personnel or active military, but occasionally the Farm recruited qualified candidates from other fields.

"Any leads on the shootings that have already occurred?" Bolan asked.

"Just the crew that you took out," Brognola said, "and

there wasn't much left of them to identify. We've got forensic teams working on it. All we know at this point was that there were four bodies in the vehicle, charred beyond recognition."

"That's it?" the soldier asked. "No other witnesses?"

"None," Price interjected. "As far as we know, no one saw anything. We've had at least 180 separate people or groups of people making coordinated hits on random victims. I don't know how that's possible."

"It's obviously possible," Bolan said. "It's happened. Making the hits wouldn't be the hard part. With the element of surprise, making arbitrary hits on random targets would be child's play for a trained sniper team. What's hard to believe is that something that would require this degree of coordination could happen under our radar, without us picking up at least some chatter. Hal, have you got anything that might help?"

"Nothing," Brognola said. "At least nothing out of the ordinary. We keep our ears open, but to be honest, the way things are today, the incendiary rhetoric has become an indecipherable cacophony. We've got everyone from ivory-tower academics to three-toed swamp runners threatening to kill the President on a daily basis, but as near as we can tell, it's all just talk. We've detained a few low-rent jihadists recently, basically guys who hooked up with the wrong people in the wrong internet chat rooms. They spout off about destroying America over their cell phones and get together to do a little target practicing on the weekends, but we haven't picked up any credible terrorist threats."

"What we've got here is credible," Bolan said, "and it shows a level of organization that would be almost impossible to achieve without alerting the authorities. At least impossible if it was planned within U.S. borders."

"You think this was coordinated outside the country?" Brognola asked.

"It had to be," Bolan said. "If this had been masterminded on U.S. soil, we'd have heard at least some rumblings about it."

"I was thinking the same thing," Aaron "the Bear" Kurtzman chimed in. Kurtzman, who had been paralyzed from the waist down in an attack on Stony Man Farm many years earlier, headed Stony Man's team of crack cyber-sleuths. Price and Brognola had been so wrapped up in their discussion with Bolan that they hadn't noticed Kurtzman roll into the room in his wheelchair.

"I've been going over everything," Kurtzman said. "I've analyzed every voice, email and text intercept we've had in the past six months, and I'm coming up with nothing. These people are displaying extraordinary communications discipline."

Bolan looked at his watch. The digital seconds were sweeping toward 3:00 p.m.—noon on the West Coast.

Seattle, Washington

OFFICER WILLIAM NELSON LOOKED at his watch. 11:55 a.m. The past hour and a half had been the longest ninety minutes of Nelson's life.

"Willie," a younger officer asked, "what time have you got?"

"Fuck you," Nelson said. He hated being called "Willie." He hated country music with a passion—he was an opera fan—and he especially hated that long-haired degenerate Willie Nelson. As a younger man he hadn't minded being called "Willie," but as the years went on he began to resent sharing a name with the country singer. But he'd been Detective Willie Nelson of the Seattle Police Department for so long now that there was no way he was going to stuff that particular cat back in a bag, regardless of how much the name irritated him. In fact, the more he tried to get people to call him "William," or even just "Bill," the more people seemed to relish calling him "Willie Nelson." Sometimes they called him worse things, like "The Red-Headed Stranger," which was more of a reference to the famous album by Willie Nelson than to his own hair, which had long since faded from shocking red to bluish white.

Three more years, Nelson thought to himself. Three more years of this bullshit and I can retire. Three god-damned more years, and then I'm retiring on a Mexican beach, where no one will call me anything but "Señor Nelson." Then these clowns can all go fuck themselves.

He might have shared a name with a famous singer, but Detective William Nelson was good police—as good as police got. Still, even with decades of experience, this was something new; the situation he was dealing with this day was beyond even his experience. In his twenty-two years on the force he thought he'd seen everything, but he'd never seen anything like this. Apparently, an army of snipers was assassinating random people across the country. Had someone suggested something like that was even possible to the detective when he woke up that morning, he would have written off the person as insane.

But it *was* happening. Nelson tapped the trauma plates in the bulletproof vest he wore. He'd sworn that he would never wear the vest. He felt that if he had to resort to that, it was time to quit the force because it meant that the bad guys had won. In spite of everything he'd seen in his years on the force, he still believed that people were basically decent. It was that belief that kept him going to work every morning, the belief that people were worth protecting. His refusal to wear the vest symbolized that belief, but this day he'd been ordered to wear the vest, and given what had been happening across the nation, he put up only token resistance.

Nelson felt a tingling in his arms, a sensation that he'd learned to interpret as a sign that something was about to go down. He didn't tell his colleagues about this sixth sense. He received enough ribbing about his name; the last thing he needed was for them to start giving him shit about his paranormal powers. In truth, there was nothing paranormal about it. Long years of experience had simply honed his ability to detect when something was slightly out of the ordinary and discern when that something might pose danger. And right now those instincts were telling him that he was in a hot spot.

No one had any idea where the snipers might hit; they only knew when—the moment the clock struck 12:00 p.m. It was now 11:57 a.m. Trying to predict where the snipers would hit was the equivalent of picking the right numbers on a lottery ticket. Nelson decided to check out Anderson Park, just east of Seattle Central Community College. It was a warm spring day, and even if he didn't find any signs of snipers, at least he'd be able to enjoy watching the college girls catching a little sun on the benches around the fountain at the south end of the park.

He parked his Dodge Charger and pulled out his binoculars, but instead of focusing on the healthy young breasts barely contained in halter tops and bikinis, he scoped out the streets and rooftops around the park.

Something caught his eye on the east side of the park, a flash of light reflecting off of something in the steeple of the church. He took a closer look, but only saw the horizontal slats that covered the windows in the steeple tower. He stared at the slats for a bit and thought he could make out a shape behind the slats. Then he thought he saw something poking out through the slats. It looked like it might be the barrel of a gun. He saw a subdued flash erupt from the end of the object and a heartbeat later he felt a blow to his forehead. Then his lifeless body slumped out the open window of his car.

Washington, D.C.

By 3:10 p.m. eastern time, Hal Brognola had received reports of thirty-seven shootings on the West Coast,

and the calls kept coming in. Even more disturbing was
the fact that the snipers had targeted law-enforcement
officials whenever possible. By 3:30 p.m. Stony Man
Farm had received reports of more than one hundred
shootings, the majority of which were law-enforcement
personnel. The final count was 129 dead, 103 of whom
were law-enforcement officers of various levels, ranging
from a meter checker to a chief of police. There were
129 more murders and zero new leads. In each case the
shooters had remained unseen, but they had gotten their
message across—they could kill with impunity, and the
only thing that the law-enforcement community could
do about it was to be fodder for their rifles.

By the time reports of shootings started coming in
from Alaska, Brognola had already flown to Washington
to meet with the President. The big Fed had seen many
different presidents dealing with many different crises,
but he'd never seen a President who seemed at a loss as
to how to proceed.

"Hal," the President said, "what do I do?"

"I wish I could help you, sir, but I honestly don't
know."

"I've got people on one side of me telling me to declare martial law," the President said. "There's a group
of people in the Joint Chiefs of Staff who have already
drawn up a contingency plan. But my instincts tell me
that's the wrong approach."

"Mine, too, sir," Brognola said. "It seems to me that
whoever is coordinating all this, their goal is to create
so much chaos that they force you to declare martial

law. You'd be serving their goal, whatever that may be, by declaring martial law."

"My thoughts exactly," the President said. "But if I don't declare martial law, what do I do? The American people expect the government to do something to stop this crisis."

"I wish I knew the answer to that, sir, but I don't. We've got our very best people working on this and for now that's all we can do."

"I understand that, Hal, but just between us, man-to-man, what do you think I should do?"

"I think you should level with the people, sir," Brognola replied. "You should go on television and tell them that we have a very dangerous situation to deal with, but that you think we need to go on with our lives. The American people need to be vigilant, but not fearful."

The President pondered Brognola's advice. "That might work for a short time," he said, "but not for long. If we have a wave of shootings tomorrow, people are going to riot. If that happens, I don't think I'll have any options but to institute the Joint Chiefs' plan."

Quantico, Virginia

WHEN REPORTS OF SHOOTINGS in Hawaii started coming in two hours after the Alaska shootings, Mack Bolan was at the FBI crime lab in Quantico, Virginia, where a forensic team pored over the charred remains pulled from the Tahoe the soldier had pursued earlier in the day. So far the team hadn't discovered much, but the corpses in the incinerated SUV were the only leads to a murder spree that had taken hundreds of victims in a matter of hours.

The coordination required to pull off something of this magnitude boggled Bolan's mind. In some cases the hits could only have been pulled off by one or two individuals, but an unknown number of them had to have been carried out in teams like the one Bolan took out. That meant that there were hundreds of organized killers roaming the country, killing at random. To have an operation of this scope take place without alerting anyone—the CIA, the FBI, the NSA and most especially the cyberteam at Stony Man Farm—seemed incomprehensible.

Bolan watched the technicians examine the wreckage of the Tahoe and felt a weight descend upon his shoulders. He'd been fighting for justice for a long time, and it seemed like every time he made a step forward he was eventually pushed three or four steps back. It was like trying to push back the tide with a straw broom. The Executioner knew that he possessed an immense reservoir of inner strength. Over the many years he had been fighting this seemingly endless battle, he'd watched countless comrades crack and break under the stress. Yet he'd always remained strong, had always been able to draw on reserves of strength that so many others seemed to lack. He hadn't thought the others weak; he just recognized that he had abilities that most people didn't possess.

Usually, Bolan had at least some sort of an idea of what he was up against; this time there were no leads.

He felt a hand on his shoulder and turned to see Patricia Jensen standing beside him. She knew very little about him—he'd purposely kept her in the dark all these years for her own safety. All she knew was that he worked for the Department of Justice, which wasn't exactly true. He had worked for Brognola in an official capacity once, many years ago, but that had not turned out well for anyone involved. These days he was more of a lone wolf. But that information wasn't something he shared with Jensen; the less she knew about the soldier, the longer she could expect to live.

The one thing she knew about him was that, regardless of everything else, he worked on the side of good. As did she. She'd returned the child to his mother earlier in the day, but instead of going home, she'd returned to the FBI lab in Quantico. Though she wasn't on the forensic team investigating the charred Tahoe, she was under contract with the FBI and had top-secret clearance at the lab. She'd become involved with crime-scene investigation, and had proved to be a particularly adept investigator, one of the top forensic investigators in the nation, in fact.

Though she wasn't officially involved with this investigation, she was lending her expertise to help out. Not that she'd been much help. There wasn't a lot left to investigate. The team had identified the vehicle, but it had been reported stolen earlier in the day. The theft was legitimate—someone had boosted the Tahoe and modified it for the shooting. The dealership placard that had been mounted in place of a license plate had obviously been stolen, but since such placards were literally worthless and were almost always thrown away after the actual license plates for a new vehicle arrived, no one had reported the theft.

That left the bodies themselves, and there wasn't much left of those to investigate. So far, all they knew for certain was that each person in the vehicle had had their teeth fixed in a manner that precluded identifying the bodies through dental records. All this told the investigators was that they were dealing with extremely sophisticated perpetrators, one with access to their own dentists. This only confirmed the vastness of the conspiracy against which they did battle.

All that was left was to perform a thorough autopsy on the bodies recovered from the wreck. If they were extremely lucky, there would be some sort of clue, something that the perpetrators hadn't counted on. They needed a break.

CHAPTER THREE

Mack Bolan awakened in Patricia Jensen's studio apartment and carefully extricated himself from her embrace. He took a quick shower and went out to see if the forensic team had discovered anything overnight. Upon stepping out of the apartment he was accosted by a team of technicians, all speaking at once.

"Quiet!" he ordered, and everyone quit speaking. "Can one of you tell me what's going on?"

"We were unable to extract dental records from any of the corpses," the woman in charge of the team said.

"I knew that last night when I went to sleep," Bolan said.

"We learned a bit more overnight. Each of the corpses had recently undergone extensive orthodontic surgery, not to repair any damage, but solely to prevent identification through dental records. But they all had one other thing in common—each corpse had been fitted with a hollow false tooth."

"Did you find any cyanide capsules in the hollow compartments?" Bolan asked.

"No, but we did find traces of cyanide. Each person must have had cyanide capsules in that tooth, but the fire destroyed the capsules."

"That means that if we capture any of the shooters alive, we'd better act fast to make sure they don't kill themselves before we can interrogate them," the soldier said, more to himself than to the woman. "Were you able to learn anything?"

"Only that one corpse had stainless steel hardware in his left leg," the woman said. "Pretty high-tech stuff for such a young man. Appears to be military."

"How can you tell?" Bolan asked.

"From the serial number on the hardware. According to production records the manufacturer shipped the hardware to the Veterans Administration hospital in Minneapolis, Minnesota."

"Did you identify the person who had the hardware installed?" Bolan asked.

"We can't legally gain access to medical records," the woman said. She gave the soldier a look that said she knew that sort of technicality might not impede him as much as it did her, but remained silent.

Bolan went back into the apartment to call Stony Man Farm on his secure cell line.

Jensen was just getting out of the shower when he returned. The apartment was set up like a hotel room, with a kitchenette between the bathroom and the bedroom area. He watched Jensen towel off her naked body, missing rivulets of water rolling off her blond hair and down her back between her shoulder blades. He stepped into the bathroom, took her towel from her and wiped off the water from her back. She was really a lovely woman, with a body that bordered on perfection. She turned around to kiss him, but instead of responding to her lips, he said, "I need you to do me a favor."

"What?" she asked, obviously disappointed. She had hoped for another session of lovemaking.

"Go out and get me a newspaper. The *New York Times.*" Bolan had no need of a newspaper, but he did need some privacy to call Stony Man Farm. It wasn't because he didn't trust Jensen, but what he needed to discuss with the crew at Stony Man was top secret. She clearly didn't appreciate being sent on such a menial errand, but she got dressed and left without questioning Bolan. He wished he'd been able to think of a better excuse for getting her to leave, but at least it had worked.

After she'd dressed and left, Bolan called Kurtzman at Stony Man and told him what he'd learned. "Can you get into the VA records?" Bolan asked.

"The problem is that the VA has been slow to switch to computerized record keeping, so most of the VA information is likely in a filing cabinet at the VA hospital in Minneapolis. But if the guy was active military when he had the surgery, which seems likely, given his age, his records should be on file with the Pentagon."

"Can you hack into those records?" Bolan asked.

"I already have," Kurtzman replied, "or at least what's left of them. They appear to have been altered." He paused. "Well, *altered* isn't exactly the correct word. *Destroyed* would be more accurate. I found a record of the hardware being delivered to Minneapolis, but no purchase order, no information on who ordered it and no information on the end user. All that information appears to have been purged from the system."

"How is that possible?" Bolan asked.

"It's not, at least in theory," Kurtzman replied. "Whoever did this had some help in extremely high places."

"How high?" Bolan asked.

"I'd almost have to say as high as the office of the President," Kurtzman said, "but that's highly unlikely."

"Where do we go from here?" Bolan asked.

"We'll start looking into possibilities at the highest level of government," the computer expert said. "And I mean the highest."

"I'll head to Minneapolis to see if I can learn anything at the VA hospital," Bolan said. "The electronic records may have been destroyed, but maybe there's still some information hidden in the physical records."

Bridgeport, Connecticut

THE FEAR EVERYONE ACROSS the United States felt as noon approached the following day hung over the country like the shimmering haze created by the unseasonably warm spring weather. Much of the country had, in fact, shut down, and work ground to a halt because many people were too afraid to leave their houses.

Jim Parkinson counted himself among the fearful who remained indoors as noon approached, though that wasn't too difficult for him since he worked at home. Parkinson really wasn't afraid of the squads of snipers that seemed to have descended on the entire nation. In fact, he was secretly grateful; the chaos couldn't have come at a better time. For the previous decade Parkinson, a British expatriate, had been embezzling huge sums of money from the publishing house for which he worked, for which he'd been the CEO for twenty years. About ten years earlier he'd been punted aside, replaced by a much younger man and given the lofty title of "Senior Vice President of Global Publishing."

Senior vice president of nothing, Parkinson thought. If he went into the offices once per month it was a busy month, and if he skipped his monthly visit, he was dead certain that no one missed his presence. He'd been replaced because the then-new owners of the company had wanted to hire someone who was more resourceful. It was at that moment that Parkinson decided to show them the meaning of the word *resourceful*. No one knew the intricacies of the publishing house's finances like Parkinson—he'd been the one who set up the system back when he'd been the company's original comptroller. He was the only person who really understood how it worked, and he also knew how to skim large amounts of money without anyone ever finding out. For the past decade he'd been siphoning off over $1 million per year and laundering it through a dummy corporation in the Cayman Islands.

Now, with the country roiling from the turmoil caused by the previous day's sniper attacks, he had the perfect opportunity to bail out, go spend the rest of his days sipping icy rum cocktails on a sandy beach of his choosing. He was at that very moment checking flight schedules, planning to get out of the country before all flights in and out were canceled. In his address to the nation the previous night, the President had said that he intended for business as usual to continue, but there were rumors that the federal government was making plans very much counter to the President's public statements. Parkinson had heard that those plans included shutting down all international airports.

Parkinson looked at the clock on the right side of the lower toolbar on his computer screen and saw that it was one minute until noon. He sat at the kitchen table of his seventh-story apartment where he had a terrific view of Bridgeport Harbor, sipping a cup of coffee while he scheduled his flight. At exactly noon he looked outside to see if he could detect any action. He saw nothing out of the ordinary. He didn't see anyone dying, and he didn't see any terrorist snipers. Most importantly for him, he didn't see the man on the roof of the building across the street, aiming a high-powered rifle at his kitchen window. And he didn't see the .30-caliber bullet that sped directly at his forehead, spraying his brains across the stainless-steel appliances and leaving more than $10 million orphaned in the account of a fictional company headquartered in the Caymen Islands.

Kansas City, Missouri

PETER SCHLETTY DOUBTED his career path. He'd wanted to be a cop since he was old enough to know what a cop was. He'd excelled in the police academy and had landed a sweet job with the Kansas City Police Department upon graduating. Up until a couple of days prior, it had been the job of his dreams. Schletty was an exceptionally intelligent person, with an IQ of 165. This made him smarter than ninety percent of the world's civilians and smarter than ninety-nine point ninety-nine percent of all police officers.

In some ways his intelligence had been a hindrance in his career as an officer because it caused him to question exceptionally stupid orders, but overall it had put him on the fast track for advancement because, frankly, most of his colleagues could politely be described as *dolts*. In his less charitable moments, Schletty conjured the word *retards,* but his politic sensibilities kept him from ever uttering such insensitive terminology aloud.

Instead, he just kept such commentary to himself and went about his work with the utmost skill and dedication. As a result, he'd found himself on the career fast track, rising through the ranks faster than most of his compatriots, earning their respect in the process. Until the past couple of days he'd felt he earned that respect, but the insane events of the past two days had caused him to doubt his own abilities.

Yesterday there had been a murder in Kansas City. That was not unusual—the city had a fairly high murder rate, double the national average, in fact. But yesterday's murder had been unlike any since Schletty had joined the force in that it had been part of a coordinated murder spree that had occurred across the entire country, from Maine to Hawaii.

Yesterday's murders had all occurred exactly at the stroke of noon, and at noon eastern time this day another wave of murders had occurred on the East Coast. In all, at least 127 people had been killed in the eastern time zone. Given that, it didn't take an IQ of 165, Schletty knew, to predict that a whole shitload of people were about to be assassinated in the central time zone. It was 11:58 a.m. central time, meaning that Schletty had two minutes to identify possible perpetrators to be of any use at all to the people he was supposed to protect and serve.

At that moment, Schletty wished he was an accountant or a store clerk instead of a cop.

SCHLETTY RODE SHOTGUN in a squad car that at that moment was crossing the Interstate 435 Bridge over the Missouri River. He usually sat at a desk; these days his duties were mostly supervisory, but after yesterday's shootings he ordered every officer on his staff out on the street, including himself. He had no idea what he was looking for, but he knew it was probably something he had never seen before. And that's exactly what he saw. At first it looked like a lump of metal on the girder of the bridge, but on closer inspection, he realized it was a man wearing material designed to make him invisible against the bridge—he wore a gray duster decorated with rust-colored patches designed to blend in with the bridge's girders.

Schletty could make out some sort of long item in the man's hands. Before he could point out the man's

location to the driver of the squad car, flame erupted
from the item in the man's hand. Schletty saw a car ahead
of him careen out of control, crash into the guard rail
and flip over into the Missouri River. Schletty watched
the figure on the bridge rappel down the girder toward
the base of the bridge. He lost sight of the figure.

"Floor it," he told the officer driving the car.

"But sir," the officer said, "we need to stop to help
the crash victim."

"He's beyond help," Schletty said. He'd seen the shot
hit its target and knew that even if they could get to the
victim in the car, he was almost certainly dead from the
gunshot wound. "We need to find the shooter."

"Shooter?" the officer asked.

"Yeah," Schletty said. "He's down at the base of the
bridge."

The officer turned on the lights and siren and accelerated around traffic. Just as they got to the south side
of the bridge, Schletty saw a gray late-model Impala
leaving the small parking area at the base of the bridge.
The officer driving saw it, too; Schletty didn't have to
tell the man to pursue the vehicle.

The squad car was unable to exit the freeway and
drive down to the road that ran parallel to the river for
another quarter of a mile, giving the shooter a good head
start. Schletty's driver was good; he drove down the embankment along the freeway, crashed through the fence
that kept animals off the freeway and slid sideways onto
River Front Road, about half a mile behind the Impala.
The squad car was an aging Crown Victoria and on its

last legs, but it still had some snort and within a mile the officer had the speedometer past 100 mph and was closing in on the Impala.

They'd just about closed in on the Impala when gunfire erupted from both sides of the road from at least four shooters. Schletty and his driver never stood a chance. As the officer driving died, his last earthly act was to push the accelerator all the way to the floorboards. The old Crown Vic accelerated hard, clipping the Impala in the left rear quarter panel and causing it to spin out of control. The Impala spun into the ditch, rolled through the air twice then crashed into a small stand of trees.

Kansas City, Missouri

MACK BOLAN PUT AWAY HIS cell phone and turned to the man beside him. Jack Grimaldi manned the controls of the Cirrus Vision SF50 jet that was taking the Executioner to Minneapolis.

"Change of plans, Jack," Bolan said. "We're going to Kansas City."

Without questioning the order, Grimaldi altered course. He'd been flying the soldier to and from battlefields around the world for years, as often as not fighting alongside him during those battles. Grimaldi trusted the Executioner like no other man on Earth, and if Bolan needed to go to Kansas City, Grimaldi would do whatever it took to get him there. But the pilot was curious.

"What's in Kansas City?" he asked.

"Another shooting site, but this time a couple of police officers spotted a shooter."

"Did they catch him?" Grimaldi asked.

"They chased him," Bolan replied, "but they were ambushed. Both officers were killed."

"Did they tag any of the bad guys?"

"It doesn't look like they got any shots off," Bolan said, "but something happened. The vehicle they were pursuing either crashed, or the pursuing officers managed to initiate a PIT maneuver." Bolan referred to the police immobilization technique in which a pursuing vehicle nudged the right rear corner of the vehicle being pursued, causing the fleeing vehicle to spin out of control. "Whichever it was, the fleeing vehicle crashed."

"Any bodies?" Grimaldi asked.

"No such luck. The scene was scrubbed clean by the time backup arrived."

"How long did it take for backup to show up at the scene?"

"Eight minutes," Bolan said. "In eight minutes they'd removed all evidence."

Price had a squad car waiting to take Bolan to the shooting scene when Grimaldi landed the plane at the airport in downtown Kansas City. Grimaldi and Bolan had seen long lines of cars leaving the city, but unlike the previous day when traffic ground to a halt after the wave of shootings, that day the downtown area was a virtual ghost town and the squad car had Bolan to the ambush scene within twenty minutes.

Normally, local officers didn't particularly like having

federal agents involved in an investigation, particularly when a cop had died. They tend to prefer to catch the perpetrators themselves in such situations, but this situation seemed different. While Bolan sensed some hostility from the officers on the scene, it wasn't the degree he'd expected to encounter. Instead, most of the members of the various law-enforcement agencies on hand—the Kansas City PD, along with the state police and representatives from various heriff's departments— seemed to appreciate any help they were offered.

The scene looked disturbingly like the one he'd run across the previous day, right down to the team of experts poring over the remains of the vehicle. Again the vehicles had been burned. The team investigating the vehicle he'd chased the day before had discovered that the vehicle had been rigged to explode in the event of a crash, with explosives strategically placed to ensure the maximum amount of destruction. Whoever was behind these incidents wanted to make certain that they left behind as little evidence as possible.

Whoever it was, they were thorough. They'd scrubbed the crime scene clean. The officers in the squad car had been torn apart by a couple of thousand large-caliber bullets, meaning that they'd gotten caught in the cross fire of what had to have been heavy-caliber machine guns, most likely .50-caliber weapons.

Barbara Price had informed Bolan that the man in charge of the operation would be Detective Kevin Maurstad of the Kansas City Police Department. Bolan didn't know what Maurstad looked like, but he had a pretty good idea that he'd be the big guy in the center of everything, the guy everyone else lined up to talk to. The soldier went up to the man who seemed to have the most control of the chaos and said, "Detective Maurstad?"

The man wheeled around, trying to identify a new irritant. He studied the tall stranger and said, "You must be the yahoo the Feds sent down to help us."

"Yeah, I'm the yahoo to which you refer," Bolan said.

Maurstad stood in a defensive stance, as if he expected Bolan to attack him. He relaxed a bit after assessing the soldier. "You don't look like the usual dipshits they send down here."

"We've been busy," Bolan offered. "We're fresh out of the usual dipshits, so they sent me instead. It looks like you've got a mess on your hands."

"Yeah," Maurstad said, "it's a class-A clusterfuck, that's for sure."

"What have you got so far?" Bolan asked.

"Not a hell of a lot. Two cops shot to hamburger in that squad car over there." He pointed at a black-and-white police car with a passenger compartment that was completely perforated. "Their squad car was blown to pieces by a .50-caliber machine gun, judging by the holes in the vehicle, most likely a Ma Deuce. There was barely enough left of the officers inside to identify them as human. We policed the area for spent .50-cal shell casings but found nothing."

"How about the shooter's vehicle? Find anything?"

Bolan glanced at the burned-out carcass of the Impala and knew what Maurstad's answer would be.

The detective saw Bolan looking at the destroyed vehicle and answered with a question of his own: "What do you think?"

"I think it looks like someone destroyed the evidence with military precision," Bolan answered.

"And military weapons," Maurstad replied. "It looks like they destroyed the vehicle with some sort of thermite antimatérial grenades."

"Probably thermate-TH3," Bolan offered, referring to a standard antimatérial grenade used by all branches of the military to destroy left-behind vehicles and weapons in a hurry.

"That would be my guess," Maurstad said.

"You were in the military?" the soldier asked.

"Marines. You?"

"Army," Bolan said. "Any bodies in the vehicle?"

"None," Maurstad said. "The shooter either got out of the vehicle on his own or someone pulled him out. We did get a serial number off the car, though."

"Let me guess," Bolan said. "Stolen?"

"As of nine o'clock this morning, yes."

One of the officers who had been scouring the edges of the ditch alongside the road came up with a rifle shell in a sealed plastic bag. "Sir," he said to Maurstad, "I found this."

Bolan let Maurstad examine the bag, and then asked to see it. Maurstad handed the soldier the evidence bag. The shell casing was a Hornady brass shell,

chambered for the .338 Lapua Magnum round. The .338
Lapua Magnum round had been developed specifically
as a round for military sniping. Its ballistics rivaled
the .50 BMG round; a good shooter could hit targets
out to 2,000 meters, and even an average shooter could
count on a 1,200-meter effective range. But the round
was uncommon in civilian use; only the most specialized gun shops carried the .338 Lapua Magnum round,
and among those that did, most didn't stock a firearm
with which to fire it.

"If you don't mind," Bolan said, "I'm going to send
this to our lab."

Maurstad clearly minded, but he just said, "You're
the boss."

Minneapolis, Minnesota

"I'M SORRY, SIR," THE administrator at the Minneapolis Veterans Administration hospital in Minneapolis,
Minnesota, told Mack Bolan, "but we can't release that
information to you regardless of how impressive your
credentials might be."

Bolan had expected as much. He knew getting the
records released would be virtually impossible, but he
had to give it a shot because the alternative didn't stand
a much better chance of success. He'd have to break into
the VA hospital at night.

The soldier looked around the administrative offices,
at the rows and rows of wide-drawer filing cabinets,
knowing that the information he sought likely rested

within one of them. One row, marked Vendors, looked especially promising. He had the name of a vendor, the ship date and the serial number. That should be enough to get him a name.

Getting in and out looked less promising. The administrative offices were on the top floor, off a twelve-story atrium around which the hospital was arranged. Several wings branched off from the central atrium area, with the head nurse of each floor posted at the end of each wing, near the edge of the atrium. It was a massive complex, one of the nicest VA hospitals Bolan had ever seen, modern and sophisticated in just about every aspect. Every aspect except record keeping, Bolan reminded himself. In this case, the Veterans Administration's antiquated record keeping turned out to be an advantage; the only reason the information the soldier needed hadn't been purged was because it hadn't been in electronic form. It was a small oversight on the part of Bolan's opponents, but so far it was the only clue the soldier had.

The hospital wasn't located in Minneapolis proper, but rather in Bloomington, a suburb of Minneapolis, home of the Mall of America. Given that the gigantic shopping center was a tourist destination, the area had an abudance of hotels. Bolan had a room in a little low-budget motel about halfway between the Mega Mall and the VA hospital; the sort of place where he could lie low for a few hours without drawing any attention.

After scoping out the VA hospital campus, which wasn't well-guarded, Bolan returned to his room to grab a nap. He set his alarm for 1:00 a.m., but he needn't have bothered; he awoke at exactly 12:55. By the time his alarm went off he'd already brushed his teeth, showered and slipped into his blacksuit. He threaded a sound suppressor onto his Beretta 93R machine pistol and sheathed it in the shoulder holster. Normally he'd also pack a Desert Eagle on his hip, but this was a soft probe. The Beretta was an old habit. There were no bad guys in the hospital; there were just hardworking healthcare workers taking care of American heroes. Under no circumstances was Bolan going to let the situation devolve into a shooting match. Stealth, quickness and silence were much more important than heavy artillery in this mission, and the bulky Israeli hand cannon would just be a liability in all of those areas.

Instead, he carried nonlethal weaponry in its place: a canister of pepper gas, a roll of duct tape, some plastic restraints and a stun gun, which the soldier intended to use only in an extreme emergency, since the device had the potential to do serious damage; it could even be lethal to a security guard with a bad heart.

Bolan also carried a pouch filled with climbing gear: rope, carbiners, belays and rappelling devices. The security at the VA hospital was light, but it was heavy enough to turn the probe into an ugly situation. Shooting his way in and out wasn't an option. To keep this probe soft, the Executioner was going to have to put his back into it.

The soldier parked his rental car, a Chevrolet Impala, about as nondescript as nondescript could be, in a residential neighborhood just west of the VA campus. The main entrance was to the east, and that put him as far away from any late-night activity as possible. Bolan scaled the ornate stone wall that surrounded the grounds with ease. The wall was strictly decorative, a pretty barrier that kept the local residents from having to accidentally see a wounded warrior.

The next climb Bolan would have to make wouldn't be as easy. The east end of the wing housing the administration offices had no windows and was featureless. The gaps in the granite covering were too narrow and too far apart to use for hand jamming and foot jamming. A granite trough, however, that served as a character line in the bleak twelve-story-tall stone surface and also masked a drainage pipe for rain that accumulated on the roof. That would provide the soldier with an avenue into the offices. He would have to make his way up to the top of the building, and then gain access through the roof entrance.

Bolan had left the offices via the stairway rather than taking the elevator. Before he'd left, he'd gone up the stairs to the roof exit, disabled the alarm and slipped a thin piece of cardboard into the doorjamb, preventing the bolt from locking. He only hoped that no one had removed the cardboard or fixed the alarm. Judging from the thick layer of dust covering everything on the stairway landing leading to the roof, he guessed it didn't see a lot of use and was probably safe.

Bolan wedged himself into the gutter, which was about eighteen inches deep and two feet wide. With his back against one side, his feet against the other, he was able to extend his legs enough to get the leverage he needed to shimmy up the gutter. Then he began the long, slow, grueling process of inching his way up twelve stories of rough granite, holding himself in place with the tension of his body while he raised one foot, then the other, then slid his back up the opposite side of the trough.

But that was the easy part. The trough ended in a rain chute that was too small for the soldier to crawl through. Instead, he was going to have to rely on a series of ornamental ridges on the overhang that jutted two feet beyond the gutter. Keeping his arms straight and perfect tension in his body, Bolan levered himself outward and reached for the lip that he had spotted in his earlier recon of the building. He trusted the lip would be in the exact spot he'd noted earlier; if his calculations were off by a single inch, he would plummet to his death, 130 feet below. When his hand connected with the ridge, he spared a millisecond to be grateful for the precision of his military sniper observation training. Using his entire body as a lever, Bolan lunged up around the overhang. His arms were melting from the abuse of climbing the wall, but he knew he only had to make it a few more feet and he was finished. Without missing a beat, the soldier used his momentum to scramble up the overhang and pulled himself over onto the roof of the hospital.

He took just a moment to rest his muscles from the strain of climbing and tied the rope he planned to use to rappel down the side of the building to a bracket holding an air-conditioning unit in place, then jogged over to the door. The thin cardboard still prevented the bolt in the door from engaging and he pushed it open. The alarm inside was still disabled. Bolan crept down the stairs with as much stealth as possible, but every footfall, though near silent, seemed to ring down the stairwell like a church bell. When he got to the next landing, the door into the administrative offices were locked. The soldier removed a small but powerful hand-held computer from a drop pouch strapped to his left leg, took out a magnetic key card connected to a USB port and attached the card to the computer. He pulled out his cell phone and sent a text message to Kurtzman saying, "Get ready—about to transmit," then swiped the magnetic key card through the slot on the scanner next to the doorway.

Moments later he received a text back from Kurtzman. Try it again. Bolan swiped the key card one more time, only this time instead of blinking red, the LED light turned solid green and Bolan entered the offices. The stairway was at the west end of the office suite; the east side of the suite was a glass window looking out at the balcony that in turn overlooked the atrium. Bolan saw a figure walk past on the balcony outside the suite and stop. It was a security guard, making his rounds. Bolan crouched behind a cubicle wall while the figure swiped a key card, opening the door into the office suite. The figure shone his flashlight around the suite, and then began walking toward the soldier.

The cubicle in which Bolan crouched had a desk

along one side and a table along another. It was part of a two-person cubicle suite, and another table separated one work space from the other. He crouched and slid under the table separating the work spaces, then slowed his breathing almost to a standstill. A large courier mailing box sat on the floor next to him. As silently as possible, Bolan placed the box between himself and the opening into the aisle that formed the boundaries in this cubicle kingdom.

He slowed his breath even more as the security guard approached the cubicle in which he hid. In his mind, Bolan formulated a plan for neutralizing the guard in the most humane way possible. When the guard stopped to shine a light into the cubicle where Bolan hid, pausing longer than he had at other cubicles, the soldier thought he was going to have to put that plan into action, but after a few moments of scoping out the scene of the crime, the security guard moved on. An interminably long five minutes later, the guard left the office suite.

After the man had moved on, Bolan extricated himself from under the table, went over to the filing cabinets and found the one marked Vendors. The cabinet was locked, but the lock was a simple blade affair that the soldier was able to twist open simply by inserting the tip of his knife into the key hole and turning. Once he figured out the organizational system, he was able to locate the vendor that had provided the hardware. He coordinated the dates of the delivery with the names of patients receiving the hardware in just moments. A bit more searching revealed that the piece the technicians had extracted from the body at the lab in Quantico—titanium braces used to reshape mangled tibia and fibula plateaus—had been installed in one Theodore Haynes, a veteran of the Iraq war from Plainfield, Wisconsin.

Bolan took out a black cloth from the drop pouch, placed it over his head like a shroud, then crouched beneath the cloth and took digital photos of all the documentation regarding Mr. Theodore Haynes. The camera was connected to his notebook computer and downloaded the images directly to a secure FTP site at Stony Man Farm. In all, it had taken Bolan less time to gather the information than it had taken the security guard to make his rounds at the office.

He replaced his equipment and was getting ready to exit the way he'd came when the security guard once again shone his flashlight through the glass separating the suite from the atrium balcony. Bolan dived behind the cover of a cubicle wall, but he worried that the security guard had seen him. The man swiped his key card, which dangled from a chain around his neck, entered the suite, handgun drawn, and made his way to Bolan's position.

The Executioner scurried around the corner of the cube wall before he could be discovered, and found that he'd backed himself into a narrow corridor without any cover. The soldier crouched and when the man rounded the corner, he sprang up, grabbed him around the neck, at the same time putting his hand over the man's mouth to stifle an outcry. He guided his target to the ground, using his own body to absorb the impact of the fall to avoid hurting the man any more than necessary. Bolan grabbed the guard's pistol in the process, and when he had the man down, he put the barrel of the pistol in the guy's mouth. What the guard didn't know was that Bolan had decocked the weapon and flicked on the safety; he had no intention of putting this innocent man in danger and regretted having to treat him so roughly, but there were hundreds—perhaps thousands—of lives on the line. There was no way the guard could know this, and he was terrified.

Bolan removed the gun and put a piece of duct tape over the man's mouth and zip tied his hands behind his back and his feet together. Then he unloaded the pistol, tossed the magazine and bullet from the chamber to one side of the room and the gun toward the other, and bolted for the stairway. He pushed open the stairwell door, only to find that several other security guards were rushing up the stairway from lower floors. The guard had to have called for backup before entering the office suite. It sounded like there were at least four men pounding their way up the stairs. There was no way the soldier could subdue that many guards without someone getting hurt; his only chance for survival now was speed.

The soldier lunged up the stairwell toward the roof, the security guards hot on his heels. He kicked the door open and ran at top speed for the rope he'd anchored to the air-conditioning unit. Grabbing the figure-eight descenders he'd clipped to the ropes, he flung himself over the edge of the roof. By the time the first of the guards had emerged from the stairwell Bolan was in a near free fall toward the ground below. He plunged down in a barely controlled descent, braking only as he neared the ground. It was hard to judge his progress in the dark, and he'd slowed his descent barely enough to keep from doing serious damage to his body when he landed.

When his feet touched the grass, Bolan pitched himself into a roll, which turned out to be a good move because gunfire from the roof tore up the turf on which he'd just landed. The gunfire tracked him as he sprang up from his roll and ran at top speed for the wall. When he reached the wall, he grabbed the top and powered over the top of it. By this time he'd put enough distance between himself and his pursuers that he only needed to worry about catching a stray bullet, but he also knew a stray bullet could kill him as dead as an aimed bullet could, so he didn't stop running until he was at his car.

He could hear sirens approaching the VA hospital. Rather than panic, Bolan calmly drove through the residential district in which he'd parked, following a route that he'd prepared in advance, one that led him to Cedar Avenue. He followed it south until it turned into State Highway 77, which in turn led him straight to his motel. When he pulled into the lot, pimps and dealers were doing business in the lot. They sized him up, decided he was more trouble than he was worth and let him pass into the motel unmolested.

CHAPTER FOUR

"So what have you got on Theodore Haynes from Plainfield, Wisconsin?" Bolan asked Kurtzman over his cell phone once he was safely ensconced in his two-bit motel room.

"Army Ranger," Kurtzman replied, "one tour in Afghanistan, two tours in Iraq, heavily decorated, had his left knee crushed when his Humvee hit an IED and flipped over. He was the only survivor. His three buddies were killed in the blast. He recovered full use of his leg, but not quite to the degree required to remain a Ranger, so he left the military."

"I'm going to take a wild guess and say he was trained as a sniper."

"Right first time."

"Anything else?" Bolan asked.

"Yeah. He's been officially dead for years. According to every record I could access, he committed suicide soon after washing out of the Rangers."

"I don't believe that," Bolan said. "I sincerely doubt that these killings are the work of some sort of undead zombie."

"There wasn't much we could tell from what was left of the bodies you brought in yesterday," the computer expert said, "but one thing we could tell was that the bodies inside the vehicle had been alive prior to the vehicle crashing, so I don't think we have to worry about zombies."

"Where is Haynes buried?" Bolan asked.

"Plainfield, Wisconsin, and I know what you're thinking. I'm one step ahead of you. Hal is having the body exhumed tomorrow morning."

"I take it that means that I'm heading to Plainfield tonight," Bolan posited.

"You take it correctly," Kurtzman said. "I've already called Jack and told him to get the plane ready."

"You pull any information off that shell casing I sent you yesterday?" Bolan asked.

"Yes and no."

"Give me the 'no' first."

"We didn't pull any prints or DNA off the brass," Kurtzman replied.

"And the 'yes'?"

"We traced the lot number on the case and found out where it had been shipped. You're not going to like this."

"Where did it go?" Bolan asked.

"McNair." Kurtzman was referring to Fort Lesley J. McNair, located on the confluence of the Potomac River and the Anacostia River in Washington, D.C., the third oldest military base in the United States. It was the home base for most of the top Army brass in the D.C. area, including the Army's chief of staff, who also happened to be the current chairman of the Joint

Chiefs of Staff. "It was part of a special production run of precision casings designed for sniper and competition use. It looks like we've got two possibilities here. One, someone at McNair is stealing supplies and selling them on the black market."

"And two," Bolan interjected, "we've got a person or persons at the highest level of the military involved in this mess. How much of this is Hal going to share with the President?"

"He hasn't decided yet," Kurtzman said. "but before you leave for Wisconsin, you need to know one more thing."

"What's that?"

"The President warned Hal that if there is another wave of killings tomorrow, he plans to declare martial law."

Plainfield, Wisconsin

NORMALLY BOLAN USED FLIGHTS to catch a nap and rest up, but the short hop from Minneapolis to Plainfield aboard the fast little jet barely allowed for a single z, so Bolan sat up front and chatted with Grimaldi, who appreciated the company.

"I've always wanted to go to Plainfield," Grimaldi said.

"Why?" Bolan asked.

"It's the home of Ed Gein," Grimaldi replied. Ed Gein had been a notorious murderer and grave robber from Plainfield.

"You a fan of serial killers?" Bolan asked.

"Not a fan, exactly," Grimaldi said, "but I find the guy fascinating. He cut off his victims' heads and stole other body parts from local graveyards. What could motivate a man to do something like that?"

"My money's on a brain disorder," Bolan offered. "That would give him more of an excuse to do what he did than most of the people we go up against. They're usually motivated by greed for wealth or power."

"You do know that he wasn't a serial killer, technically, right?"

"I have to admit I'm not up to speed on the particulars of Wisconsin's second most famous cannibal."

"Gein was only tried and convicted for one murder," Grimaldi said. "Back then prosecutors exercised a little more common sense than today. They figured since he got life for one killing there wasn't a lot to be gained by spending the money to try him for the other murders. Can you imagine a time when such logical thought ruled the day?"

Bolan thought it was a rhetorical question and remained silent.

"You know that you poking around here digging up bodies might bring back some bad memories for the old-timers who were alive back when Geins was doing much the same thing," Grimaldi said.

"I'm not any happier about having to dig up a local war hero than the folks around here will be, but we don't have a choice. And we don't have much time."

The sun had yet to rise over the eastern horizon when

Jack Grimaldi brought the Cirrus Vision SF50 jet in for a landing at the Plainfield International Airport, an extremely pretentious name for a facility that consisted of two dirt runways and a steel shed. It wasn't a fit place to land a jet, even a small jet like the SF50, but a seasoned pilot like Grimaldi had no problems. He brought the little hot-rod jet in as easily as most pilots would bring in a small two-seat Cessna.

Brognola had arranged for a federal agent to meet Bolan at the airport. It wasn't hard for either party to find the other. The Cirrus wasn't only the first jet of the day to land in the airport, but it was also the only jet to ever land there. And if the vehicle driven by the federal officer—a gunmetal gray Crown Victoria sedan—wasn't a dead giveaway, his conservative dark suit was. Besides, he was the only person waiting at the airport. The agent, a somber Nordic-looking fellow named Tracy Anderson, said, "It'll be another hour or so before we finish exhuming the body. Want to stop for breakfast?"

Bolan accepted the agent's offer.

"It looks like we've got a few options," Anderson said as they cruised the town's main drag, along which stood several diners and cafés. "Any of them look promising?"

"Pick that one," Bolan said, pointing to the diner that had the most big pickup trucks parked out front. A lot of pickups usually meant that the place had the best food, but it also meant that it was a spot where the locals congregated, and Bolan hoped to use this opportunity to learn a bit more about Mr. Haynes.

Rather than taking a booth, Bolan, Grimaldi and the agent sat down at the counter, where the soldier could have better opportunities to interact with the locals. Sure enough the local sitting next to Bolan struck up a conversation before the waitress had even poured them a cup of coffee. "Mighty nice weather we're having for this time of year," the man said. The weather was always a safe ice breaker and a favorite topic of conversation in northern states.

"It's close to perfect," Bolan replied. "Summer's come early this year."

"It's global warming," the man said.

"Yep," Bolan replied.

"My name's Myron," the man said, extending his weathered hand. "Myron Haynes."

"Matt," the soldier replied, using his undercover name, "Matt Cooper."

"You in the military?" Haynes asked.

"Was," Bolan replied. "Now I'm doing some contract work for the Department of Justice."

"What are you guys doing about those shootings that have been going on the past couple of days?"

"Everything we can," Bolan replied.

"Well," Haynes said, "we ain't had none around here. What are you investigating in these parts?"

"I hate to ask you this," Bolan said, "but are you related to Theodore Haynes?"

The man got quiet. Then he said, "Everyone around here is pretty much related to everyone else. Our family trees are more like family wreaths. Teddy was my cousin's boy. Damned shame what happened to him."

"Yeah," Bolan said, "it sure was."

"Not that we didn't expect the boy to come to a bad end. He was in trouble from the time he was ten years old. Earlier than that, even. He stole his parents' car when he was twelve. When he went in the army, we thought that might turn him around. And it seemed to. He'd done good in there, made sergeant, but when he come out, he was worse than ever. He got into the drugs real bad. I think that's what made him go and kill himself."

"What kind of drugs?" Bolan asked.

"Oh, I don't know. Drugs is drugs, I suppose. I imagine he was doing meth—everyone around here was doing meth, it seems like. And I know he had a problem with prescription pain pills ever since he got out of the VA hospital. He got caught robbing the drugstore in town once, but they let him go because he was a war hero. If they'd locked him up then, he might be alive today." The man paused for a response, and Bolan gave a slight nod of his head, which passed for conversation in rural areas, and the man continued, "Then again, maybe he'd be just as dead in prison. He was messed up with those damned Slaves."

"Slaves?" Bolan asked.

"Satan's Slaves," Haynes replied. The Satan's Slaves were a mid-sized motorcycle club, located primarily in the upper Midwest, and they currently controlled Minneapolis. The Twin Cities of Minneapolis and St. Paul had been the territory of the Hellions, one of the biggest outlaw motorcycle clubs in the world, but the Hellions had imploded following a series of arrests that had decimated the club. Since nature abhored a vacuum, the Slaves had filled that vacuum and now controlled the area, at least temporarily, until the Hellions could regroup and regain control. The Slaves had a reputation for over-the-top violence, as if they were trying to overcompensate for being a second-tier club by living out an extreme example of the motorcycle gang stereotype. They were also much more political than most motorcycle clubs; they harbored extremist political views and were associated with a number of white supremacist organizations.

"Those guys are bad news," Bolan said. If given the choice, the soldier would have taken the Hellions over the Slaves any day. He had run up against members of the Hellions before, and they were definitely no angels, but the Hellions were a motorcycle club in which some of the members happened to be criminals, whereas the Slaves were an outright criminal organization. Maybe even more than criminal—the Slaves were known to be active in a number of hardcore white supremacist organizations, and Bolan had heard rumors that the club had been involved in terrorist activities against minority groups. The Hellions weren't exactly civil rights activists themselves, but in general they tolerated their neighbors. They tended to police their territory, especially in the neighborhoods around their clubhouses, which tended to be located in the seediest parts of the cities in which the Hellions operated, but they were equal opportunity haters. If someone caused trouble on Hellion turf, that person usually ended up enduring a beating whether he was black, white or any other hue found in the natural world.

"You're telling me," Haynes said. "You know what I think? I don't think Teddy killed himself."

"Oh?" Bolan said. Haynes definitely had the soldier's interest by this point.

"Hell, no," Haynes said. "I saw him the night he died. We had a few beers down at the tavern. He was in a good mood. Then some of those damned Slaves rode up and he left with them. Next thing you know, they found him in his trailer house with his head blown off. He was holding his own shotgun and it sure as hell looked like he'd shot himself, but that could have been anyone in Teddy's bed without his head."

Normally, Bolan would have dismissed such talk as the desperate grasping of a bereaved relative, but in this case he happened to know that Haynes' suspicions were correct. He thought about this while he took the last bite of his hash browns, but his thoughts were interrupted by the ring of Agent Anderson's cell phone.

"We'll be right there," Bolan heard Anderson say.

BOLAN CONTEMPLATED WHAT he'd learned on the ride to the cemetery. After they'd overseen the loading of the remains into the van that would transport them to the federal crime lab in Minneapolis, Anderson returned Bolan and Grimaldi to the airport. As soon as the plane was airborne, Bolan called Kurtzman to debrief.

"What have you learned about the supposed Haynes suicide?" Bolan asked.

"There was no autopsy," Kurtzman stated. "The death certificate was signed by a general practitioner at the local clinic, a fellow named Lee Klancher who was eighty-eight years old at the time. A year later he was diagnosed with advanced Alzheimer's disease, so the odds are good that he didn't do the most thorough examination."

"We can be certain of one thing," Bolan said. "That headless corpse we pulled out of the ground just now wasn't Theodore Haynes."

"I think we're one hundred percent on that one," Kurtzman replied. "But that begs the question, who was it?"

"My guess is someone that the Satan's Slaves wanted to eliminate," Bolan stated, "or at least found expendable."

"The Slaves are involved in this?"

"I think so. At least, they're the only lead I have right now. See what you can find out about them."

Washington, D.C.

"What do you think I should do, Hal?" the President asked.

"I think declaring martial law would be a mistake, sir," Brognola told the man.

"I believe you're right. Once we go down that road, nothing will ever be the same. But my national security adviser and the Joint Chiefs of Staff don't believe we have any other option. People are screaming for us to do something. They're afraid to leave their houses. People aren't going to work. Food, fuel and medicine aren't being delivered. The economy has nearly shut down."

"We're doing everything we can to solve this situation, sir."

"Please, Hal, tell me that you're close to finding the shooters."

"I wish I could, sir, but I can't lie to you."

"Then I'm going to have to declare martial law."

"Sir," Brognola said, "once you've turned the United States into a police state, it will never again be a beacon of freedom. I know this is supposed to be a temporary state of affairs, but what guarantee do you have that bringing the military in will stop the shootings? You're risking turning these terrorist attacks into something resembling an insurgency. I think recent history has shown us how long an insurgency can drag on."

"My instincts tell me you're right, Hal. But what do we do? If I don't go along with the Joint Chiefs, I'm risking a low-grade insurgency in my own administration. They're adamant about declaring martial law."

"Well, sir, far be it from me to tell you what to do, but you are their boss. You are the commander in chief."

The President pondered Brognola's comments and said, "If I give you three more days, do you think you can wrap this thing up?"

"We'll give it everything we've got."

"Fair enough," the man said. "We'll meet in three days.

I pray to God that the purpose of that meeting will be for you to debrief me on the capture of the terrorists. In the meantime, please keep me informed every step of the way."

"Yes, sir."

Minneapolis, Minnesota

BOLAN DOWNSHIFTED THE black Mustang as he approached the Slaves' north Minneapolis clubhouse, located in an industrial area along the west bank of the Mississippi River. The twin tailpipes barked with authority as the 412-horsepower V-8 picked up revs on the downshift. The soldier hadn't wanted such a flashy car, but he needed something fast. The only cars the Farm had been able to line up that met his performance criteria were this Mustang, a red Corvette and a yellow Porsche 911 Turbo. Of the bunch, the Mustang was the slowest, but it was also the least conspicuous. At least it was black, and it had something resembling a backseat so the soldier could keep his war bag within easy reach.

It was almost noon and there was hardly another vehicle on the road. As expected, there'd been another wave of shootings up and down the eastern seaboard at noon eastern time, but this day's kill rate was down somewhat. People weren't moving around much, especially at the stroke of noon. Still, the body count was climbing. Most of the victims had been officers from various law-enforcement agencies, since they were pretty much the only people out at noon, but a few stray civilians had also been killed. Some were people who simply refused to succumb to the fear of the terrorists that was paralyzing the country, but several had been killed in their own homes, shot through windows and doorways. This new development was worrisome; taking out a target inside a building required much more skill than simply shooting someone out in the open and indicated that the skill level of the opponents Bolan faced was of the highest order.

It looked like Teddy Haynes wasn't the only terrorist with military sniper training. It seemed inconceivable that military veterans could be behind this, but that appeared to be the case, and judging from the access needed to scrub the identities of the shooters this clean, there had to be military involvement at an extremely high level.

As hard as that fact was for the soldier to swallow, he found it even more unlikely that some sort of paramilitary operation could involve a group of people such as Satan's Slaves. Bolan slowed even more as he rolled past the Slaves' clubhouse.

The Slaves had taken over the building the Hellions had used as their clubhouse when they'd controlled this territory. It was an old garage that had once served as the headquarters for a taxicab company. Bolan had studied the layout of the place from photos and blueprints that Kurtzman had sent him and knew that getting in would be no easy task. The layout had been designed to keep the taxicabs and employees safe in what was one of the most crime-ridden neighborhoods in the entire Midwest. Several years earlier the city had earned the nickname "Murderapolis," and it had earned that moniker because of killings that had, for the most part, occurred within twenty blocks of the clubhouse. The taxi company's headquarters had been a virtual fort, with razor-wire fences, thick brick walls and entrances that were well-controlled and easily defensible.

Bolan didn't expect any activity outside the clubhouse since it was almost noon and the city seemed virtually deserted, but when he drove past the clubhouse he saw a group of five men beating another man senseless in the vacant lot adjacent to the Slave's property. The men doing the beating all wore Slave cuts—the sleeveless denim jackets on which club members displayed their colors or club patches.

So much for inconspicuous, Bolan thought. He flicked off the traction-control switch, downshifted again and pushed the accelerator to the floor. The rear tires broke loose in a cloud of smoke, and he power slid the Mustang onto a concrete slab that had to have been the driveway of whatever structure had once occupied the vacant lot. Before the car came to a complete stop, Bolan threw open the driver's door and bolted toward the group of men, crossing the thirty-foot distance in several long strides. The five assailants had barely had time to look up from their victim before Bolan was on top of them.

The Executioner snap-kicked the man closest to him in the head, which jerked back at an impossible angle. His neck broken, the man toppled to the ground. Two of the other men stopped beating the victim and brought the broken pool cues they'd been using as clubs to bear on Bolan. Before the wooden sticks could contact the soldier's skull, he reached up and grabbed them both, one in each hand. Bolan flipped the cue in his right hand around so that he was holding the fat end of the club and speared its original owner through the eye with the jagged broken end. The soldier felt the bone in the eye socket give way and the cue penetrate the man's brain pan. Two down, three to go.

By this time, the remaining assailants had turned their attention from the man on the ground and attacked Bolan. With the pool cue in his left hand Bolan whacked the man closest to him across the temple, and the man went down, but this left Bolan vulnerable to the other two attackers. One of them, a burly giant with a long red beard and even longer hair, tackled him, knocking him flat on his back, while the other one smashed a cinder-block-size fist into the soldier's face. Bolan brought a knee up into the groin of the man who'd tackled him but was unable to avoid another blow from that oversized fist. This time the soldier saw stars. He knew he had to end this fight soon, or his attackers would end it for him.

But ending the fight would be a challenge. Bolan's knee to the groin had slowed his attacker, but the man was tough and it hadn't taken the fight out of him. Bolan kicked the man in the jaw, driving him up and away. The other attacker tried to drive his fist into Bolan's face one more time, but the soldier managed to twist to the side and avoid the blow. As he did this, he reached down and pulled a custom-made eight-inch bowie knife from a sheath in his boot and in one sweeping motion he brought the knife around in an arc and drove it through the man's ribs, just below his armpit. He pulled out the blade and a geyser of blood erupted in its wake. Bolan had severed the man's aorta as well as both his pulmonary arteries; he'd bleed out in a matter of seconds.

Knife in hand, the Executioner turned to face the final assailant, but the man standing over Bolan held something in his hand that trumped the soldier's bowie knife: a Ruger Super Redhawk Alaskan revolver. Judging from the diameter of the bore in the barrel staring down at Bolan's face, the revolver was chambered for a .454 Casull cartridge.

The man pulled back the hammer and aimed the sights of the stubby revolver on a spot that looked to be directly between Bolan's eyes. Just as he seemed about to pull the trigger, the soldier detected movement behind the man. An instant later a steel pipe swung through the air and caught the Slave on his temple. Bolan heard the crunch of breaking bone and saw the man's eyes roll up in his head. He collapsed, revealing the bloody figure of the beating victim.

"We have to get out of here," the man said. "There's twenty or thirty more where these guys came from, and they'll be out here any minute." Bolan didn't need any more explanation than that and both men raced back to the Mustang. By the time the doors to the clubhouse opened and men started pouring out, Bolan had rowed through three of the Mustangs six gears and the speedometer needle had hit 100 mph. Someone from the club house managed to fire off a few shots at the fleeing Ford, but by that time Bolan was already three blocks away.

When they were out of sight of the clubhouse, Bolan asked his passenger, who appeared to be taking inventory of his injuries, "Are you hurt bad?"

"I think I have some broken ribs," he said, "but I'll live. You okay?"

Bolan rubbed his swelling jaw. "Nothing an ice pack won't take care of. What did you do to those guys to make them want to kill you?"

"It's not what I did," the man said. "It's what I am."

"What's that?" Bolan asked.

"A Hellion."

"What were you doing at the Slaves' clubhouse?"

"I wasn't there by my own choice," the man said. "They grabbed me at a bar in Anoka and brought me here."

"Were you wearing Hellion colors?" Bolan asked.

"No. I wasn't trying to commit suicide, if that's what you're asking. But they know who I am, and apparently they knew where to find me."

"Were they going to kill you?"

"I suspect that was their plan," the man said. "I appreciate your putting a stop it."

"Don't appreciate anything just yet," Bolan said. "I've got some questions for you, and if I don't like your answers, you might wish I'd never broken up your little tea party back there."

"You a cop?"

"Do I look like a cop?"

The man pondered the soldier's question a moment. "You just killed three Slaves, and the two we left breathing looked like they'll be sucking their meals through tubes for the rest of their lives. If you're a cop, you aren't like any of the cops I ever saw."

"If you don't tell me what I want to know," Bolan said, "you're going to wish I was a cop."

"Look, man, you saved my life and you just took out a bunch of Slaves. Even if you were a cop, you'd have my respect. I'll tell you anything you want to know. Where do you want me to start?"

"How about you start with your name?"

CHAPTER FIVE

After Bolan had tended to the wounds of the injured Hellion, whose name was Neal Trembley, though his biker name was Animal, and safely deposited him in a room in the same Bloomington motel where the soldier was staying, he called Kurtzman to see if they'd learned anything from the body they'd exhumed earlier in the day.

"What did our corpse have to tell us?" Bolan asked.

"It was not our boy Teddy Haynes," Kurtzman said, "but we already knew that. We're waiting for a conclusive DNA match, but it appears the body was the former president of the Minnesota chapter of the Hellions, a certain Bryan Trembley, though most people knew him by the name Dirt. The FBI has him listed as a fugitive. We're not one hundred percent sure that it's Trembley, but we're sure enough that I'd bet money the FBI can scratch Mr. Trembley from its most-wanted list."

"What was he wanted for?" Bolan asked.

"You name it. Human trafficking, for starters. Apparently, the Hellions were bringing in girls from Eastern Europe and forcing them into prostitution." Bolan said nothing. The soldier's own sister had been the victim of forced prostitution. It was a subject he took very seriously.

"It gets even more sordid," Kurtzman continued. "The Hellions apparently were running some sort of welfare scam using these girls. Not only were they profiting from the women as sexual slaves, but they were collecting government checks for them, too."

"Were any Hellions convicted of any of this?" Bolan asked.

"Yeah, five of the top guys. They almost beat the rap, though. They presented a pretty good case that they were set up by the Slaves, that the Slaves were really the ones running the prostitution ring. The trial was a genuine spectacle, but in the end the jury didn't have a lot of sympathy for a bunch of greasy, long-haired bikers."

"What's your take on it?" Bolan asked.

"You know as well as I do that damn near everyone who's ever gone to jail claims to be innocent, Striker, but you know better than anyone that the system can be gamed. The Slaves don't seem like the type of organization that would have the clout needed to manipulate the system to that degree, though."

"They could if they had the right people backing them," Bolan said.

"You mean like the type of people who could organize hundreds of random assassinations across the country with military precision?" Kurtzman asked.

"Yeah, I mean people like that."

"You think our bad guys are using the Slaves to help carry out their dirty deeds?"

"It looks that way, Bear. At least we have five less of them to worry about."

"I heard about that," Kurtzman said. "We picked up the chatter on the Minneapolis police radios. They were slow to respond to your afternoon soiree at the Slaves' clubhouse because they were responding to sniper attacks."

"How many were there?" Bolan asked.

"In the central time zone or in Minneapolis?"

"Both."

"There were sixty-nine in the central time zone, almost all of them cops. There were two in the Minneapolis metro area, one cop and one member of the Minnesota National Guard, an Iraq War veteran." Again the soldier was silent. "Anything else to report?" Kurtzman asked.

"Yeah, I need you to get me some information on another Hellion. He goes by the name Animal, but his real name is Neal Trembley. Probably a brother or cousin of our misidentified corpse."

Kurtzman didn't respond, but Bolan could hear him clacking away at his keyboard as he pulled up information. Finally, he said, "Brother. He was in the club, too. You have something on him?"

"I have him," Bolan said. "The Slaves I took out were in the process of beating him to death when I tried to scope out their clubhouse. What do you know about him?"

"He's a felon, but not for anything serious. He and some buddies stole a car. They took it for a joyride and then they brought it back, freshly waxed and with a full tank of gas. They even left a $50 bill on the dash. It's kind of funny, really, but the owner of the car didn't think so. Trembley was convicted of grand theft auto. He did six months in the state pen in Stillwater."

"Just six months?" Bolan asked.

"He got time off for good behavior. Worked his ass off in the prison laundry. The report says he was a model prisoner. He joined the Marines after he got out, served in the Corps for eight years and worked his way up to staff sergeant. When he got out he started a carpet-laying business with his brother. That was fifteen years ago, and except for a couple of speeding tickets, he's been spotless ever since."

"Are you serious?" Bolan asked. "How does a member of the Hellions get by without being busted for something?"

"It wasn't for lack of trying. Everyone from the Hennepin County Sheriff's office the NSA has had him staked out at one time or another. He got in a few fights over the years, but for a member of a motorcycle club, the guy's practically a Boy Scout."

"He never got caught up in the sting that brought his brother and the other Hellions down?"

"You know something, Striker?" Kurtzman asked. "The more I look into this, the odder that whole thing seems. This human trafficking business was a little out of character for the Minneapolis chapter of the Hellions. Don't get me wrong—these guys weren't the reincarnation of Mother Teresa or Gandhi or anything like that.

Members were involved in occasional small-scale drug busts every now and then, mostly for selling a little grass, but they were busted at about the same rate as any other group of blue-collar workers. Most of what I'm seeing here indicates the Hellions were a motorcycle club that really did focus on riding motorcycles. Or at least the Minneapolis chapter was."

"Was Neal involved in the investigation?"

"He was originally a target, but he came up clean. I'm telling you, Striker, there's something fishy about this whole thing. Look into it some more and let me know what you find out."

BOLAN THREADED THE SOUND suppressor onto the barrel of his Beretta 93-R and kicked open the door to Neal Trembley's room. He put the barrel to Trembley's head and said, "Tell me everything you know about the Hellions' involvement in human trafficking."

Trembley remained unfazed. "I would if I could, mister, but I don't know shit about it. I'd be willing to swear on our mother's grave that my brother didn't know shit about it, either, and I'm pretty damned sure the five guys they sent to Leavenworth didn't know any more about it than we did."

"Are you saying you were set up?"

"That's exactly what I'm saying," Trembley said.

"Tell me why I should believe you, Neal."

"I really don't give a shit if you believe me or not. If you're going to gun me down in cold blood, I guess I won't be any worse off than if the Slaves had killed me back at their clubhouse."

Bolan looked Trembley in the eye. If the biker was lying, he was one of the best liars Bolan had ever met, but gut instinct told the soldier that Trembley was telling the truth. He holstered the Beretta. "So tell me your side of the story."

"There's not much to tell," Trembley said. "My brother and I just wanted to ride with the club. The Hellions were our life, especially Bryan's. We ran our own business. We laid carpet, and made pretty good money up until the economy took a dive."

"So you decided to supplement your income with a prostitution ring?" Bolan asked.

"Hell, no," Trembley said. "We just sucked it up. Work slowed up, but we were still doing all right. We had low overhead. We lived together in the house we'd inherited from our parents, so our housing was paid for. Our bikes and other toys were all paid for. Once the economy turned sour we maybe only worked two days a month, but that just left us more time to ride motorcycles and go fishing. We still had enough money for gas, bait and beer."

"How about the other club members?"

"Some of them were hit pretty hard, especially the ones with families and mortgages."

"Any of them get involved in prostitution?"

"I don't believe they did," Trembley said. "Some of them were growing a little weed for extra money, but they were just growing a few plants in their basement.

I'm not talking about any kind of industrial grow operation. Mostly guys were just doing what they could to get by. A couple of members even dropped out of the club because they had to sell their motorcycles."

"So why are five of them rotting away in prison for running a prostitution ring?"

"That's a question that's been haunting me," Trembley said. "I know each of those men almost as well as I know my own brother. They were club officers. We elected them because they are solid men, people we could trust with the club's treasury, such as it was. I've known most of them since high school, and the last damned thing they were was pimps."

"Can you prove that, Neal?"

"No, but my brother thought he could. He was just about to go to the police with some information when he disappeared."

"What do you think happened to him?"

"I expect pretty much what would have happened to me if you hadn't come along."

"Do you know what your brother knew?" Bolan asked.

"In the broadest sense," Trembley said. "He said he had proof that the Slaves had set us up. What that proof was, I don't know. Dirt called me on his cell phone. He said it wasn't safe to talk, but we were supposed to meet at a bar in Wisconsin. He said he knew what the Slaves were up to, and said it was big. That was the last I ever heard from him. I went to the bar, but he never showed up."

"I'm afraid I have some bad news about your brother, Neal," Bolan said.

"You telling me he's dead?" Trembley asked. "Hell, I know that. If he was still alive, he'd have contacted me somehow."

"I think we found his body," Bolan said. "We're waiting for positive identification."

"Who's 'we'?"

"You know who the Slaves are?" Bolan asked.

"What kind of a dipshit question is that?" Trembley asked.

"All you need to know is that 'we' are on the other side, which would make us on your side, according to my calculations."

"Do you at least have a name or something I can call you?" Trembley asked.

"Call me Matt."

"That works for me. Could you do me one favor?"

"Depends," Bolan said.

"Call me Animal. I hate being called Neal."

"So, Animal, you feel well enough to get a little revenge on the Slaves?"

"Hell, yes. What have you got in mind?"

"We need to catch one so we can have a few words with him. We need someone pretty high up. Know anyone who fits that bill?"

"I'd like to get my hands on Pete Tressel, the chapter president, but no one's seen him in almost a month. If he's still in town, he's hunkered down at the clubhouse."

"You must know the layout of the clubhouse as well as anyone," Bolan said. "Is there any way in?"

"No normal way," Trembley said. "Going in through a door or a window would be suicide. But I know a way in, provided you don't have any problems with oversized rats."

"I'm not squeamish," Bolan said.

"There's a storm sewer that runs right under the property. It empties into the Mississippi. There's an old storage room underneath what used to be another garage building. Now it's just a concrete slab we used to park our Harleys on. There's a floor drain in the storeroom that empties straight into the storm drain. It's just barely big enough for a person to squeeze through."

"Is the storeroom attached to the main clubhouse?"

"There's a short tunnel that connects it to the basement, but we boarded it up because rats kept coming up through the drain and getting into the clubhouse. The thing is, there's a panel in the boards that snaps out. It's big enough for a person to get through. Dirt and me put that in there. We figured it might come in handy sometime."

"Do you think the Slaves know about that room?"

"No reason they would. Only Dirt and I knew that you could still get in there. And I'm damn certain Dirt didn't tell them about it, even if they tortured him."

"How can you be so certain?"

"How would they know to ask him?" Trembley said. "Besides, I'm sure they had more important things to talk about."

"Where would Tressel be located?" Bolan asked.

"Probably in the basement apartment. You going in there?"

"That's the plan," Bolan said.

"I'm coming with you."

"Can you handle a gun?"

"I'm a little rusty," Trembley said. "I lost my gun rights when I became a felon. I haven't handled a firearm since I was in the Corps, but yeah, I think I remember the basics—don't point it at anything you're not willing to destroy and keep your finger off the bang switch until it's time to shoot."

"Do you have any preference for weapons?"

"I'd take an M-4, given my druthers."

"That might be a bit cumbersome in a storm sewer," Bolan said. He reached into his war bag and pulled out a pair of FN P-90s. "Think you can handle one of these?"

"Hell, yeah," Trembley said. "I've always wanted to try one of those."

Bolan pulled a pouch filled with fifteen loaded P-90 box magazines from the war bag and divided them up. "You're not going in," Bolan said.

"The hell I'm not."

"I need you to watch my back. You're going to stay just outside the storm drain and cover me when I go in. I'll have enough to worry about with what's in front of me. I don't need any surprises coming up behind me. I'm giving you five magazines, I'm keeping ten. Now tell me what I can expect to find inside."

"Expect to find at least two dozen Slaves. Maybe three dozen. It seems like they've been fortifying their ranks since all this shit started. It looks like they've brought some talent in from out of town."

"What's the layout?" Bolan asked.

"Assuming you get into the clubhouse alive, you're going to find yourself in our recreation room. There'll be a stairway leading upstairs, and a hallway that leads to the apartment. The apartment has six bedrooms. We used it when we picked up some girls or we got too drunk to ride home. Sometimes a club member who'd fallen on hard times would live there. If you make it that far, you can be certain that Tressel will be well guarded."

"Anything else you can tell me?"

"There's a bathroom in the hall. Otherwise I think we've covered most of the bases in regard to the basement."

"Good. Now all we need is a boat to get to the storm drain."

"I've got just what you need," Trembley said.

BOLAN AND TREMBLEY UNLOADED Trembley's bass boat at the docks just south of Plymouth Avenue, about a mile south of the storm drain that ran under the Slaves' clubhouse. It was a gaudy boat, metallic red with sponsorship stickers all over it. It turned out that the Trembley brothers had been semiprofessional fishermen. When they weren't working or riding motorcycle, they were most likely competing in bass fishing tournaments. Gaudy or not, the boat had a 200 horsepower Yamaha outboard engine, making it an ideal getaway vessel.

Bolan wore a pair of dark green cotton cargo pants and a loose-fitting gray long-sleeved shirt made of fabric that provided protection from the sun's rays and also cover for his heavy load of weapons and the Kevlar vest he wore beneath his shirt. A big-brimmed hat made of similar material covered his head. In other words, he looked pretty much like everyone else who might be out on the river fishing under the warm afternoon sun. Trembley dressed much the same way.

The boat landing was on the east bank of the river, opposite the clubhouse. Trembley barely had time to rev the boat's engine before they'd crossed to the west bank and had to drop the throttle. Once on the west bank, Trembley engaged a silent electric trolling engine and slowly made his way north along the bank toward the storm drain. Both men cast spinner bait toward the shore, as would anyone fishing for smallmouth bass on the river. Bolan had a couple of bites in the five minutes it took them to silently glide toward the storm drain, and Trembley reeled in a football-size smallmouth.

Once they got to the storm drain, Trembley dropped anchor and switched rods to one rigged with a bobber and a marabou jig. He cut off a chunk of a leech and began fishing for crappies. Meanwhile, Bolan, after having made sure they weren't being watched, slipped into the six-foot-diameter pipe and made his way to the drain on the clubhouse property. He found the drain, which was connected to the main storm drain by a short length of pipe that was about two and a half feet in diameter, just barely wide enough for the soldier to squeeze his broad shoulders through.

Bolan grabbed the rim of the drain pipe, careful not to cut his hands on the rusty corrugated steel, and pulled himself up toward the grating that covered the top of the opening. The grating was lodged in place, but Bolan was able to loosen it without making too much noise. When he pulled himself up into the storeroom, rats scurried in all directions. He pulled out a small flashlight and found the tunnel leading to the basement of the main clubhouse. It wasn't much of a tunnel, extending three feet from the storeroom to the basement. The tunnel ended in a wood-framed wall. From what Trembley had told him, the soldier knew that the panel was virtually invisible on the basement side, but on the unfinished tunnel side he could clearly make out the outline of the removable panel thanks to the four metal prongs stuck into grommets that held it in place.

Bolan reached into a pouch on his belt and pulled a small round object that was connected to an earpiece by a thin wire. He held the round end up against the wood panel and listened through the earpiece. The device amplified sound, and he could hear someone moving around on the other side of the wall. He listened as the footsteps ascended a staircase, leaving the room in silence.

The soldier slowly pushed the panel until the metal prongs were out of the grommets and then just as carefully set the panel down inside the basement. He looked out into a recreation room, with a pool table, foosball table, dartboards and a pinball machine. A bar extended along one wall, and couches and comfortable-looking chairs were strewed around the room. A stairway extended toward the main floor of the two-story brick building.

Once inside the room, Bolan replaced the panel as carefully as he'd removed it. A hallway led away from the rec room, the soldier moved toward the apartment Trembley had told him about. He figured he'd be a lot more likely to find Tressel hiding somewhere down there than upstairs, where all he'd most likely find would be twenty or thirty heavily armed sociopaths hell-bent on killing him. A doorway in the side of the hallway opened into a bathroom, and at the far end Bolan saw a large door beneath which a thin ray of light seeped out into the darkness of the basement. He held the listening device to the door and heard voices on the other side.

"We got to get Pete a piece of ass," one of the voices said. "He's going crazy down here."

"Well, get him one, you idiot," the other voice said. "It's not safe for him to go out and find one himself, not until we kill every last one of those Hellions. As long as one of them is still breathing, Pete's got to stay put. And you know what they'll do to us if something happens to Pete."

"Don't go talking about that," the first man said. "I don't even want to think about what those crazy bastards are capable of doing. I've seen enough already, and they're just getting started."

"You know we got to do what we got to do," the second man said. "If this is what it takes to take our country back from the blacks and the Jews, then it's what we got to do. You can't go getting soft on us now."

"I think some of them are Jews," the first man said.

"You shut your mouth. Anyone hears you say that, you're a dead man. Anyway, it don't matter none. They're paying us good money." The two men quit talking just when Bolan was beginning to find their conversation interesting. He listened for a while longer and heard a door open and another man walk into the room.

"Will one of you retards go and get me another case of beer?" he asked.

"Sure thing, Pete. And we're working on getting you a piece of ass, too."

"About damned time," Pete said. "I've been beating my dick like it owed me money. I swear, I'm so goddamned sick of being stuck down here, I'm about to kill myself. If I have to watch another damned episode of *Ice Road Truckers,* my goddamned head is going to explode. 'Oh, look, they're going out on the goddamned ice again…' Motherfuckers should live in Minnesota. We drive on the fucking ice every damned day in the winter."

"Amos says this whole thing is almost over," the first man said.

"The day I take his word for anything is the day I start riding a goddamned Suzuki," Pete said. "Now get me some fucking beer and shut your fucking mouth about what Amos said. And don't forget about the piece of ass. Don't you dare send Annie down here. Last time I banged that sloppy bitch, I got the fucking clap."

Bolan heard one of the men walking toward the door, and he ducked into the bathroom, keeping the door open a crack so he could see when the man went past his position. A lumbering blond with his bare torso nearly covered in tattoos made his way past the bathroom door. When he'd just moved past the opening, Bolan opened the door, grabbed the man around the head, covering his mouth, and pulled him back into the bathroom. As soon as he had all six-feet and five-inches of the big biker's frame into the small bathroom, he sliced the man's throat from ear to ear with his bowie knife. He gave the man's nearly severed head a twist as he spun the dying carcass toward the porcelain toilet at the opposite end of the room. By the time the corpse landed at the base of the fixture, the geyser of blood erupting from its neck had sprayed every surface on that half of the room.

Bolan searched the body, finding a wallet and a key ring, then rinsed as much of the blood as he could off of his hands, arms and face, and went back into the hall. He unholstered his silenced Beretta and tried the doorknob. The door was locked. He selected what looked like a house key from the key ring he'd pulled off the corpse and tried it in the door. The key worked the tumblers and this time the door handle turned under his hand. He carefully stepped into the lit room.

The soldier crept into the living room of the apartment Trembley had described. A big biker who bore a striking resemblance to the one Bolan had just killed sat reading the latest issue of *Skin* magazine. He didn't look up from his magazine when he asked, "You forget something?" When Bolan didn't answer, the biker looked up to see the sound-suppressed muzzle of the Beretta pointed straight at his forehead. Before he could let out a yelp, Bolan squeezed the trigger. The gun made a muffled chugging sound that wasn't quite as loud as the sound of the biker's brains splashing against the wall.

"What the hell's going on out there?" came a voice from one of the rooms at the rear of the apartment. "You spilling my beer?" The voice was getting closer as it spoke. Bolan stepped to one side of the hallway that led to the rear of the apartment and watched as Pete Tressel walked into the room. He saw the gory mess that had recently been one of his fellow club members leaning against the wall in a big pool of brains and blood and said, "What the fu—" Before he could finish mouthing his expletive, the soldier brought the butt of his Beretta crashing against the back of the man's head and laid him out cold.

Pulling a roll of duct tape from another pouch on his belt, Bolan bound and gagged the man in a matter of seconds. He heaved Tressel, who was quite a bit smaller than the other two bikers, over his shoulder and trotted for the entrance into the storeroom. He removed the panel in the wooden wall and was putting Tressel down inside the tunnel when he heard feet coming down the steps. He dropped the biker onto the concrete floor and spun, drawing both his Beretta and his Desert Eagle in the process. When the first man descending the steps saw Bolan, he raised a pistol, but before he could get a shot off, the Beretta chugged twice and the man fell down the steps, dead.

Behind him, at least five or six other bikers rushed toward the Executioner. Flicking the Beretta's selector switch to full-auto, Bolan sprayed the men with the ammunition remaining in the magazine. Two of the men fell, but the others kept coming, and behind them it looked like at least a dozen more men were joining in. Bolan emptied the magazine of the .50-caliber Desert Eagle in his left hand at the men, but his left hand was his weak hand and he missed as many men as he hit. Still, he'd taken down four more Slaves and bought himself enough time to bring the FN P-90 into play. Bolan sprayed the men with a dozen high-velocity 5.7 mm rounds. Several more men went down, and those who remained standing ducked for cover. This gave Bolan enough time to roll into the storeroom and pull Tressel from the line of fire.

By this time the men upstairs had regrouped and were charging down the steps. Bolan pulled the pin on an M-67 fragmentation grenade, lobbed it into the room and ducked behind the wall for cover. The explosion blew the wall covering the short tunnel to pieces. The various body parts mixed with the remains of the wooden wall told Bolan that the grenade had been effective, but he also knew he had only moments to make his escape, before the bikers responded with heavy artillery of their own. He lowered Tressel into the drain—the wiry little man fit through the hole much more easily than Bolan did—and was going down himself when another group of Slaves started firing into the tunnel. Bolan dropped down, grabbed his cargo and ran as fast as he could for the river.

He'd almost reached to the boat when he heard the sound of footsteps echoing through the storm drain. He reached the opening, heaved Tressel down into the bass boat, then turned and fired. Two men running toward him dropped, but he heard more footsteps coming. Bolan jumped into the boat, which Trembley had already started, and heaved another M-67 grenade as far down the drain as he could throw. "Go!" he shouted at Trembley.

The biker didn't need to be told twice. He slammed the throttle wide-open, and the overpowered bass boat shot off across the water like a rocket. They were about thirty yards from the storm drain when the grenade went off, shooting flames, shrapnel and bloodied body parts out over the river.

Just when Bolan thought they were going to get away, they heard the sound of personal watercraft engines firing up. A small dock extended out from the clubhouse property. Bolan hadn't noticed any boats moored at the dock, but the Slaves had to have had a few Jet Ski-type vehicles sitting on shore. Bolan saw four such personal watercraft leaving the dock and heading their way. He reloaded his P-90 and waited for them to get within shooting range.

"What should I do?" Trembley asked.

"Don't go straight for the dock," Bolan said. "We need to lose these guys before we head to shore. You think you can manage that?"

"No problem. Just hang on." Trembley pointed at Tressel's unconscious form and said, "Make sure we don't lose him."

By this time the fast little personal watercraft were closing in on Trembley's bass boat. His boat was fast, but nothing like the little watercraft. When the lead watercraft was in range, Bolan fired a short burst from the P-90 and the rider flew off the back of the vehicle. The other watercraft broke formation. "Hang on!" Trembley yelled as they passed under a railroad bridge at top speed, heading straight for the V-shaped dam that stretched across the river just south of Nicollet Island. Just before they got to the dam, Trembley cranked the wheel of the boat and did a high-speed one-eighty, then slammed the throttle wide-open. He headed straight for the three remaining personal watercraft, causing the pilots to scatter once again. Two of them were able to regain control of their vehicles, but a third was going too fast and was unable to stop before flying over the dam. The dam was a two-stage affair; the current between the first and second stage was so powerful and turbulent that no one could survive in it.

By the time the other two had regrouped and caught up to the speeding bass boat, Trembley was under the railroad bridge north of Hennepin Avenue. When he passed under the bridge, he cut a sharp right around the wooden pilings below the lift section of the bridge, then went back under the bridge, through the main channel used by barges.

When they were under the bridge, Bolan shouted, "Kill it."

Trembley dropped the throttle and the boat stopped. The soldier lined up his sights and as soon as the first little watercraft appeared around the piling, Bolan put a bullet through the pilot's head. Then he did the same with the pilot of the second water vehicle.

"What now?" Trembley asked.

Bolan could already hear sirens in the distance. "Now we get the hell out of here before the cops come."

The two men left the boat at the docks south of Plymouth Avenue. They also left Trembley's truck and boat trailer parked at the adjacent Boom Island Park. By this time Tressel was starting to wake up. Rather than clubbing him again and risking doing serious damage to whatever was left of the Slaves' leader's brain, the soldier used a sleeper hold to put him down again. They tossed him in the trunk of the Mustang and took him to an abandoned north Minneapolis garage owned by Trembley's uncle. Before they removed the prisoner from the trunk of the Mustang, Bolan took his war bag, a cooler, a camp stove and a few other supplies into the garage.

"What's that for?" Trembley asked.

"It's tools to get our boy Tressel to talk."

"You're going to torture him?" Trembley appeared to be concerned about the Executioner's methods for interrogation.

"No, well, not really." Bolan's answer didn't appear to alleviate Trembley's concerns.

"So what exactly are you going to do?"

"It's a little trick I learned from a movie."

CHAPTER SIX

By the time Tressel regained consciousness, he was hanging from the rafters of the abandoned garage. A shackle held each of his wrists, connected by a chain that ran over one of the rafter beams. A large man held a stainless-steel pancake flipper over the flame of a Coleman camp stove until it glowed red hot. The man had the coldest blue eyes that Tressel had ever seen. When the biker thought about what the tall man intended to do with the pancake flipper, be became so afraid that he lost control of his bladder and a stream of urine ran down his leg.

"You're pissing yourself already?" Bolan asked. "I haven't even gotten started on you."

Tressel looked away from the big man and saw other instruments of torture lined up on a workbench. He saw a large ice pick, some cutting shears and a blow torch among other things. Then he saw Neal Trembley standing in the shadows. "Fuck me," he said to himself.

Bolan walked up to the man and punched him in the stomach, swinging him around so that he faced away from the soldier. The punch had been designed to deliver maximum pain while inflicting no serious damage. Bolan hated to use brute force against an incapacitated opponent, but this relatively harmless punch would psychologically prepare Tressel to believe the charade the soldier was about to perpetuate. He hadn't let Trembley in on the charade because its effectiveness depended in part on Trembley's disgusted reaction.

With Tressel facing away from him and unable to see what he was doing, Bolan pulled a pack of dry ice from the cooler, along with a fresh steak. With one hand he put the dry ice on the small of Tressel's back while at the same time he held the piece of steak up near the dry ice and pressed the red hot pancake flipper onto it, searing the meat and producing the smell of burned flesh. Tressel screamed as though he'd been burned, which, in his mind, is exactly what happened.

"Who are you?" Tressel shrieked. "Are you a cop?"

"You ever meet a cop who would do this to someone?" Bolan asked, once again pressing the dry ice into Tressel's back and searing the steak with the superheated pancake flipper.

"Why are you doing this?" he asked.

"Fun, mostly," Bolan said. "I'm a busy man. I have to take my entertainment where I can find it. But I do plan to ask you a few questions, eventually. If you live that long." He lit the blow torch and touched it to the steak at the same time he reapplied the dry ice pack to Tressel's skin. The steak started to smoke, producing a sickening smell. "I hope you didn't pay too much for these tattoos. They're garbage. I'm doing you a favor by burning them off."

"For the love of God, please stop!" Tressel screamed.

"Stop? I've barely started." Bolan picked up a pair of ice tongs. "Do you want me to try to peel off what's left of your club tattoo as a souvenir?" He poked at the frost-bitten skin that had been beneath the icepack and Tressel's screaming started anew.

"That's not helping," Bolan told him, looking at the bloody-but-razor-sharp blade of his bowie knife. "You scream like a little bitch, I might just have to perform a little impromptu surgery to make you a real bitch." Bolan walked around in front of Tressel and cut off the button on his blue jeans. With the tip of his knife, Bolan began slicing the urine-soaked jeans off Tressel, nicking the biker's skin now and then for effect, but taking extra care not to seriously cut him.

The wet jeans fell away, leaving Tressel wearing just his underwear. "Briefs," Bolan said. "I would have pegged you for a boxer man." Bolan inserted the knife into the leg of the underwear, just millimeters from Tressel's genitals, and in one motion sliced through the fabric, leaving the Slaves leader completely naked. "It looks like your balls are trying to crawl up inside your cavity," Bolan said. "This might take a little longer than I expected."

The entire time, Tressel had been shrieking and begging. Now he said, "Please, don't. I'll tell you whatever you want to know."

"Who's Amos?"

"Please," Tressel pleaded, "anything but that."

"That information is the only thing that's going to stop me from turning you into a castrato," Bolan said.

"Castration looks pretty good, compared to what he'll do to me if I talk."

"Suit yourself," Bolan said and ran the tip of the bowie knife across the wiry little biker's testicle.

This was too much for Tressel and he snapped. "Okay. I'll tell you everything I know about Amos. It ain't much."

"Start talking."

"Okay. First off, he's a Jew. I don't mean a Jew like your garden-variety New York Hebe. I mean he's a real Jew, you know, from Israel."

"Does he have a last name?" Bolan asked.

"Probably, but I don't know it."

"How'd you hook up with him?"

"He found us. Well, he found the Texas chapter of the club. That's the original charter chapter, where the club was founded. Mel Schmidt, the president of the Texas chapter, he's the one who put Amos in contact with us."

"What did Amos want from you?"

"Not much. Mostly he wanted us to drop off a body in Wisconsin."

"You mean Bryan Trembley?"

"Yeah."

"He also wanted you to kill Trembley?"

"Yeah, but he didn't have to twist our arm on that one."

"What did Amos offer you in return?"

"Money. Lots of money. And territory. He promised

that he'd get rid of the Hellions and help us take over Minneapolis."

"When did you first start working with Amos?"

"Almost three years ago. This whole thing took a long time to put together."

"What else did Amos tell you?"

"Not much," Tressel said. "He wasn't the talkative type. He said he'd get rid of the Hellions. He kept his word so we kept ours."

"Do you know anything else about this Amos character?"

"I don't know this for a fact, but I heard he's got a bunch of black guys working for him."

"What do you mean?" the soldier asked.

"I mean I heard he hired a bunch of blacks. You know, gangbangers."

"What for?"

"How the hell should I know? You asked me what I know about this guy, and I'm telling you."

"I'm not sure what you've given me is enough for me to allow you to keep your testicles intact. Did you ever meet any of his associates or overhear any conversation he might have had?"

"I swear, I've told you everything I know. I only met the dude in person three times, and then only for a few minutes at a time."

"And there's nothing unusual that you remember about him? Did he ever take a phone call while you were meeting with him?"

Tressel thought about it a bit. "Yeah, once he got a call. I didn't overhear much of it, though."

"Did you hear the name of the caller?"

"Sort of, but not really. It sounded like some kind of Jew name, the kind where it sounds like you're clearing phlegm from your throat when you say it."

"Do you remember anything about the conversation?"

"I do remember him saying one strange Jew word. He said something about 'the Irgun.'"

For a second Bolan thought he'd misheard Tressel. Bolan hadn't heard the name "Irgun" for years. Short for Ha'Irgun HaTzva'i HaLe'umi BeEretz Yisra'el, which was Hebrew for National Military Organization of the Land of Israel, the Irgun had either been a paramilitary freedom-fighting organization or a group of terrorists, depending on one's point of view. The Irgun had been instrumental in the creation of the modern nation-state of Israel, but they had accomplished this through the same brutal methods that Islamic terrorists now employed against Israel, including bombing hotels and slaughtering entire villages of Palestinians, including women and children.

The reason the Irgun were no longer heard from was because they'd been absorbed into the legitimate Israeli Defense Forces at the start of the 1948 Arab-Israeli war. The Irgun eventually evolved into the Herut party, which was the predecessor to the modern Likud party. Though Israel officially declared the Irgun a terrorist organization after achieving nation status, membership in the organization held no stigma for former Irgun fighters. In fact, many former Irgun leaders went on to be national leaders in Israel. With such legitimate clout there was little incentive to maintain a violent terroristic organization like the Irgun. Bolan could only think of a few reasons why anyone would resurrect the organization, none of them good.

"Are you certain Amos used the word *Irgun?*" Bolan asked.

"I probably heard the son of a bitch say maybe fifty words total. Like I said, he didn't talk a whole lot. But I'm damn sure I heard him say *Irgun* over the phone once. I thought he was talking about some kind of fancy-ass Jew gun."

Bolan was about to prod Tressel for more information when automatic gunfire erupted, punching holes through the clapboard walls of the garage. Bolan and Trembley both took cover, Trembley behind an old tow-truck parked in one corner of the building and Bolan behind a steel tank. Tressel wasn't so lucky—bullets hit him from every direction, spinning him around on his chain like some kind of crazy marionette.

BOLAN ESTIMATED THE LOCATION of the shooters based on the angle between the holes that were appearing in the clapboard walls and the shots that were hitting Tressel's now lifeless body. He returned fire with the P-90, spraying half a magazine through the wall just about where he estimated the shooters were located. His Hail Mary shots had to have had some effect, because the volley of gunfire coming into the building stopped.

No sooner had the shooting stopped than a black Cadillac Escalade burst through the overhead garage door. The door was old, its wood rotting away, and it presented the big SUV with very little resistance.

Bolan and Trembley opened up on the Cadillac, taking out both the driver and the front-seat passenger before either had a chance to return fire, but the two men in the backseat were able to get shots off at the soldier and his partner. Bolan ducked out of the way, but Trembley took several rounds in the chest, knocking him on his back.

The Executioner put a short burst into the man who'd shot Trembley, then ducked as the other shooter once again returned fire. Trembley rolled over and put a short burst through the head of the last shooter in the vehicle.

"Are you okay?" Bolan asked Trembley.

"The body armor did its job," Trembley said, "but getting shot didn't do my broken ribs any favors. You okay?"

Before Bolan could answer another wave of gunfire erupted from outside the door. The soldier triggered a burst through the collapsed door, but ran out of ammunition.

"Fire at them while I reload," he told Trembley, who had just reloaded his P-90. The biker triggered short bursts and the soldier joined him as soon as he had a fresh stick magazine snapped in place atop the P-90. "How's your ammo holding out?" Bolan asked.

"I've got two full sticks left. You?"

"The same. The way they're coming at us, that won't last us five minutes." The soldier could see his war bag lying beneath the table holding his supposed instruments of torture. "Cover me," he yelled. Trembley fired off a burst from his P-90 and Bolan lunged across the room, grabbed the bag and rolled under the old wrecker for cover, bullets chasing him the entire way.

From his point of view under the wrecker Bolan could see his assailants' position; they were firing from behind an Escalade that was a virtual twin to the one that had burst through the door, right down to the chrome twenty-one-inch rims. Bolan pulled an M-203 grenade launcher from the bag. The launcher was designed to be mounted under the barrel of a rifle, specifically the M4, but John "Cowboy" Kissinger, the in-house weapons expert at Stony Man Farm, had modified this one with a pistol grip so it could be used on its own. Using the SUV that had crashed through the door as cover, Bolan crept forward until he was behind the Cadillac.

"Fire another burst," Bolan commanded, and Trembley sprayed a burst of bullets out the door. While he fired, the Executioner rolled out from behind the Escalade and fired a high-explosive grenade at the SUV outside, then rolled back. Judging by the strength of the explosion, followed by a secondary blast—probably the sound of the SUV's gas tank exploding—he'd scored a direct hit. The soldier crept around the Escalade and peered through the wreckage of the garage door. Bodies lay scattered around the burning vehicle, along with assorted body parts. Most of the bodies had been torn to pieces, but a couple were still partially intact, and judging from the screams, at least one of them numbered among the living.

Bolan ran toward the man screaming on the ground, making sure that no one else was still capable of attacking. One of the attackers who'd been lying on the ground rolled over and tried to aim his pistol at the soldier. His hand was too damaged to hold the gun and he dropped it, but not before Bolan's had instinctually put a round through the man's head. The soldier noticed that each of the shooters had worn some sort of red item of clothing—sweatshirt, baseball cap, bandana. They were members of the Bloods street gang.

The screamer was in a bad way. Both his legs had been blown off. He'd soon bleed out, but Bolan hoped to get some answers from him before he died. He grabbed the dying man by the hair and lifted his head so that he could look the man in the eye. "Who sent you here?" he asked.

"Omar. Omar sent us."

"Why?"

"He said we had to kill you white boys holed up in a garage."

"How'd he know we were here?"

"How does Omar know anything? He just knows, that's all." The man's eyes started to glaze over and he lost consciousness.

Bolan ran back to the garage, grabbed his war bag

and said, "Come on! Let's get out of here before the cops come."

"Do you realize that's the second time you've said that today?" Trembley asked as they jumped into the Mustang. "Is this something you do on a regular basis?"

"It's a situation that sometimes comes up in my line of work."

"That's some line of work you've got. What is it you do again?"

"Pretty much this."

"You ever heard of a guy named Omar?" Bolan asked Trembley as they sped away from the urban battlefield.

"I know of a couple Omars, but since those assholes who just attacked us were Bloods, my guess is that you mean Black Omar. I don't know him, but I know who he is—the head of the Rollin' 30s Bloods. They own north Minneapolis. I don't consider myself any more or less racist than the next guy, but I really, really hate these assholes. I'm telling you, these guys are some serious pieces of shit, and Omar's the biggest piece of shit in the shit pile. They initiate fourteen-year-olds by having them kill someone for the club. Last year a fourteen-year-old and two sixteen-year-olds were sentenced to life in prison because the sixteen-year-olds had forced the fourteen-year-old to beat a seventeen-year-old kid to death with a shovel as part of the younger kid's initiation into the club. That's how they initiate members. They call it a jump in. Omar was the guy who came up with this system. I don't know the guy personally, but I've seen him around."

"Do you know where we can find him?"

"No. You probably figured out that the Hellions weren't real tight with the Rollin' 30s. About the only interaction we had with them was when we beat a bunch of their asses after they pulled some shit near our clubhouse. All I can tell you is where they hang out. I have no idea whether or not Omar is there."

BOLAN AND TREMBLEY ROLLED past the Bald Kitty Klub, the north Minneapolis strip joint where Trembley had said they'd find the Rollin' 30s Bloods hanging out. Judging from all the red being worn by the people milling around the parking lot, it looked like they'd come to the right place. "This whole thing is crazy," Trembley said. "We've got some shadowy Israeli working with Rollin' 30s Bloods and Satan's Slaves. I can't imagine a situation where the Slaves and the Bloods would be working on the same side. I never knew anyone who hated black people more than the Slaves. Look, I'm no hypocrite. Me and my brother never had any problem with black folks, at least any more problem than we ever had with white folks, and I know that some of our club brothers weren't as understanding, but they weren't even in the same class as the Slaves. We might not have been card-carrying members of the NAACP, but compared to the Slaves we were regular Martin Luther Kings. The Slaves make the Ku Klux Klan look racially tolerant."

"I've been wondering about that myself," Bolan said.

"Another thing I can't see is the Slaves working with an Israeli. I'm telling you, the Slaves are seriously into that white power crap. I think they consider themselves more of a Christian militia than a motorcycle club."

Bolan thought about Trembley's comments. He'd been thinking much the same thing himself, but he said nothing. This whole thing was tied in with the sniper attacks somehow. The soldier had no idea what was going down, but he knew it was big. For something this big to happen right under the noses of every security organization on Earth required a conspiracy at such a high level that the soldier didn't know who to trust. It was time to talk to someone he knew he could trust: Aaron Kurtzman. He dialed the computer expert's secure line, wondering just how secure it might really be.

"Give me some good news, Striker," Kurtzman said by way of a greeting. "You're turning Minneapolis into a war zone. Please tell me that all this mayhem is getting us closer to catching the snipers."

"We're getting incrementally closer, Bear," Bolan said. "I need you to get me any information you can on an Israeli who's operating in this area, guy named Amos."

"Amos what?"

"Amos is all I've got. The only other thing I can tell you is that he's somehow linked to the Irgun."

"Very funny, Striker. The Irgun has been defunct for over half a century."

"I know, but it seems this Amos character has resurrected the name."

"That doesn't sound good."

"It's a whole pile of not good, Bear. This guy's a

smooth operator. Not only did he have the Slaves on his payroll, he's got the Rollin' 30s Bloods working for him."

"You're talking about the Slaves in the past tense," Kurtzman said.

"I wouldn't write them off completely, but their leader, Pete Tressel, is no longer among the living. Cut off the head, the body's probably not going to be very effective. Speaking of the Slaves, I need you to bring in one Mel Schmidt. He's the president of the Texas chapter of the club. He's the one who hooked up the Minneapolis chapter with this Amos."

Kurtzman paused while he typed on his keyboard. "Got a squad car headed to his house right now. I'll let you know the instant we have him."

"You might want to send in a specialized squad," Bolan said. "He might have a false tooth like our charred friends in Maryland. In the meantime, I need you to send the blueprints for the Bald Kitty Klub, a strip club on Broadway in north Minneapolis. Include any construction permits filed with the city."

Kurtzman typed loudly on his keyboards and said, "Check your in-box. They should be there."

"Thanks, Bear. You got any other news for me?"

"I was hoping you'd ask," Kurtzman said. "The LAPD thinks they might have a lead on one of the shooters."

"You've got my interest," Bolan said.

"An off-duty cop was eating lunch in a restaurant on the tenth floor of the Thompson building on Wilshire Boulevard. He was looking down at the top of a parking ramp and saw someone fire a shot from inside the vehicle. The shooter took out a cop. It was a white SUV that looked like it had been modified like the vehicle you chased. The cop called it in and they followed the vehicle with a helicopter to a salvage yard in Long Beach. They've had the place staked out all day. No one has gone in or come out. They're going to raid it any minute."

"Keep me posted. If they get anyone, I want to interrogate him. Same goes for Mel Schmidt. Let me know the second you have him in custody."

"There's one more thing you need to know," Kurtzman said. "I've been watching you on the Minneapolis PD's CCTV system. You're being followed."

"You mean the black Lincoln?"

"Yeah," Kurtzman said.

"I've had my eye on her for a while now."

"Her?"

"Yeah, her. She's been following us since we left the garage."

"She's been following you since you got out of the boat this afternoon," Kurtzman said.

"Then she's good. Sounds like a professional."

"You'd better lose her anyway."

Bolan didn't respond. Instead he shifted down two gears and took off down Broadway. He watched as the black Lincoln LS tried to keep pace, but the Mustang was much more powerful than the older vehicle and after a few hard corners Bolan had shaken his tail. "She's history," he told Kurtzman.

"Watch your back, Striker."

"Will do."

"Who was that?" Trembley asked. "Your boss?"

"A friend. I don't have a boss."

"Bullshit," Trembley said. "If you're not working for anyone, what are you doing out here? And where did you get all the cool toys?"

"You've seen the way I work," Bolan said. "Would you want to be my boss and be responsible for what I do in the field?"

"Fair enough. I guess I'm just glad you're on my side."

Bolan made a second pass by the strip club. "There's no way two white boys like us are going to just waltz into that joint," Trembley said. "How are we getting in?"

"We're not. I'm going in alone. I need you to wait out in the car and be ready to get out of here in a hurry."

"I know the drill," Trembley said. "Before the cops come."

BOLAN CIRCLED AROUND THE BLOCK a couple of times to confirm the layout that Kurtzman had sent him was more or less correct. The only two ground-level entrances of the two-story building would be heavily guarded; the soldier needed to find another way in. His best chance appeared to be a second-story balcony that opened into a hallway that ran through the upstairs office area, but climbing up to the balcony would be out of the question since it was in plain view of the parking lot, which was a beehive of activity. Dozens of people milled around the lot, smoking grass, selling dope, turning tricks or just plain loitering.

Instead, Bolan intended to drop down to the balcony from the roof of the building. He parked the Mustang just outside the unlit alley that ran behind the Bald Kitty Klub and had Trembley get in the driver's seat. Then he pulled his blacksuit from the trunk and changed into his work clothes. He loaded the gear he thought he'd need into pouches on his utility belt, made sure he had a full load of ammo for both his Beretta and his Desert Eagle, then crept through the shadows toward the back of the strip club.

When Bolan got close to the rear of the building he heard voices in the shadows.

"On your knees," a man's voice said.

"I will, baby," a woman replied, "but first give me a hit off that pipe."

"Shut the fuck up and get busy," the man said. Bolan heard the sound of a cigarette lighter igniting and saw a flame flare up in front of a man's face. A whitish chunk of material in a glass pipe began to smoke, and the man held the pipe up to his mouth and breathed in the smoke. When Bolan's eyes adjusted to the new light source, he made out the outline of a woman kneeling in front of him.

"Please, baby, I'll do you real good," the woman said. "Just give me a hit off that pipe."

The man pulled a pistol from his back pocket and placed the barrel of the gun against the top of the woman's head. "Hit that dick or I'll blow your head off."

This was all Bolan needed to see. He aimed at the man's forehead and pulled the trigger of his sound-suppressed Beretta. The pistol chugged once and a small hole appeared in the man's forehead. A much larger hole appeared in the back of his head, and brains and blood sprayed against the brick wall the man leaned against. The woman looked up and said, "Please don't shoot me."

"Go," Bolan said. "You start running and if you turn around in the next ten blocks, I'll do to you what I did to him." The woman took off running, but not before she stooped to retrieve the crack pipe from the bloody corpse. Once she got moving, she ran remarkably fast for a woman wearing six-inch spiked heels.

When she was gone Bolan removed a small grapple hook connected to a length of rope and swung it up to the roof. When he was sure the hook was secure, he scaled the wall. He walked as softly as he possibly could across the roof, not wanting to alert anyone on the second floor to his presence, and looked over the edge of the roof to see if the balcony was clear.

It wasn't. A man with a red do-rag leaned on the balcony railing, smoking a joint. Bolan could see a handgun bulging from the rear waistband of the gangbanger's low-slung pants. The soldier untied the cord from the grapple hook and fashioned a slipknot at one end. He lowered the noose until it dangled just inches above the man's head and gave it a spin, opening up the slipknot. The man looked up to see what was making the sound above his head. Bolan dropped the noose around the man's neck and jerked him up. The man clawed at the rope choking off his air supply and kicked wildly on his way up, but by the time Bolan pulled him over the roof he was unconscious. The Executioner held the cord tight until he was certain the man had stopped breathing. When the man was no longer a threat, lowered himself down to the balcony.

Bolan peeked around the edge of the doorway that led into the hallway and saw the coast was clear. He crept inside and stopped in front of the door that, according to the plans Kurtzman had sent, opened into the main office. The hallway and office area were secured from the rest of the building with a reinforced door and soundproofed walls. Bolan guessed there were more guards on the outside of the reinforced door but the man he had just taken out appeared to have been the only guard on this side door. He placed his listening device against the door of the main office and heard voices inside.

"Man, this is bad, Omar," one man said. "The only bodies they found at the garage was our boys. Whoever these white boys are, they're some bad motherfuckers. We ain't up against no normal rednecks here. It ain't like we fighting the Slaves, or even the Hellions. This is some badass shit."

"You saying we tell the Jew we failed?" another man said. Bolan figured it had to be Omar. "You want to tell him yourself, Sharod? Because I sure as hell ain't going to be the one to tell him. We need to send some more of our guys out to take care of those two white boys."

"Who?" Sharod asked. "Who we going to send? Those two white boys already killed fifteen of our best men."

Make that seventeen, Bolan thought.

"If they couldn't bust caps up the asses of a couple of white boys, they wasn't our best men," Omar said.

"I'm telling you, Omar, these ain't no ordinary white boys."

"Don't matter none," Omar said. "We don't follow through on his orders, the Jew's going to kill us both. You know that."

"At least we killed that biker trash Tressel," Sharod said. "He's the one the Jew really wanted dead."

"He said he wanted all three of them dead. I dropped outta school in the seventh grade, but I got enough math to know that thirty percent ain't no great average. What are we going to do? The Jew's going to kill us both."

Bolan kicked down the door and went in with both his guns drawn, one pointing at each man in the room.

"Get him, Sharod," Omar shouted, but Bolan squeezed the trigger of his Beretta and Sharod fell to the floor, half his face obliterated.

"I don't think Sharod's going to be much help," Bolan told Omar.

"What do you want?" Omar shouted. "You want money? I got more money than you can spend."

"You can keep your money," Bolan said. "I only want some information. Who's the Jew?"

"Fuck, man, you might as well shoot me now, because I say one word about that shit, I'm deader than dead."

"I swear," Bolan said, "you help me get the Jew, I'll make sure you're safe."

"No way, man," Omar said. "Ain't no place on Earth that the Jew won't find me. I've seen the kind of artillery you brought to the party. You connected, no doubt, but you ain't connected like the Jew's connected."

"You might be surprised."

Omar looked at Bolan. "I suppose I ain't got no options. The Jew's going to find out you come and see me. I'm dead already."

"So tell me, who is the Jew?"

"His name is Amos."

"I knew that already. You're going to have to do better than that. Do you have his full name?"

"No, but I know something I bet your people don't know."

"And that is…?"

"He's working with the U.S. military. He's got boys in the Pentagon."

"How do you know this?"

"The Jew likes dark meat, if you know what I mean. He's been banging one of my girls. She overheard him talking on the phone. She's a smart girl. She figured out he was talking to some high-up military dude. When he went to sleep, she got the number off his cell phone. I got some people work for Verizon, had them track the number. It belonged to a goddamned Air Force general."

"Did you get his name?"

"Yeah, it was Joe Clement."

Joe Clement was the commander of Bolling Air Force

Base in Washington, D.C., the home base of Air Force
One. Clement also represented the Air Force in the Joint
Chiefs of Staff. This was big stuff. As much as Bolan
hated to help out an animal like Omar, he'd given the
man his word. "We've got to get you to someplace safe,"
he told the gangbanger.

"I hope like hell there is such a place," Omar said.

"Let's go out the back," Bolan said. "I have a car waiting." Omar led the way to the secure door opening to
the stairway down into the club. He opened the door to
reveal two heavyset guards sitting on overstuffed chairs
placed one on each side of the door. One of them was
enjoying a lap dance from a particularly lovely black-
haired stripper. She was white, but dark-skinned. Bolan
thought she looked vaguely familiar. When the guards
saw Omar come through the door, they jumped up,
knocking the petite woman to the floor.

"We sorry, Omar. We was paying attention, we
promise, but this little bitch was just working that tight
ass."

Omar looked at the men. "Don't let it happen again.
Now Sharod is taking care of some important business.
Don't let no one, and I mean no one, go back there. Got
me?"

"We got you, Omar."

Bolan followed Omar down the stairs. The stripper
followed the pair down. "Tell your girl to shove off,"
Bolan said to Omar.

"She ain't mine," Omar said. "I never seen the bitch
before."

Bolan looked back at the woman, but she'd disap-

peared into the crowd. The soldier scanned the crowd,
but before he could spot her they'd reached the back
door. Omar opened the door and Bolan heard the muffled crack of a rifle report. Omar fell to the floor, a fist-
sized hole through his torso right about where his heart
had been. Another shot rang out, but the Executioner
had already taken cover behind the brick wall, gun in
hand. The shot struck a bar patron who was standing
too close to the door and he, too, fell to the floor, his
leg nearly severed at knee level.

By this time the cacophonous din in the room had
fallen to a hushed murmur. Even the DJ had stopped the
music and quit talking.

"Everyone get out the front door!" Bolan yelled loud
enough for people to hear. Everyone began to leave,
but the lap dancer from upstairs appeared on the other
side of the door from Bolan. She held a compact Glock,
either a 9 mm or a .40 caliber, in her hands. Where
she'd kept that hidden in her skimpy stripper outfit was
anyone's guess. She popped out from behind the door
frame and fired in the direction from which the sniper
had attacked.

CHAPTER SEVEN

Isaac Madhoff chose the code name "Amos" because he had to carry so much responsibility, and now he once again found himself shouldering the responsibility to clean up a mess because the people he'd delegated responsibility to had proved incompetent. Madhoff put the finishing touches on the camouflage around his impromptu sniper hide on the rooftop of the abandoned store. The Minneapolis metropolitan area was filled with empty commercial real estate, but the north end of the city, which was predominantly populated with blacks, had been especially hard hit. Entire blocks of old two- and three-story buildings were boarded up and unused. Madhoff's people had once owned the majority of these buildings, but they'd had the sense to sell out before the gangs had completely taken over.

Madhoff adjusted his camouflage, which was nothing more than a dark gray tarp over his prone body, and surveyed the rear of the Bald Kitty Klub through the night scope of his M-25 sniper rifle. Judging from the body lying on the ground behind the building, the big stranger who was rampaging through the city had already made his way inside. This man presented the first real stutter bump in Madhoff's until-then unimpeded path toward fulfilling his life's work. Madhoff couldn't understand how the man had connected the sniper attacks with the Satan's Slaves. At first Madhoff thought the attack on the Slaves was just interclub warfare, orchestrated by the Hellions as revenge for what the Slaves had done to their club, but when the big man had kidnapped Tressel, he knew that this was part of something bigger.

When the tall stranger had identified the link between the Slaves and the Rollin' 30 Bloods, Madhoff knew for certain that the big man was on his trail.

How much the stranger knew remained to be determined. For that matter, who he was and who he represented were complete mysteries to Madhoff. He had ears in most intelligence agencies in the world. He knew every aspect of the investigations into the sniper attacks being conducted by every major intelligence agency operating in the United States, both foreign and domestic. Every investigation except the one being conducted by this murderous intruder. He'd never seen such an effective operative in the field. He clearly worked for someone, but that seemed inconceivable. Madhoff knew everyone, yet he didn't know this stranger or the name of the organization he worked for.

For such a capable organization to even exist without Madhoff's knowledge represented the first major miscalculation in the entire plan. And it was proving to be a serious miscalculation. It was bad enough the stranger had interrogated Tressel. The biker was an idiot, a man who had attained power by stupid brute strength rather than by wits and resourcefulness. The only information that Tressel could give the stranger was Madhoff's code name and the fact that he was an Israeli. That in itself would be of little help to the stranger.

Should the stranger speak to Omar, that might present a very different situation. Omar wasn't the simpleton that Tressel was. Omar controlled his territory as much by manipulation and intelligence as by brute strength, and the man had resourcefulness and a capacity for abstract thought that Tressel lacked. Madhoff had been very careful not to provide Omar with any more information than was absolutely necessary, but he suspected the wily gangster had ways of getting information. Madhoff was especially worried that his own weakness of the flesh might have compromised the plan.

Madhoff's only option at this point was to eliminate both the stranger and Omar. He took a tremendous risk by going out in the field himself and performing the task, but it was the only way to accomplish the job in the necessary time frame. Madhoff hadn't had direct contact with any of the sniper teams operating throughout the country, and he needed to keep that status quo intact. The teams needed to believe that their direct superiors were in charge of the attacks; if they had any inkling that a foreign national was behind the master plan, especially an Israeli, most of them would abandon the cause. They were motivated to action by their belief that they were setting the stage for the Second Coming of Jesus, a belief that would be sorely tested should they learn that a Jew was pulling the strings behind the scenes.

Personally, Madhoff considered all religions to be

nothing more than primitive superstitions, including his own. Madhoff found the fact that the three religions squabbled incessantly among themselves amusing, given that in many ways all three embodied the same ancient mythology, a mythology that was basically an evolution of the Zoroastrian myths. The stories common to all three modern religions such as the great flood were all part of the oral storytelling tradition of the Sumarians, Persians and Egyptians. Even the magical figures of the three religions, people such as Abraham, Mohammed and Jesus, had their counterparts in such characters as Gilgamesh, Zoroaster and Osiris. How a rational person couldn't see that each of these mythological systems was just an evolution of earlier superstitions seemed fantastic to Madhoff.

At least Judaism was the least immature of the three religions that had evolved from the superstitions of the Semitic tribes of the Near East. It made sense; Judaism was the oldest of the lot, having been around much longer than Christianity and Islam. Islam, being the youngest, was by far, in his opinion, the most barbaric. In Madhoff's estimation, Islam was so primitive that its very existence was a threat to Israel's nationhood. This is why he'd devoted his life to the utter and complete destruction of every Muslim state on Earth, an ambitious goal, to be sure, but one that was now within Madhoff's reach. In a matter of days he would be able to use the military might of the United States against the Muslim world without any restraint whatsoever.

Israel's manipulation of U.S. policy toward Muslim

nations was practically an open secret. Israeli operatives had used the so-called "Neocon" movement within the previous administration to manipulate the nation into going to war under false pretext, resulting in the successful removal of Saddam Hussein. They had attempted to do the same with regards to Iran, but public sentiment in the U.S. had turned against both the war in Iraq and the administration that had coddled these Neocons.

Madhoff thought the failure to get the U.S. military to attack Iran symbolized the ultimate failure inherent in working through established channels of power. He preferred the more direct approach of seizing power and exercising it with complete autonomy. He found a certain amount of irony in the fact that he, a man who despised the concept of religion, was using religion as a tool to manipulate people into doing his bidding.

Madhoff had enlisted the services of some of America's top generals and admirals in all branches of the military, including seated members on the Joint Chiefs of Staff. He had singled out these men because of their devout fundamentalist Christian beliefs. All of the men sincerely believed that the Second Coming of Christ was imminent, but like many fundamentalist Christians, they interpreted the Bible literally, and like many, they believed that rebuilding the Jewish Temple on the Temple Mount in Jerusalem was a prerequisite for the return of Christ. The trouble was that the Temple Mount was partially under Muslim control, and the Muslims weren't too keen on the rebuilding of the Jewish Temple.

Madhoff had convinced his coconspirators that if

they helped him obliterate the Muslim world, he would reward them by building the temple, and of course he planned to do just that, but he labored under no delusions that doing so would bring back something that never existed in the first place. Whether or not his coconspirators would ever realize that they'd betrayed their country for a superstition was of no concern to him. Most likely they'd do all sorts of mental gymnastics to explain the failure of Jesus to appear on command. They had lots of practice at that sort of thing.

Though he concealed it well, Madhoff had almost as much contempt for Christians as he had for Muslims. He considered Christianity only marginally less savage and primitive than Islam, but since they were enemies of his enemy, he considered them his friends, at least until his plans had reached fruition. Until then, they made excellent tools.

Ideally, his allies in the military would have been the ones handling this operation rather than Madhoff himself, but to pull sniper teams from the next day's planned attacks and redirect them to this assignment would have taken too much time. It would have required Madhoff to contact his people in the Pentagon, who would then have to make contact with a sniper team and relay the instructions. This would have taken half the night; by the time a team was ready, the stranger and Omar would have been long gone. The only option was to do the hit himself.

Madhoff thought the odds were better than ninety percent that if the stranger was able to get Omar to cooperate with him, they'd exit through the back door of the club. He patiently watched as a steady stream of blacks came and went through the back door, either going out to smoke cocaine or receive oral pleasure from the dancers inside, dancers who were thinly disguised prostitutes. When a patron brought out a particularly comely prostitute of African descent, Madhoff's attention deviated from the task at hand. He had to fight the urge to watch the action, and force himself to keep his scope trained on the door lest he miss his marks. Occasionally, his predilection for dark-skinned women overcame the discipline instilled in him when he received his sniper training in the Israeli military, and his scope seemed to gravitate toward a sexual tryst as if of its own accord.

Each time this happened, Madhoff forced his scope away from the copulating couple and back on the rear exit of the building. On one such occasion he returned his scope to find his targets opening the door. Flustered from almost missing his marks, Madhoff's sniper discipline suffered and he fired off his shot a split second too early; he'd intended to wait until both men were through the door so that he could drop them both before either had a chance to find cover, but he fired before the big stranger was all the way through the door. His shot found its mark, killing Omar, but the stranger was able to dive for cover before his rifle had finished cycling a round. When he reacquired his target, the stranger was almost behind the wall. He fired a shot in desperation, but missed the stranger, instead hitting an innocent bystander.

Then something completely unexpected happened. One of the strippers, a Caucasian, popped out from behind the door frame opposite from where the stranger had taken cover and fired off shots from a handgun. Although the distance between his position and the door was well over a hundred yards the bullet from the handgun hit the brick wall just inches from Madhoff's hide. He fired a shot at the woman, but she'd ducked for cover before he was able to get her in his crosshairs.

With his location known, Madhoff had no choice but to flee from his hide. Never before had he failed to complete a mission, yet he had to leave this one only partially complete. A combination of anger and shame burned within the Israeli, anger at his adversaries for having outwitted him, shame for the fact that his failure had been caused by his own weakness.

San Leon, Texas

SERGEANT ZACHERY MILLER HAD been on a lot of hairy assignments in his years with Houston's SWAT team, but he'd never had as bad a feeling about an assignment as he had this night. His squad had been sent down to San Leon, a little bedroom community jutting into Galveston Bay just southeast of Houston, on what should have been a fairly routine assignment: bring in Mel Schmidt, president of the Texas chapter of the Satan's Slaves motorcycle club. It wasn't the first time they'd had to arrest a member of the club. It wasn't the first time they'd had to arrest Mel Schmidt himself, for that matter. But the instructions for this assignment were the oddest Miller had ever received in all his years on the force: make certain the subject didn't commit suicide.

The Texas chapter of the Slaves was the oldest in the country, and also the largest. The club had been founded in San Leon by Schmidt's immediate predecessor. The Texas chapter held so much clout that the president of the Texas chapter served as the informal president of all chapters. Miller had a long history with the club. He'd encountered all sorts of bizarre situations when arresting members of the Slaves motorcycle club. He'd found his subjects drunk, stoned, in the middle of group orgies. He'd busted Slaves who put up a little fight, and he'd busted slaves who'd put up a big fight, but he'd never encountered a Slave who was suicidal.

What's more, he was supposed to make certain that Schmidt didn't have a cyanide capsule hidden in a hollow tooth. Miller had never encountered that kind of crazy James Bond shit before. What the hell did they think Schmidt was? Some sort of Russian spy? Schmidt was a lot of things, most of them not good. He was mean, brutal, and as far as Miller was concerned clinically insane. Schmidt was on a real white power trip and often spouted off Nazi shit, talking about a master race and creating a white Christian nation. A lot of bikers had swastika tattoos on their bodies and wore Nazi paraphernalia just for shock value—with Schmidt, it was a genuine philosophical statement. Miller thought

Schmidt's whole attitude was a little ironic and comical. After all, Hitler would have sent a dirtbag like Schmidt off to the camps with the Gypsies and the Jews. Hitler preferred his henchmen to wear neatly pressed brown shirts, not greasy, sweaty denim club cuts.

Hypocritical or not, Miller knew that Schmidt was extremely dangerous. A twice-convicted felon, Schmidt couldn't legally own guns, but he and the rest of the Slaves had been rumored to have been stocking up on heavy artillery. Miller suspected that had something to do with why he was being sent to get Schmidt, though he was only supposed to bring the Slave in for questioning. That was the oddest part of the assignment—sending a SWAT team to bring a subject in just for questioning. Well, the oddest part next to the hollow-tooth-with-cyanide-capsule part. Whatever the hell was going on was pretty damned peculiar and Miller didn't like it one bit.

There were some beautiful homes in San Leon, but they were all along the waterfront; go inland just a few blocks and the city degenerated into a cesspool of broken-down trailer homes sitting amid the rubble of junk cars, broken appliances and other white-trash detritus. One such cluster of trailers served as the un-likely headquarters of an international motorcycle club. If these people were the criminal masterminds they were often portrayed as being by the media, they should have had more opulent digs. Many of them did, in fact, own beautiful homes, but it made little sense to advertise any potentially ill-gotten gains by flaunting an expensive clubhouse; hence the trailer enclave. It made sense.

On a level that Miller found to be of more immediate concern, the trailer site also gave the Slaves a tactical advantage. It may not have been much to look at, but the site was easily defensible—every abandoned vehicle, boarded-up shed and even broken appliance presented a possible sniper hide, a subject that was on every law-enforcement official's mind these past few days. Miller had brought ten of his best men on this assignment. Normally, a team of two men would go out to pick up a subject for questioning, at most, but SWAT teams weren't normally sent out to pick up subjects for questioning. As often as not when a SWAT team was sent out after a subject, that subject came back in a body bag.

Yet this time Miller's assignment was to specifically bring the subject in alive, which would be no easy task. His team had studied plans of the compound based on real-time satellite imagery provided by the Department of Justice, which in itself was unusual. Miller had worked with the Feds before, but in those instances he'd been assigned to assist arrogant field agents who viewed him and his team as marginally useful, at best, and more often simply ignored his team's presence altogether. Now the Feds were not only utilizing Miller's team as a resource, but they were providing assistance of the highest quality. All of which contributed to Miller's unease.

Miller checked his watch. According to the drill,

his men would be in place and ready to go in exactly twenty-nine seconds. The veteran officer watched the seconds tick away, waiting to give the go-signal over the subvocal microphone attached to his neck. It was a very cool new toy, a microphone that attached directly to the user's neck and allowed the user to speak to the rest of his team without opening his mouth. He had been given these as part of this assignment. It took a little practice, but once he'd mastered the equipment Miller couldn't imagine not using the system. He hoped he wouldn't have to return the equipment when he got back from the assignment.

If he got back from the assignment. At exactly 11:42 p.m. central time, Miller gave the go command and his men moved into the compound. As expected, the property was patrolled by a pack of extremely vicious-looking dogs, mostly pit bulls or some sort of pit-bull crosses. When the men approached the fence surrounding the compound, they aimed their suppressed M-4s at the animals and began shooting them over the fence. Miller was a dog lover and it genuinely bothered him to kill these dogs, innocent animals who were just doing their jobs, but they presented a deadly menace to his men. Any fully functioning normal-sized human male could kill any lone canine in hand-to-hand combat. Sure, the person would be chewed to bits, but unless the animal got lucky and tore an artery, the human would ultimately be the victor, thanks to a much larger brain and opposable thumbs. The trick was to ignore the claws and control the head, ultimately breaking the jaw, and then the neck.

But add more than one animal to the mix, and the advantage turned toward the canines. Canines were pack animals and worked in teams. A pair of wolves could kill a bear; a human presents little challenge for them. Because of that, Miller's team had no choice but to eliminate the patrol dogs. The suppressed rifles popped away as Miller's men killed every animal they could see moving. Even with the suppressors the sound of the rifles was much too loud to Miller's ears.

Apparently, it was too loud for other ears, too. The thunderous boom of an unsuppressed rifle rang through the air and Miller watched one of his men go down with a large wound in his neck, just below his face shield. The man's neck was one of the few parts of his body not protected by body armor. The shooter knew what he was doing.

When one of their number went down to gunfire, the men ducked behind the cover of the fence. It was a crude affair made of corrugated metal nailed to posts and would provide no protection from a high-powered rifle, but at least it shielded the team from the shooter's line of sight. One of Miller's men attended to his wounded comrade while the others moved to predetermined positions. "I'm calling for backup," Miller said.

"Officer down," he said into his portable radio, giving their location. In truth, Miller hadn't expected this level of resistance. After all, he was just bringing in a subject for questioning. And it was a subject he knew personally, one he'd arrested before. Schmidt might have been a crazy white supremacist, but he wasn't a fool. He wouldn't commit what amounted to suicide just to avoid being brought in for questioning. Yet the Slaves had been prepared for all-out war, which was the situation Miller now found his team in. This whole thing was just plain crazy.

"Did anyone see the shooter's location?" Miller asked through his throat microphone.

"I did," said one of the men. "There's an outbuilding between the second and third trailer. The top of the building seems to be made of heavy steel. The shot came from a slot in the steel."

"Send a grenade into the shed," Miller said. The man who'd seen the location of the shooter popped up and launched a round from the M-203 grenade launcher under the barrel of his M-4 into the shed. The grenade exploded on impact and the poorly constructed shed collapsed in flames.

No sooner had the man ducked back down than bullets rained down on his position from multiple locations. He'd had the sense to roll away from his position as soon as he ducked out of sight, which saved him from having to put his body armor to the test.

Since the mission was already totally screwed up and his team had lost the element of surprise, Miller turned on the PA system of his portable radio and announced, "This is the Houston Police Department. We have a warrant to bring in Mel Schmidt for questioning. He is not under arrest. Send him out and there will be no further gunfire."

Whoever was guarding the complex responded by opening fire in the direction from which Miller's announcement had emanated. One of the shooters scored a lucky shot through the corrugated steel, hitting Miller in the shoulder. Miller's armor prevented serious damage, but the impact broke his collarbone.

"What now, boss?" asked his second in command.

"Now we bring in the big guns." Miller had positioned three of his snipers in key locations that allowed them to triangulate the entire compound. "Kill anything that moves," he ordered. He knew he was supposed to get Schmidt alive, but the Slaves had crossed a line and shot a cop. They knew that, and there was no way anyone in the compound was going to be taken as long as they had enough life in their bodies to pull a trigger.

Nathan Jones, the most experienced sniper on Miller's team, fired. Moments later Jones spoke through radio: "Subject is down and not moving."

"The subject's location?" Miller asked.

"At your two o'clock, sir, approximately ninety meters from your location."

"Subject's description?"

"White male, armed with a bolt-action hunting rifle with what appears to be a night scope. It's not our boy Schmidt."

"Any other activity in the compound?"

"Yes, sir. A bunch…"

Jones's voice was drowned out by a loud explosion.

The Slaves had responded by launching a grenade of their own from deep inside the compound. "Is anyone hurt?" Miller asked. One by one the men let Miller know they were okay.

While the men were responding, Jones fired again. "Took out the Slave with the grenade launcher," Jones said. "I can't be certain, but it didn't look like it was Schimdt."

Meanwhile, one of the men hadn't responded. "Has anyone seen Anderson?" Miller asked.

"He was attending to Parker," another of the men said. Parker was the officer who had been shot earlier.

"Oh, man," another officer said. "I can see them both. They're not moving, and there's blood everywhere."

"Damn it!" Miller said, this time opening his mouth and speaking aloud, which made his voice sound like thunder through the subvocal microphone. "Let's throw everything we've got at these assholes. Jones, give us a report on the activity in the compound."

"There's not too much to report. I spotted some activity in the center of the compound, but couldn't get a clear shot at anyone. Wait…." Miller heard a shot, and then Jones's voice returned. "I just shot a man armed with an AR-15-type weapon moving between two of the trailer houses. It doesn't appear to be Schmidt. He's too young."

"What's our best route for entering the property?" Miller asked Jones, who had a much better view of the property than did Miller and his remaining men.

"The original plan still looks the best, but be careful.

I see movement…." Jones fired another shot, and then in the space of half a heartbeat he fired a follow-up shot. "Two men were moving toward your position from behind the nearest trailer. I tagged them both. Both are down for the count. It looks like there's more activity back there…."

Before he could finish speaking another shot rang out, but this time the shot came from inside the compound. "Jones," Miller asked, "did you see where the shot came from?" Jones didn't respond. "Jones! Report back." Silence.

"I can see Jones's hide from my location, sir," said Jason Nestle, one of the other snipers. "He's been shot, sir. He's not moving."

"Did you see the location of the shooter?"

"No, sir."

"Wilson," Miller said to the other sniper, "did you see anything?"

"I think so, sir. I'm trying to see…." Another shot rang out, this time from Wilson's position. "I got him, sir. I got the son of a bitch who shot Jones."

"Can either of you see any activity in the compound?"

"We're catching glimpses of motion, sir, but nothing definite," Nestle said. "Hold on. Something's happening." Before Nestle could let Miller know what was happening inside the compound, the men inside charged Miller's position with automatic weapons ablaze and all hell broke loose.

"Go full-auto!" Miller ordered his men and they began to fire back at the charging bikers. By this time

Miller had just five men left at the fence, plus two snipers. There were between twenty-five and thirty members of the Slaves charging their position. The snipers were able to take out some of them before they reached the fence and the officers had the advantage of wearing full body armor, but that still left their arms and legs exposed and two of Miller's men went down with serious wounds. The officers and snipers were able to take out two-thirds of the attackers, but that still meant nine or ten men reached the fence alive. Miller and his men made a brave stand, taking out the remaining men with the help of the snipers, but when the shots died down Miller and one of his officers were the only two men left standing.

"Nestle, report," Miller commanded, but heard no response. "Wilson, report."

"Here, sir. Nestle's been shot. While you were fighting at the fence, someone shot him from inside the main trailer."

"Is there any other activity in the compound?" Miller asked.

"The only thing left alive appears to be the shooter inside the trailer. What now sir?"

Miller could hear the sirens of the ambulances and squad cars coming to their assistance. "Now we wait for the cavalry, and then we're going to smoke Mr. Schmidt out of his rat's nest. If he doesn't have a cyanide capsule in his teeth, he's going to wish he did."

THE STRIPPER IN THE Bald Kitty Klub squeezed off a surprisingly accurate shot at the sniper. The sniper returned fire, but the stripper had already ducked behind the brick wall for cover. The woman was most definitely a pro, and not of the streetwalker variety. Bolan was dealing with some sort of highly trained operative. When things settled down he'd have to find out who she was. If he lived that long.

The sniper's return fire caught one of the guards from upstairs in the throat. The pair of guards had run down as soon as the shooting started and were attending to Omar, though it was far too late to help the man. The guard who took the bullet soon joined his boss in the ranks of the dead, but the other pulled a gun and started firing toward the sniper's position. When no return fire rained down on the remaining guard, both Bolan and the female operative concluded that the sniper had fled. Both simultaneously chanced a look out from behind their respective side of the door frame.

The sniper had shot from the roof of a building on the other side of a vacant lot behind the strip club. Bolan caught a glimpse of a figure moving toward the back of the roof and took off in that direction. The female operative followed, doing a fair job of keeping up in spite of the radically spiked heels she wore. Bolan couldn't help but notice that her shoes constituted the single most concealing part of her outfit. Her G-string bikini bottom left little to the imagination when viewed from the front and even less when viewed from behind. The small swatch of fabric that covered her chest could barely have held a dollar's worth of pocket change, much less her breasts, which, while firm, clearly were natural, judging from the way they bounced as she ran. Bolan had no idea who this person was, but everything about her spelled trouble on multiple levels. Some of those levels intrigued him, but others worried him.

They got to the rear of the building just in time to see the taillights of a dark full-sized SUV disappearing out the entrance of the alley. "I've got a car on the next street over," Bolan said to the woman, and the two sprinted for the street where the soldier had left Neal Trembley and the Mustang.

"Get in the back," Bolan said to Trembley when he was close enough for the man to hear him over the burble of the idling V-8 engine. Bolan jumped in the driver's seat and the woman dived into the passenger seat.

"Well, hello," Trembley said to the woman.

When she didn't respond, he said to Bolan, "Friend of yours?"

Bolan, who'd already dropped the car into gear and was tearing off in the direction the SUV had gone, answered, "No idea." He looked at the woman, who was about as talkative as the Glock she held in her hand, and wondered just who the hell she was.

He had a lot of questions for her, but right now he was preoccupied, driving through north Minneapolis in the middle of the night at 130 mph. He rounded the corner just in time to see the brake lights of the SUV light up. The vehicle disappeared around a corner. Bolan dropped the transmission down to Fifth gear and floored the accelerator. The speedometer approached 150 before he tapped the brakes. He slowed as much as he could before he got to the next corner, but it wasn't quite enough. The cornering forces overwhelmed the Mustang's traction control and the rear end stepped out, the tires smoking and screaming in protest. Filmmakers loved this form of cornering because it looked dramatic and exciting onscreen, but in reality it was one of the slowest ways around a corner, burning up precious momentum. Fortunately the powerful 5.0-liter engine had excessive horsepower in reserve and Bolan was able to get back up to speed and gain some ground on the SUV before it once again disappeared down an alley.

The soldier took the corner into the alley much more proficiently, losing a lot less momentum, but he didn't seem to be gaining ground on the SUV, which had emerged from the alley and turned onto a southbound street. Bolan once again had the speedometer needle approaching 130 mph before he reached the street. He braked hard. Smoke from the brake pads filled the vehicle and he could feel the brakes losing power, but he slowed enough to not lose traction in the corner and he accelerated hard down the street.

By now Bolan could make out the vehicle—a Jeep Grand Cherokee. It had to be an SRT8 version, judging by the way it was accelerating. The 6.1-liter Hemi in the Jeep cranked out 420 horsepower. The 412-horsepower Mustang would still be faster because it weighed nearly one ton less than the big Jeep, but with its 420 pound-feet of torque, the Jeep could accelerate at least as hard as the Mustang on a city street, making the job of catching it a challenge. Bolan's advantage was the Mustang's manual transmission, and the soldier worked it for everything it was worth.

Bolan closed up the distance with the SUV with more ease than he'd expected. It was too easy, in fact, and the soldier smelled a trap, as did the scantily clad woman in the passenger seat. She had her Glock in a high-ready position and was scanning the surrounding area. She saw what he was looking for, a glint of a machine-gun barrel poking out from an overturned garbage bin. "At your 1:30!" she yelled to Bolan, who also saw the trap. Just before the barrel of the gun began to spit flame, the soldier jammed on the emergency brake and spun the car around one hundred and eighty degrees. Fifty-caliber bullets tore up the rear of the car, causing the back window to shatter. Bolan dropped the shifter into third and popped the clutch, the accelerator buried to the floor. The tires broke loose in a thick cloud of white smoke, obscuring the vehicle from view. When the tires gained traction, the Mustang shot off in the opposite direction with neck-breaking force.

Bolan kept the throttle pinned as he rounded the corner, but one of the bullets caught the inside rear tire just before he could disappear from the shooter's line of sight. The blowout sent the car into a spin, and the vehicle looped twice before smashing into a streetlight. Everyone in the car had managed to put on their seat belts at some point during the chase, and when the car hit the light standard, airbags deployed in every direction. Bolan pulled his bowie knife and cut himself free from the airbags and seat belts. His passenger had done likewise, pulling a stiletto dagger, but Trembley wasn't moving in the backseat. One look told the soldier why— he'd taken a .50-caliber round in his leg. The leg was gone, and the pool of blood on the floor of the Mustang told Bolan that Trembley had most likely bled to death before the car had hit the streetlight pole.

"He's gone," his passenger said. "We'd better get out of here ourselves. What should we do?"

"Let's do the last thing they'd expect," Bolan said. "Let's try to catch whoever was manning that Ma Deuce back at the garbage Dumpster."

CHAPTER EIGHT

San Leon, Texas

After Sergeant Zachery Miller had helped get the wounded and dead into ambulances and replenished his ranks with officers sent in as reinforcements, he turned his attention to the lone gunman in the trailer. After his men had been ambushed, Miller's emotions had taken over and he was planning to throw everything he had at Mel Schmidt. He hadn't cared one whit about any orders regarding Schmidt's being taken alive; he cared only about revenge.

But now that he'd had time to cool off his training took over and mentally he was back to the original mission: bring Schmidt in alive, at any cost. Miller watched the last ambulance cart away the bodies of his slain comrades. At any cost, he thought to himself, even this. Miller hoped this mission was worth the tremendous sacrifice. His new squad—he didn't even know some of the men's names—cleared the outbuildings to make certain there would be no more surprises and surrounded the main trailer. When everyone was in position he took out his bullhorn and said, "Come out, Mel. You're surrounded. You don't have a chance."

"Goddamned right I don't have a chance!" Schmidt shouted from inside the trailer. "I'm a dead man no matter what happens."

"I promise," Miller said, "if you come out unarmed, with your hands up, we won't hurt you."

"Who are you?" Schmidt shouted.

"Sergeant Miller."

"Zachery Miller?"

"That's right."

"So they sent the big guns out to get me," Schmidt said.

"Come out and we won't hurt you," Miller repeated.

"It's not you I'm worried about!" Schmidt shouted. "It's the Jew."

"The what?" Miller asked. Schmidt couldn't have possibly said he was afraid of "the Jew."

"The damned Jew," Schmidt shouted.

"What Jew?"

"Calls himself Amos, but that sure in hell ain't his real name."

"Don't worry, Mel," Miller said. "We'll protect you from anyone, Jewish or otherwise."

"You think you can do that?" Schmidt shouted. "Then you're a bigger damned fool than I always figured."

Miller's patience was wearing thin. The night had been a complete clusterfuck, and he'd lost almost all of his best men. Now he had to try to reason with some sort of anti-Semitic lunatic. He couldn't imagine how this night could get any worse. If it had been his decision, he'd have lit the trailer on fire and he really wouldn't have cared if Schmidt had become an outlaw barbecue, a biker-kabob, but he had a job to do, and right now that job entailed engaging a madman who appeared to be about to go off on a racist rant.

"I swear," Miller said, "if you surrender, we'll keep you safe from the Jews."

"Goddamn it," Schmidt shouted, "I didn't say the goddamned Jews. I said *the* Jew. I'm talking about one guy, and he is one seriously bad motherfucker. If he decides to take me out, and I goddamn guarantee you he will. Ain't nothing you or me can do about it, ain't nothing every goddamned cop in Texas can do about it."

"If this Jew is that powerful," Miller said, "don't you suppose he already knows we're here?"

"I reckon he does," Schmidt said.

"Then you are already well and truly fucked, my friend. You might as well surrender and take your chances with us because you don't have a chance in hell out here on your own."

Schmidt thought about what Miller said. He knew the cop was right, but he also knew there would be nothing the cops could do to protect him. Even if they locked him up in solitary confinement for the rest of his life, the Jew would find a way to get at him. Still, if his odds of getting killed in prison were ninety-nine percent, they were better than one hundred percent on the outside.

At least in prison it would be quick. Schmidt had seen what Amos did to people who crossed him. Hell, he'd helped Amos do it once. Of all the twisted, obscene things Schmidt had done in his life, what he'd helped Amos do to a snitch was the one thing that haunted him. They'd skinned a man alive.

No, if given a choice, Schmidt would rather be taken out by a shank in the prison yard than endure the slow death the Jew would provide for him once he realized that Schmidt had been compromised.

Not that he had a lot of options in the matter anyway; the cops had him surrounded. He would either go out in a body bag or he'd go out in chains. At that moment the body bag seemed like the preferable option, but apparently the cops wanted him alive or they'd have taken him out by now. It made sense; the cops would want to question him about the Jew, which was why they came here and also why the Jew would most certainly kill him.

There was always the option of death by cop— Schmidt could charge the cops with his guns and go down in a blaze of glory. But even though that would be the easiest and most painless way out, he just wasn't willing to commit suicide. He almost wished he hadn't taken out the cyanide pill that the Jew had put in his false tooth. That would have been an even less painful way out of his current predicament, but Schmidt had feared he'd accidentally dislodge the pill and swallow it in his sleep. If the Jew had known he'd taken it out, Schmidt would have been dead already. The Jew was right, it turned out—sometimes suicide really was the best solution, but it didn't matter. Schmidt had a reputation as a tough guy, but when it came to suicide, he just didn't have the sand to take his own life. He laid down his guns and shouted, "I'm coming out!"

He came out of the trailer with his hands over his head. Before he set foot off the cinder block steps leading up to the trailer, the cops had grabbed him and slammed him to the ground. His hands were cuffed, and Miller was over him reading him his rights almost the moment he hit the ground. Agents swept through the trailer making certain the place really was empty and began collecting evidence. In all the commotion, no one heard the pair of incoming AGM-114 Hellfire missiles. They hit the compound almost at the exact spot where Miller stood over Schmidt. Each missile's twenty-pound blast-fragmentation warhead exploded upon impact, killing Schmidt, Miller and everyone else within a hundred-yard radius.

Minneapolis, Minnesota

ISAAC MADHOFF THOUGHT he'd made a clean getaway, but just as he was about to relax and slow down he saw headlights coming his direction. Given that he was going well over 100 mph, the vehicle approaching him had to be moving even faster, leaving little doubt that he was being pursued. At least the vehicle wasn't displaying flashing lights, so it wasn't a police officer. At least not a police officer of the usual variety. He still had no idea who the tall American was or who employed him. Judging from the way he'd tortured that idiot Pete Tressel, this strange interloper wasn't part of any normal military or civilian police or intelligence agency with which Madhoff was familiar, or at least any American agency. The Americans were even bigger fools than the Israelis when it came to limiting the effectiveness of its operatives.

Madhoff entertained the possibility that the tall stranger was an operative for another government, perhaps the Russians or one of the Eastern European countries, who were much more bloodthirsty than their Western counterparts, but that, too, seemed unlikely. Madhoff had eyes and ears in every agency on Earth capable of fielding such an effective agent, and he knew of no one matching the description of this man. This left the almost fantastical possibility that the American worked for the U.S. government in some sort of freelance capacity, but the existence of an organizational structure that could field a man like this without Madhoff's knowledge seemed virtually unthinkable.

Still, the Israeli had heard rumors of such a man over the years; a tall, dark-haired soldier who operated outside the restrictions of the law. This renegade had been credited for wreaking havoc across the globe, disrupting everything from terrorist plots to human-trafficking rings. Madhoff always considered this person to be a mythological figure that the weak and the simple-minded could blame for their failures. Now he was starting to think these stories might at least hold a grain of truth.

Madhoff would have to learn the identity of this stranger. He thought he knew the identity of the woman posing as a stripper, though: Sarah Westerberg, a Mossad agent who'd been investigating Madhoff's operation. She'd been looking into the Irgun's activity for several years. She hadn't learned anything concrete—she didn't know what was going on, who was involved or even that the Irgun had re-formed—but she knew something was going on, and she'd discovered just enough information to keep her on the trail. The woman was smart; the fact that she was in Minneapolis attested to the fact that she knew more than she should. Madhoff would have to deal with her as well as with the big American.

Madhoff hadn't wanted to resort to that. Westerberg was a good agent, a genuine patriot, and she'd done a great deal in the service of Israel. Madhoff had even met her on several occasions, at official dinners when he'd served in the Knesset as a member of the Likud party, and once when Ze'ev had brought her to the beach— she and Ze'ev had once been an item. Ze'ev Hazan was Madhoff's top lieutenant in the field and one of the people who'd helped revive the Irgun movement. He was also a stone-cold killer. He'd been in the Mossad, but had retired because he thought Israeli intelligence was going soft, buckling to public pressure to use less effective methods. In truth, the Mossad was glad to be rid of Hazan, even though he was one of the most deco-rated agents in the agency's history. In an agency known for resorting to ruthless methods, Ze'ev was too ruth-less even for the Mossad. The agency considered him a loose cannon, and when he retired, those in charge of the agency had breathed a collective sigh of relief.

Had they known what Hazan would do in his retirement, they would have breathed less easily. He was a formidable opponent, one who no one in the Mossad relished going up against. This is what made him so effective in the field, and Madhoff was grateful for the man's assistance. He didn't share the Mossad's squeamishness about Hazan's methods. To the contrary: he found them brutally efficient and appreciated the expediency with which the man dispatched those who stood in the way.

That may have been why Westerberg was here, in fact. She and Hazan had broken up many years ago, but perhaps Hazan had done something that aroused her official curiosity. She was a charming young woman, beautiful and smart. Too smart, it turned out. When things settled down, he'd have to mine his sources of information and find out exactly why she'd come to Minneapolis. There might be some follow-up housecleaning he'd need to attend to once the mission was completed.

Madhoff gunned the powerful engine in his Jeep and watched the needle climb to 130 mph, but still the car gained on him. He couldn't tell what sort of vehicle was pursuing him, but it was clearly driven by a talented driver, which meant a lot more than the type of vehicle when it came to urban pursuit. He wasn't going to outrun him in an SUV weighing nearly three tons, regardless of its vaunted Hemi engine, so he needed another plan. He pushed a button on his steering wheel marked with a telephone icon and an electronic voice said, "Phone ready," followed by a beep.

"Dial Ze'ev," Madhoff ordered, clearly pronouncing the name as two separate syllables to avoid confusing his robotic phone operator.

"Dialing Ze'ev," the voice replied.

Madhoff heard the phone ring over the speakers of the vehicle's stereo system, followed by Hazan's voice saying, "Yes."

"I'm being followed," Madhoff said. "I'll be passing your position in approximately two minutes. You know what to do." He hung up the phone. Madhoff wondered if Hazan would hesitate if he knew that he was about to ambush his former flame. Madhoff doubted that it would be a problem. Hazan wasn't a slave to his emotions. He'd earned his reputation for ruthlessness in the Mossad, and Madhoff expected his second in command to display that ruthless efficiency in just a few moments when he eliminated the occupants of the car now chasing him. He didn't think a former love connection with one of those occupants would be an impediment.

He'd placed Hazan along his escape route just for a contingency such as this. The former Mossad agent had set up a hide along a narrow section of the route where anyone pursuing Madhoff would be a sitting duck for his preferred weapon, an M-2 heavy machine gun.

Madhoff careered around one corner, just about losing control of the big vehicle but not quite, and accelerated hard toward an alley. Still the big American was on his tail. He lost control of the Jeep as he turned too quickly into the narrow alley and the SUV slammed up against the brick wall of the building on the passenger's side of the vehicle. In spite of the sparks flying Madhoff didn't slow down; instead, he accelerated harder and slid out onto the street in a four-wheeled drift, heading straight toward Hazan's position.

He'd barely regained control of the Jeep when he passed his subordinate's hide. He couldn't see anything to give the Israeli away except for the tip of the gun barrel poking out from behind an overturned garbage Dumpster, and he wouldn't have seen that unless he'd known what he was looking for.

Madhoff had the Jeep up to 140 mph when he roared past Hazan's hide. By this time the American had emerged from the alley and was gaining on him. Which was fine by Madhoff; it would give him a better view of Hazan's ambush. The American's vehicle—Madhoff could now see it was a black Ford Mustang—approached the hide and Madhoff saw the M-2 belching flame from behind the garbage Dumpster. The Ford spun around one hundred and eighty degrees, creating a huge white cloud of tire smoke. Hazan continued to fire at the vehicle, but it was hard to see what was happening in that great cloud of smoke.

Madhoff had to assume that Hazan had the situation under control and leave the scene. That was how they'd planned it, and both men knew better than to deviate from the plan because of fear or worry. Even though Madhoff couldn't visually verify that the target had been taken out, he fled the scene at top speed.

Long Beach, California

ERIC VON HOLT COULDN'T shake the sense that something had gone wrong. The day's mission seemed to have gone off without a hitch, like the others, but something just didn't feel right. He went over the events of the day. He'd set up his hide before dawn, as he'd done on the other days. He'd been the only one on top of the parking ramp in the early-morning hours and over the course of the morning only a handful of cars came and went. After 11:00 a.m. there was no movement at all; people had already been trained to go into hiding well before noon. People were almost becoming complacent. That was why they were going to switch it up starting the following day.

Most of the others worked in teams, as they'd been trained to do in the military, but von Holt preferred to work alone for this mission. He'd been trained to work sniper missions with a partner, as had the others, and when he'd been a marine sniper, he liked working in teams, but this was different. This was something he needed to do alone.

It made sense for most of the others to work in teams. There was a reason that military snipers worked in two-man teams, and those reasons were as valid for this work as they were for any other sniper work. It especially made sense for the snipers working out of vehicles to work in teams. They needed at least one person to drive the vehicle while the sniper shot through holes drilled somewhere in said vehicles. Some of the snipers even worked in multiple-member teams, but von Holt thought that was amateurish. He'd heard that one of the four-man squads in Maryland had been killed.

That worried von Holt. Four men doubled the odds of being captured compared to traditional two-man teams, and they quadrupled the odds compared to the lone snipers like von Holt. He believed in their cause with every fiber of his being, but at the same time he was terrified of being caught.

Still, increasing the odds of being caught wasn't why von Holt preferred to work alone. The truth was—and this was nothing von Holt could ever admit to his superiors—he preferred to work alone because he was afraid that if he had a partner he might display doubt about the mission. Doubt would be interpreted as a sign of weakness, and any sign of weakness would be terminated with extreme prejudice. If his superiors thought he was a weak link, he would disappear in a heartbeat.

But he did have doubts. That first day, when he'd lined up the first target in his scope, he almost couldn't squeeze the trigger. He'd killed plenty of people in both Afghanistan and Iraq, but the truth was he didn't consider them people. Rather, he thought of them as targets, heathens who worshipped a false god. People had tried to explain that the Muslims worshipped the same god as his God, but von Holt knew better. They might call their heathen god by the same name, but von Holt knew that they didn't worship Jesus, and he knew damned well that the only way into heaven was through Jesus. He'd known that since he was a small boy going to church.

He had absolutely no qualms about killing anyone who didn't worship his savior Jesus Christ the Lord.

He'd shown incredible zeal for killing heathens in the course of multiple tours of duty in both Iraq and Afghanistan, but that hadn't counted for much when the Humvee he was riding in hit an IED in Anbar Province back in early 2007. They'd claimed he'd injured his head and he'd been given a medical discharge. The Corps had been his life, all he'd ever wanted—besides salvation, of course. When he'd been kicked out of the Corps, he felt like his life was over.

But it turned out that someone had noticed his enthusiastic service to his country, an Air Force general who went to the same church as he did while he was getting doctored at Walter Reed after the explosion. After he'd been given the boot from the Corps, the general—his name was Joe Clement—had taken von Holt under his wing. They'd gone to prayer meetings together, gatherings where they met a lot of like-minded folk. Sometimes the meetings got a little radical, with folks talking about some pretty crazy things that needed doing before Jesus could come back. After a while those things started to sound less crazy. The deeper he got into the group, the more sense it made, the more he started to feel at home.

Part of that was because most of the people in the group were former snipers. That seemed a little odd in hindsight, but at the time it made sense. While snipers weren't ostracized as they had been in earlier wars, they were still a breed apart in all branches of the military.

Because of that, they tended to socialize with one another more than they did with nonsnipers. General Clement himself had trained as a sniper, so he fit right in. The group grew tighter and tighter.

One day a group of them went out on a field trip and von Holt found himself in a Chevy Suburban filled with a bunch of former snipers. They went way out into the West Virginia countryside, and when they finally got somewhere on the other side of the middle of nowhere, they stopped for a prayer meeting. But it wasn't like any other prayer meeting they'd ever had. This one was the most fire-and-brimstone prayer meeting von Holt had ever been to. General Clement had talked about how they were all living in the end of end times, and how Jesus needed to come back right that moment, but he couldn't because Satan had taken over the world's governments. Satan controlled everything from the Bilderberger Group down to the local dog catcher, to hear General Clement tell it, each and every one of his minions was colluding to keep Jesus from coming back. By doing this, Satan was keeping each and every Christian from experiencing the glory of the Rapture.

General Clement said the only way to beat Satan was to form a righteous Christian army, one willing to take on not only the enemies of the country, but the enemies of Jesus himself. He asked each man there if he was willing to die for Jesus. Of course each of them was more than ready; they'd been willing to die for a lot less than Jesus over in Iraq and Afghanistan. In fact, von Holt wasn't one hundred percent sure what they were risking their lives for over there, but that wasn't something he gave a lot of thought to, then or now. He'd gone over there because that's where the Corps had sent him, and when the Corps told him to do something, he did it.

But now he was starting to see that the Corps was really just another pawn of Satan. If Satan controlled the government, and the government controlled the Corps, then Satan controlled the Corps. That would explain the shabby way the Corps had disposed of von Holt once they'd deemed him irreparably broken. That realization rocked von Holt's world. In the past it would have made him suicidal, but at that moment he had General Clement beside him, offering him a better way. He said that if every man there would commit to his cause, together they could bring about the Second Coming of Jesus. There was nothing any of them desired more than the Second Coming of Jesus, so it wasn't a hard sell on the general's part.

That day each of their lives changed. Every day the general revealed a bit more of his master plan. Maybe if he'd told them the plan all at once, many of them—perhaps most of them—would have left and likely reported the general to the authorities, but the general was too smart for that. He acclimated the men to his ideas slowly, like they were all frogs in a pot of water on the stove slowly acclimating to the heat. By the time the water started to boil, it was too late for the frogs to escape and they were cooked.

The general was a smart one, no doubt. He'd involved

each of the men in increasingly illegal activities, until they'd all become felons, but he made it seem like they were doing God's work in the process. It would start out small—they'd steal mail from some Jew or Muslim or other heathen's mailbox and get credit cards and check routing numbers, things like that. Then they'd make false check blanks with those routing numbers and use them to buy truckloads of televisions and other electronic equipment, which they'd sell to help finance their Christian revolution. Then the activities became darker. They'd beat young Muslim men senseless if they caught them out walking in the park or some other deserted place. These beatings got increasingly more violent, until they actually started to kill people.

None of the men in the group were prone to over-thinking things. Each was shrewd in ways that made them good snipers, but none were what you'd call intellectuals. Still, it eventually dawned on them that at some point they'd crossed a line and that they couldn't go back. Not that any of them wanted to; General Clement had a way of making them truly believe that everything they were doing, they were doing in the name of Jesus. Ultimately the end—the return of Jesus Christ the Lord—would justify the means.

By the time General Clement explained his final plan for bringing about the Second Coming, each of them was in too deep to protest, even if they'd wanted to. Like the others, von Holt truly believed they were doing Jesus's work, that they were doing what needed to be done to bring about the Rapture. And even if they hadn't, each of them knew that if he got cold feet, he would end up under a ton of garbage in a West Virginia landfill. Each of them had already disposed of at least one body in just that manner, so they knew what was in store if they backed out.

They'd trained for the mission for more than two years before the first day of shooting. They'd worked to improve their stalking skills, their ability to blend in with the landscape and not be seen, and their shooting skills. When they were ready, they were dispatched to various parts of the country. Mostly they'd been sent to their home towns, where they were to blend in and assimilate into their communities. Secretly, though, they continued their training. They'd selected their potential hides, and had gone through multiple dry runs, spending entire days at a time in their hides.

As the time to implement the plan approached, General Clement arranged for each of them to officially disappear. Mostly he'd made each disappearance look like a suicide. This was a fairly brilliant plan on the general's part because the suicide rate among returned Iraq and Afghanistan veterans was so high that no one questioned when another of them took his or her life. Most of the time a body had been discovered at the suicide scene, one that was officially identified as one of the general's Christian soldiers. General Clement's soldiers needed to disappear in a hurry after the faked suicides so von Holt never really knew how Clement got the body placed, how he managed to have that body falsely identified or who was doing the grunt work, but he had his suspicions. On occasion several greasy, long-haired bikers had attended prayer meetings. They were members of the Satan's Slaves motorcycle club, which seemed pretty odd, given that Satan was the enemy against whom von Holt and his comrades fought, but General Clement had assured his people that the outlaw bikers were really on the side of Jesus.

Once Clement's Christian soldiers had gone underground, time seemed to drag on without end. The men holed up in a series of safe houses set up in out-of-the-way places, with nothing to do but pray and play gin rummy or cribbage, or, if they were lucky enough to be in a facility with cable, watch television. It was the longest six months of von Holt's life.

Finally, the day came to set the plan in motion. Although he'd prepared for this event like he'd prepared for nothing else in his life, when the time came for von Holt to take his first shot he almost couldn't do it. It wasn't because he hadn't killed before. He had, many times in Iraq and Afghanistan, and on more than one occasion during his training for this mission. The reason he had so much trouble squeezing off that first shot was because he knew there was a good chance that his target was a Christian, just as he was. When the clock struck twelve o'clock noon on that first day, he almost couldn't make himself take that first shot. He'd stared at the blond-haired head in his scope for what seemed like ages, though he knew it couldn't have been for more than thirty or forty seconds. It couldn't have been much longer than that, because he'd fired his round and was already packing up his gear when his watch indicated 12:01 p.m.

Each day it got a little easier, though, and this day's target had been the easiest yet. It helped that the target was a police officer. It seemed as if everyone was an agent of Satan anyway, at least to hear General Clement tell it, but it seemed to von Holt that as government servants, police officers were even closer to Satan than the rest. It got to the point where it didn't even bother him to kill a police officer, as he did this day. He'd taken a police officer out the previous day, too, since about the only people out on the street at noon anymore were police officers.

But that didn't matter. That day had marked the end of phase one of the operation: the sniping phase. The next day they were going to initiate phase two: the bombings. Whereas each soldier was now taking out one victim at a time, the next day they would start taking out victims by the dozens, or even hundreds. The body count was about to increase at least twentyfold.

Starting the following day, the plan was to detonate bombs in crowded public places simultaneously. The bombs would go off at 3:00 p.m. eastern time and 9:00 a.m. in Honolulu. Everyone had learned to expect attacks at noon, and Clement's men had carried that motif as long as they possibly could, in part to further train people to expect attacks at that specific time. It made them lazy and complacent.

When the first wave of sniper shootings failed to occur at noon the next day, people would think the threat was over. As the day progressed, they'd start to genuinely believe the nightmare had ended. By the time the bombs went off simultaneously, from New York City to Honolulu, people would have already become comfortable in their sense of relief. Although the explosions, which would take place in crowded office buildings, shopping malls and any other sort of space in which large numbers of people gathered, would be far more deadly than the sniper attacks when it came to total body counts, they would be even more devastating from a psychological standpoint. They would come just as people began to experience the euphoria of the sniper attacks ending and would bring them down so hard that they would not stand for anything less than the government declaring total martial law.

If, for some reason, the President failed to declare martial law immediately after the first wave of bombings, General Clement had planned a second wave of bombings to take place three hours after the first. After the first wave of attacks most people wouldn't expect another wave until the next day. Even though the modus operandi of the attackers had obviously changed completely, people's expectations almost always lagged behind the reality of a situation. They were simply slow to change gears. A second wave of attacks on the same day would be so jarring that should the President resist the call for martial law after the first wave, he'd find it impossible to resist after the second wave. One way or another, the United States would be under martial law within twenty-four hours.

Which was, of course, General Clement's aim all
along. Once the President declared martial law, Clement
and a few other top generals intended to stage a coup and
take over the country. Because the media would be under
the control of the government in a martial-law situation,
few people would even know that the President had been
removed from power because Clement would keep him
on as a figurehead. The President would still be the face
of the government to the masses, but he would be under
Clement's direct control, a mere puppet doing and saying
whatever Clement wanted him to say.

And what the President would tell the people was
that the attacks were the result of Muslim fundamen-
talists, and that the United States had no option but
to declare war on the Muslim world. After the chaos
sewn by the terrorist attacks, the people of the United
States would not only accept the President attacking
the Muslim world, they would demand it. Within hours
Muslim countries from North Africa to Indonesia would
be laid to waste. This would, of course, bring the world
to an economic standstill, but General Clement assured
his men that this wouldn't stop them from finally setting
the stage for the return of Christ. Their plan for paving
the way for the return of Jesus was to reclaim all of
Jerusalem for the Israelis so that Israel could rebuild
the temple on the Temple Mount, which was what had
to be done before Jesus could come back to Earth. And
there was only one way to do this—bomb every Muslim
nation on the planet. Once Clement and his men took
over the federal government, they intended to hit every

major Muslim country with nuclear weapons. Otherwise there was no way in hell that the Muslim nations would allow the Israelis to rebuild the temple on the Temple Mount.

It said so right there in the Bible, von Holt knew, in the Book of Daniel, Daniel 9:27 and Daniel 12:11, to be exact. God said that: "He (Antichrist) will…put an end to sacrifice and offering. And on a wing of the temple he will set up an abomination that causes desolation, until the end that is decreed is poured out on him… From the time that the daily sacrifice is abolished and the abomination that causes desolation is set up, there will be 1,290 days."

Now how in the hell was the Antichrist going to do all this in the temple if there wasn't any temple? von Holt wondered.

The answer, of course, was to rebuild the temple. It seemed a little odd to go to all that trouble to create a place where the Antichrist could go about his business, but that's what it said in the Bible, and von Holt wasn't any more likely to question the instruction found in the Bible than he was to question the orders of his superiors when he'd been in the Corps. Like the rest of the men, von Holt had thrown his back into the assignment and they had just about succeeded in their cause. One, maybe two more days tops, and they'd be in a position to help bring back Jesus.

And all this would be set in motion the very next day. Clement and his compatriots would have a short window of time in which they could bring about the

Rapture, but von Holt felt confident that the great man would succeed in this sacred duty.

So far everything had gone pretty much according to plan. As far as his own role went, von Holt had performed flawlessly. He'd taken every precaution and taken out every target. Compared to Afghanistan and Iraq, this had been the easiest mission of von Holt's life. Still, he couldn't shake the sense that something had gone wrong that day, though he couldn't figure out exactly what that might have been. He was positive no one had seen him go to or leave his hide, and he was certain that he hadn't been followed to the salvage yard at which he'd spent most of the past year, yet he had a bad feeling, like someone was rubbing sandpaper lightly across his skin. He'd learned to trust those feelings in the military; that's why he was still alive. The last time he'd felt like this was that day many years ago when his squad had driven over the IED.

The flashing light on the panel up by the closed-circuit television monitor confirmed von Holt's worst fears; he looked up on screen and saw that he had visitors.

CHAPTER NINE

Minneapolis, Minnesota

Bolan grabbed his war bag from the vehicle and ran toward the ambush site, the female operative hot on his heels. They ran through the shadows along the wall of the building that stood between them and their ambusher or ambushers. Bolan thought the hide looked too small for more than one shooter, but he mentally prepared for more.

He glanced around the building and saw that the machine-gun barrel no longer protruded from under the garbage Dumpster. When he determined there was no sign of movement, he ran for the bin, the barrel of his Desert Eagle leading the way. Not that he expected to be fired upon. The shooter would be thinking from the position of offense and thus expecting his target to be thinking defensively, but Bolan had long ago learned that the best defense was often offensive action. If the shooter's goal had been to kill Bolan, he—or she— would have come after them to confirm the kill, but the goal had clearly been to end the soldier's pursuit of the original sniper. The machine gunner had clearly ac- complished that task, which meant that the next logical action the shooter would take would be to clear out as fast as possible.

And that's exactly what had happened. The only avenue for an unseen escape was down a narrow alley that ran between two buildings almost directly behind the overturned garbage Dumpster. Bolan glanced around the corner and saw a figure at the far end of the alley throwing what had to have been the machine gun into the box of a pickup. The soldier aimed his Desert Eagle at the figure and squeezed off a round. He hit his target. The powerful .50-caliber bullet knocked the man to the ground, but before Bolan could get off another shot someone fired back at him from inside the pickup.

Bolan ducked behind the building on the left side of the alley while the shooter in the pickup fired off several more rounds. When the shooting stopped, the soldier's new partner popped out from behind him and emptied her Glock at the vehicle. Bolan could hear the thumps of her rounds hitting the sheet metal of the pickup's bodywork. When her gun locked open she dived back behind the cover of the wall. "I hit both tires on this side of the vehicle," she said. "Now what?"

"I'm open to suggestions," Bolan said.

"Where does that alley lead?" she asked.

Bolan had already pulled out his handheld computer and pulled up a live satellite feed of the scene. "It takes a ninety-degree turn to the west and then ends at North Fourth Street."

"Let's head them off," the woman said, taking off toward North Fourth Street before Bolan had a chance to respond. Somehow she'd produced a fresh magazine for her Glock.

The two rounded the corner just as the pockmarked truck emerged from the alley. Bolan fired two rounds from his Desert Eagle and the windshield shattered right about where the driver's head had been. The truck veered up onto the sidewalk and crashed into a glass storefront. The entire cab of the vehicle disappeared into the store.

Bolan and the woman sprinted toward the pickup, guns drawn, but stopped when the barrel of what looked like an M-2 heavy machine gun appeared over the side of the pickup box. An arm reached up and pull the charging handle. At the sight of this, both he and the woman hit the pavement. The person in the box of the truck fired off a good part of a belt of ammo in their direction, but because the gun wasn't secured to the vehicle the shots went wild; the big gun was a beast to control when it was mounted on a pintle or tripod; when it was being fired unsecured, it was impossible to control, even for the most powerful of men.

The gun fired until the belt ran out. Bolan and the woman returned fire, but the shooter in the pickup had to have been well-trained because he loaded up another belt and cocked the firing handle before Bolan even emptied a magazine from his Desert Eagle. Once again the soldier and his partner tried to bury themselves in the pavement.

Bolan only hoped that the bullets didn't hit any innocent victims, though he knew that given the range of the .50-caliber rounds the weapon fired, the odds were that some innocent person would be hurt or more likely killed; the half inch chunk of lead that the weapon spit out wasn't likely to just leave a flesh wound. The soldier knew he had to end this battle immediately. He really wanted to bring the shooter in alive, but the situation was too dangerous.

The shooter in the pickup didn't get off more than part of a belt of ammo when the gun quit firing. The barrel was probably overheating because the weapon had jammed. Bolan knew a trained operator like the person in the truck could clear a jam in just seconds, so he didn't have much time to waste. He reached into his war bag and pulled out his M-203 grenade launcher. He loaded a high-explosive round into the weapon's breech and fired at the pickup. When the round hit the box of the pickup it exploded with such force that the shock wave washed over Bolan and the woman.

The initial explosion was followed almost immediately by an even larger explosion as the gas tank blew. By the time Bolan and his partner arrived on the scene, the building had already begun to burn. He could hear sirens in the distance.

"Let's get out of here," the soldier told the woman.

"My car's three blocks east of here," the female operative said. The pair began to run back in the direction from which they'd come, but a police cruiser tore around the corner and skid to a stop on the street in front of them.

"Freeze!" a voice shouted over the squad car's PA system.

Bolan could see the officer in the driver's seat and

his partner opening their doors. He could hear another car approaching from behind, so that direction was cut off, too.

The duo stood next to a storefront that had plate glass from floor to ceiling, much like the one that the pickup had crashed through. Bolan grabbed his fellow warrior and pulled her tight against his chest. Then he flung himself backward through the plate-glass window, shielding the petite, nearly nude woman from most of the glass. He hit the floor still clutching the woman to his chest, rolled over and jumped upright. The pair was running for the back of the store as soon as their feet hit the floor.

The soldier saw a door leading toward the back of the store. He didn't even slow as he approached it; instead, he jumped and kicked it down. They had crossed half the storeroom behind the door before the cops had gathered their wits enough to begin pursuit. Bolan could hear them in the front room of the store, which appeared to sell some sort of sports shoes, mostly.

At the back of the storeroom the Executioner spotted what he hoped he'd see: a door that led back into the alley from which they'd originally came. But this door was a much different proposition than the one leading to the storeroom. This was a heavy steel door with serious locks; even Bolan wouldn't be able to just kick his way through this door, so he leveled his Desert Eagle at the lock and fired several rounds into it. Then he emptied his magazine into the doorknob and the accompanying bolt.

He approached the door, hoping that his shots had done the trick—if not, his knee would likely suffer irreparable damage. He leaped at the steel slab and gave it a flying kick. The door resisted for a moment, but before the shock of the impact could work its way into Bolan's joints it gave way and the door swung open into the alley.

The duo raced out into the alley. They could hear a squad car approaching them, but it hadn't yet rounded the ninety-degree corner. The fleeing pair ran toward the street, but they could hear cars coming from that direction, too. Bolan looked up and saw a fire escape just beyond his reach. Without saying a word, he grabbed the woman and hoisted her above his head.

She understood the situation and swung up onto the fire escape. Bolan jumped atop a garbage bin under the fire escape and pulled himself up beside her. The two scrambled up the fire escape and disappeared over the top of the roof just as squad cars appeared at both ends of the alley.

"Now what?" the woman asked. So far most of her end of their conversations had mostly consisted of her saying just that.

Bolan surveyed the landscape. There was a building on the other side of the narrow alley about fifteen feet away from the roof upon which they stood. The roof of the building was about eighteen inches lower than the roof upon which they stood. The woman saw Bolan eyeing the gap between the buildings.

"Think you can jump that far?" he asked.

"Not in these," the woman said, removing her stripper shoes. "Let's go." The woman ran toward the edge of the building and jumped. She made it across the gap to the other roof with inches to spare. With his much longer legs, Bolan had less trouble. The two ran toward the east along the roof of several buildings that were attached to one another. The roofs were more or less the same height, and they could jump up or down to the next building. When they encountered another alley, the woman leaped across to the other building, which was perhaps a foot or two farther than the last one had been. This time the woman barely made it. One of her feet landed on the roof, but the other slipped down along the wall of the building. If she hadn't grabbed the concrete lip of the building with her hands, she would have fallen to the pavement thirty feet below.

Bolan and the woman ran to the edge of the roof and found themselves looking down at a wide street.

"There's my car," the woman said, pointing to an older Lincoln LS. When he saw the car, he realized why the woman looked vaguely familiar—she was the woman who had been tailing him all day. The soldier mentally chastised himself for not figuring that out earlier, but things had been happening pretty fast since he'd first encountered her in the Bald Kitty Klub and he hadn't had a lot of opportunity for reflection. Besides, he had to admit that he'd been a bit distracted by the scantily clad woman.

The Executioner reached into a drop pouch and pulled out a length of cord with a metal clip at one end. He attached the cord to a heavy piece of cast-iron drainpipe and tossed it over the edge of the building. It reached down to a point about five feet over the sidewalk. That would work.

"Can you climb?" he asked the woman, though he knew full well she'd be able to climb down after seeing her in action. Instead of answering him, she just looked at him like he was something she'd scraped off the bottom of her shoe.

"Okay then," he said, and let himself over the edge of the building. He scaled his way down to the bottom of the rope, jumping the final several feet once he ran out of cord. The woman did the same.

They could hear sirens approaching by the time they reached the car. Once again the woman impressed Bolan by producing a set of keys from some hidden fold in the wisps of fabric that passed for her clothing. She definitely had aroused his curiosity. She drove away from the chaotic scene purposefully but calmly, moving quickly, but not in a manner that would attract attention. Once she'd put some distance between herself and the action, she increased her speed and practically flew through north Minneapolis.

When she got to the Camden neighborhood, she pulled into a driveway, hitting a garage door opener clipped to the sun visor of her car. The door on the garage that was attached to the older ranch-style house rose and she drove the car inside. The woman got out of the car and Bolan followed suit, wondering where exactly they were. Most likely some sort of a safe house, he figured. This woman was clearly an operative for some intelligence agency, probably the Mossad, judging from the very faint Israeli accent he detected in her voice.

Bolan stepped out of the car to find himself face to barrel with the woman's Glock. "Put your hands on the roof of the car," the woman ordered. "Now!"

Long Beach, California

ERIC VON HOLT LOOKED at the wall of monitors that covered every angle approaching the property that surrounded the salvage yard. The place was a virtual fortress; it was designed to be highly defensible, but it also could be considered a prison, depending on whether you were inside looking out or outside looking in. Right now he was inside looking out, and he was looking at what appeared to be a well-equipped team of federal officers surrounding the building site. He hit the alarm button, alerting everyone in the compound that they were under attack.

They'd planned for such a contingency, though in actuality von Holt knew the plans had been more for the benefit of alleviating everyone's fears than for repelling an attack. Only he had been privy to the real plan for protecting the site.

The salvage yard served as more than a safe house for several of the sniper teams; it was the factory in which General Clement's men were building many of the bombs to be used in the attacks in Southern California. Most of the explosive devices they'd built were already out in the field. The cops were too late to stop any of the bombings that would occur the following morning, but they still had quite a few explosive devices that needed to be placed for the secondary attacks, should that become necessary.

Most of the devices to be used in the secondary attacks were now with the units that would place them. The only devices that were still in the compound were the ones that von Holt and the three other teams staying in the compound were supposed to place later that night. Failing to place four explosive devices in the secondary wave of attacks would hardly cause Clement's mission to fail, but there was more at stake here. There was a lot of incriminating evidence in the place that could lead back to the general. Clement had a plan for cleansing that, but before von Holt resorted to implementing that plan, he intended to fight off the intruders to the best of his abilities.

There were eleven others in the compound besides himself—three two-man sniper squads, four technicians who built the bombs and Minnie, a young woman who took care of the cooking, cleaning and other duties in the compound. She was something of a prostitute, von Holt supposed, but so was Mary Magdalene. General Clement was a warrior, a Christian warrior to be sure, but a warrior nonetheless, and he understood the needs of a warrior, especially when that warrior was a young man.

Like the young men she serviced, Minnie was also a Christian warrior, in her own way. She believed in the general's cause every bit as much as did the men and she sacrificed herself for the needs of those men. In all truthfulness, von Holt got the feeling that it wasn't much of a sacrifice on her part; she seemed to enjoy servicing the men as much as they enjoyed her company, but von Holt wasn't complaining. Minnie was the only thing that made the long months trapped inside the compound bearable for him. It appeared that on this night she was about to make the ultimate sacrifice.

Even though he knew it could have been any of the sniper teams that led the law to their safe house, von Holt couldn't shake the feeling that he'd been the culprit. He'd done everything by the book, but when he'd left his hide, something hadn't felt right.

Maybe he just felt guilty about not being part of a team. When he'd chosen to work alone instead of with a spotter, he knew that he was taking more of a risk than the others, and even though General Clement had approved of that decision, the knowledge that he might be putting the Second Coming of the Lord Jesus Christ at risk had weighed heavily on him ever since. But he'd conducted that day's mission as meticulously and thoroughly as he had all the others. He hadn't seen anyone who might have spotted him, but then he lacked the extra pair of eyes that most of the others had.

Not that it mattered. He knew that ultimately no one was getting out of the compound alive that night, not from either side. He watched the others man their stations; even Minnie had an assigned post. Her role might only have been that of a concubine, but concubine or not, she had the soul of a true Christian warrior. She was one of the first team members in place and doing battle against the intruders, just as von Holt had expected.

The officers on von Holt's video display had to have had good intel on the layout of the compound. Their initial assault had been well planned; they'd surrounded the compound and attacked the main building site, which consisted of four large fabricated metal sheds clustered together in the center of the compound. They moved with the precision of a well-practiced team, getting into position and then attacking simultaneously from all sides. They appeared to be some sort of FBI SWAT team. They were well-equipped and wore what looked like the best body armor available. Von Holt recognized it because it appeared to be the same body armor that General Clement had supplied to the men in the compound. This was both a positive and a negative—each side was well protected, but each side also knew the vulnerability of the other side, since they shared that vulnerability.

The defenders had the advantage of familiarity with the layout of the compound, and that layout had been specially designed to repel just such an attack. A series of concealed catwalks connected all four buildings. They opened out onto numerous shooting stations that offered protection and concealment while at the same time allowing clear shooting lanes in all directions. The defenders could move around unseen from shooting station to shooting station, maximizing their effectiveness.

But the attacking officers had the advantage of numbers. Overwhelming numbers. The Feds weren't screwing around—they'd sent in at least one hundred officers to capture or kill twelve people—or rather twelve terrorists, at least in the minds of the federal officers. Von Holt wondered how many of them were good Christians who would join forces with General Clement if they'd only known the righteousness of the general's cause. Unfortunately, there wouldn't be time to convert them; at the moment von Holt and his compatriots had their hands full trying to fend off forces that outnumbered them by nearly ten to one.

Von Holt's men—and Minnie—were doing their best to even the odds; they'd taken out nearly a dozen officers before one of their number went down. The first of Clement's Christian soldiers to get taken out of action was Michael Burk, a former Marine sniper who'd served with von Holt in Iraq in 2004. In von Holt's opinion, Burk was weak because he'd become addicted to painkillers after being wounded near Fallujah. Supposedly Burk was off the drugs now, though von Holt never quite trusted him one hundred percent. Ultimately, it didn't matter. When von Holt looked at the video monitor and saw Burk take a round through the neck, he knew that all the drugs in the world wouldn't do anything for the rapidly dying man.

Tim Osborne was the next to go. Anderson and Burk were old friends. They'd known each other since junior-high school and had enlisted in the Marine Corps together. They'd even gone through sniper training together and had hoped to work as a team, but Burk had been sent to Iraq and Anderson had been shipped off to Afghanistan. Anderson was a quiet, good-natured guy, but when his back was against the wall, he was a real fighter. A spidery little guy, he moved from location to location between shots, never giving the attackers a chance to get a fix on his location. Von Holt watched him take out ten officers before one of them finally put a bullet through Anderson's chin.

Von Holt wished he could grab a gun and join his comrades in warding off the attackers, but his role in an event like this had been carefully choreographed. His job was to stay in the control room until the last possible chance for repelling the attackers had been exhausted. Even then he would never leave the control room; when all hope had been extinguished, his job was to push a small button hidden underneath a dummy potentiometer, a button none of the others in the compound knew existed. This button would set off a fifteen-ton bunker-buster bomb in the center of the facility, a behemoth designed specifically to penetrate Iran's underground nuclear research facilities. It was the most powerful nonnuclear bomb ever built and would reduce the entire compound to a large crater and everyone in it to a fine red mist. General Clement had appropriated this bomb from the Air Force, as he had most of their other equipment.

Apparently, the invasion wasn't going as well as the officers had hoped. After taking out four more of the defenders, including, unfortunately, Minnie, the officers pulled back and regrouped. Perhaps they thought that they faced more opponents than they really did, but in reality they just faced more effective opponents than they were used to opposing. In reality, there were just four people left to fight them off, and, of course, von Holt himself.

Whatever alterations the officers made in their plan of attack had to have been minute, because they appeared to be using the same basic approach of surrounding the building. The tactic hadn't been particularly effective the first go around, but it was more effective this time simply because they faced fewer defenders. Still, those remaining defenders fought as though the fate of the world hung in their hands, which, of course, it did. They knew that they were paving the way for the return of Christ.

But von Holt knew that none of them would live long enough to see that. The defenders took out another dozen officers, but eventually the last of them fell beneath the overwhelming assault. Before the last shot was fired, von Holt had pulled the dial off the dummy potentiometer and popped it out of its socket, revealing the real control button underneath. When the last of his men went down, he pushed the button, killing everyone and everything within a quarter of a mile of the blast's epicenter.

Minneapolis, Minnesota

BOLAN STARED DOWN the barrel of the .40-caliber Glock. It was a subcompact model designed for easy conceal-ment and was hardly bigger than the Walther PPK that James Bond carried in the Ian Fleming novels, but at that close a distance it seemed disproportionately large, obscuring the soldier's view of the scantily clad beauty wielding it. He watched her elegant finger squeeze the trigger and knew that the striker-fired weapon was cocked and ready to fire.

"I said hands on the car roof," she repeated. "Now." Bolan complied.

He assumed the position and the woman removed his weapons. "I don't know who you are," she said, "I don't know who you're working for and I don't care. I saw what you did to that biker at that garage. I know he was the scum of the Earth, but to torture him that way means you are no better."

"You realize we're on the same side," Bolan said.

"We might be working for the same people, but I'm not on the side of anyone who would do such a thing to another human being."

"I faked the torture," he said. "I used dry ice and a piece of steak to make Tressel believe I was torturing him. It was crude, but I didn't have much time and there are hundreds, maybe thousands of lives at stake."

"You torched the meat and made Tressel think you were burning him by applying dry ice? Clever."

"If you appreciate that, then you can appreciate the fact that we haven't got much time. I don't know how much you know about what's going on. I don't know enough myself, yet, but I do know that it is huge, much bigger than the sniper attacks we've experienced so far. And I know that whatever this is all leading up to is about to go down any minute. We need to work together and we need to work fast."

"How can I be sure that you won't do to me what it looks like you did to that ignorant biker?"

"Because I would have done it by now," Bolan said. "I took a lot of risks to keep you alive and out of jail."

The woman looked at him without moving or saying a word, but Bolan could tell she knew he was right. After a couple of moments, she put the gun down the front of her G-string bikini bottom into what had to have been a Thunderwear-type deep-concealment holster. She caught Bolan staring at her as she did so.

"Men," she said. "You are simple, doglike creatures. You will undress a woman with your eyes, you'll ogle our breasts, our legs and our asses, but you're not comfortable staring at that particular region of our anatomy. You're afraid that if you see some sort of unsightly bulge there, you'll have to deal with the fact that you've been aroused by a member of your own sex. Since you'd rather not know this, that's the one place you avoid staring. That's why the crotch makes an ideal place for a woman to carry her gun."

"Speaking of guns," Bolan said, "can I have mine back?" The woman hesitated a moment, then returned the soldier's weapons.

"Now tell me," the woman said, "who are you? Or at least who are you supposed to be, since I imagine that whatever cockamamie name you give me will be your cover identity."

"I'm Matt Cooper," Bolan said. "Or at least I'm supposed to be."

"Let me guess," the woman said, "military, or more likely retired military, contracted to do security work?"

"For the record, yes."

"Off the record?"

"Who are you and who do you work for?" Bolan asked, changing the subject.

"Sarah Westerberg," she said, "and I'm pretty damned sure I don't need to tell you who I'm working for, but for the record I'm a translator for the Israeli embassy in Washington, D.C."

"Let me guess—you've come to Minnesota on vacation to do some sightseeing? See anything interesting?"

"Plenty," Westerberg said, "but I suspect not as much as you've seen."

"Have you seen Amos?" Bolan asked.

"Maybe," she said. "It would help if I knew what Amos looked like."

"What do you know about him?"

"Just that he's got his tentacles into the Knesset pretty deep. That, and that he's possibly the most dangerous man on Earth. I assume you're here investigating the sniper attacks?"

"That would be a safe assumption," Bolan said.

"And I assume that's what led you here?" she asked. The soldier just nodded yes. "What else do you know?"

"Not much," Bolan said, which was the truth. "I've

got bits and pieces of information and none of it makes much sense. What do you know about this Amos?"

"Other than what I've already told you, nothing."

"What led you to Minneapolis?"

"Ze'ev Hazan," Westerberg said.

Though he'd never worked with Hazan, Bolan knew him by reputation. He'd been something of a loose cannon in the Mossad and the crew at Stony Man had kept tabs on him. "I thought Hazan had retired."

"My, you know a lot about the inner workings of Israeli intelligence," Westerberg said. "I'm very curious to know more about your 'contracting' operation, but I believe you won't be sharing those details anytime soon."

"You believe right. Why are you investigating a retired Mossad operative?"

"We have reason to believe that Mr. Hazan is not quite the retiring wallflower he pretends to be."

"What reason would that be?"

"For starters, Mr. Hazan appears to be working with this mysterious Amos. Also, I think he may well have been the fellow who ambushed us with the heavy machine gun."

"Do you have any clothing here?" Bolan asked.

"Yes. Why?"

"Because we're going to investigate the ambush site."

"How are we going to get access? The place will be crawling with police officers."

"Because we're going in as federal officers, but that

won't happen with you looking like a two-hundred-dollar hooker. You need to put on your dowdiest official-looking suit."

"I resent that," Westerberg said. "I think I look like at least a five-hundred-dollar hooker. What will you wear? You can't go in wearing that goofy-looking catsuit."

"I'll take care of that."

"What will we use for identification?" Westerberg asked.

"I'll take care of that, too. Now go change clothes."

When she was gone Bolan called Kurtzman. "Is Hal there?" he asked. Even though it was 3:00 a.m. eastern time, Bolan knew the odds were that Brognola would be working during a crisis like this.

"What have you got for me, Striker?" Brognola asked.

"What do you know about General Joe Clement?" Bolan asked.

Brognola was silent for a moment. Rather than the strong, silent type, the big Fed was more of the loud, explosive type, and long, silent pauses weren't his typical modus operandi, so Bolan knew this was something big. Finally he said, "Clement's gone underground."

"You've been watching him?" Bolan asked.

"Watching him? Hell, we were getting ready to arrest him."

"For what?"

"Suspected arms trafficking," Brognola said. "He's been linked to the disappearance of a tremendous amount of ordnance. We suspect that he's been selling it to the cartels in Mexico. We would have arrested him two days ago, but when the shit hit the fan with these sniper attacks, we put the plan on hold. As you might guess, arresting a member of the Joint Chiefs of Staff is a delicate operation, especially when he happens to be in charge of the Air Force base where they park Air Force One. Plus the general's a pillar of the community. He's extremely active in his church and does a lot of work with wounded vets. When we finally got our ducks in a row and went to get him, he'd disappeared."

"Well, I think this pillar of the community might be at least one of the perps behind the sniper attacks," Bolan said. "Any idea where he's gone?"

"None," Brognola said. "We've had him under constant surveillance for weeks. He hadn't left his house since the sniper attacks began. A lot of people have been staying at home, so there's nothing odd about that, but when we went in to get him, we found no trace of him."

"Did you get any computer records from his residence?" Bolan asked.

"Nothing. The place had been scrubbed clean, which is what we would have expected if he really was an arms trafficker."

"I don't think he's an arms trafficker," Bolan said. "I think he's some sort of terrorist mastermind, and we need to find him as soon as possible."

"We're already on it," Brognola said. "What else have you learned?"

"The woman who was following me is Sarah Westerberg. Mossad. Find out everything you can about her."

"I've already started investigating," Kurtzman piped in. "I've hacked into the Mossad's computer system and pulled her file. She looks like a heavy hitter. Cute, too. What's she doing in Minneapolis?"

"She's here tailing Ze'ev Hazan."

"That name's a blast from the past," Brognola said. "I thought we'd heard the last of that bloodthirsty bastard."

"I think we may have," Bolan said. He gave Brognola and Kurtzman the condensed version of the ambush and their escape. "Find out everything you can about him. I think he's the key to figuring out who this Amos is. I need to investigate the crash scene and I need you to help us get in there, Bear. Get us a car—this time make it a government Crown Vic, complete with all the goodies—flashing reds in the grille, police radio, full war load. I'll also need some clothes, a nondescript suit like a federal agent would wear. And I'll need federal agent identification for both me and Westerberg. Create a file on her. Her identity doesn't have to stand up to investigation by the press, it just needs to help us get access to the accident scene tonight."

"I suppose you need that all tonight?" Kurtzman asked.

"I need it within the hour. We have to get to the scene before the local cops destroy any possible evidence that can help us end these terrorist attacks."

"Can you handle that, Bear?" Brognola asked Kurtzman.

"Does a yeast infection itch?" Kurtzman replied.

"I'll take that as a yes," Brognola said. "Striker, I'm afraid I've got some bad news for you. We weren't able to bring Schmidt in alive."

"What happened?" Bolan asked.

"Our men met heavy resistance. There were a lot of casualties on our side, but we took out all the Satan's Slaves except for Schmidt himself."

"So you got him?"

"We had him, at least for a few minutes. Then the entire compound was attacked."

"By whom?" Bolan asked.

"Not 'by whom,'" Brognola said, "by what. The compound was hit by missiles."

"What? Are you kidding me? Missiles in Texas?"

"I couldn't be more serious. Within minutes of apprehending Schmidt the compound was taken out by a pair of AGM-114 Hellfire missiles."

"How is that possible?" Bolan asked. "Were they shot from a Predator?"

"Worse." Brognola said. "They came from a Reaper. The drone was running too high and too fast to be a Predator." The MQ-9 Reaper was the latest development of the MQ-1 Predator unmanned aerial vehicle, the remote-operated drone aircraft used in places like Iraq and Afghanistan. In place of the 115-horsepower engine used in the MQ-1 Predator, the MQ-9 Reaper featured a 950-horsepower unit, which allowed the Reaper to fly four times as far, four times as high and four times as fast as the older Predator. The Reaper was state-of-the-art technology.

"How did anyone get their hands on a pair of Hellfire missiles, much less a Reaper?" Bolan asked.

"We were wondering that ourselves," Brognola said. "And where'd they get the skilled personnel to operate the thing? It looks like it might have something to do with our friend General Clement."

"Tell me you got something from the California lead," Bolan said.

"I wish I could," Brognola said, "but the results there were even worse than the results from the Texas raid."

"Worse than a pair of Hellfire missiles being fired from state-of-the-art military flying machines?"

"Yeah," Brognola said. "Just when the agents raiding the salvage yard thought they'd quelled all resistance, the compound exploded."

"If it didn't get hit by missiles, what happened to it?"

"Judging from the size of the crater, it was booby-trapped with an MOP." An MOP was an acronym for Massive Ordnance Penetrator, or bunker-busting bomb. "A GBU-57A/B, by the looks of it."

"You can't be serious. I thought the GBU-57A/B was still under development."

"It is," Brognola said, "but it's in the final stages and is just about ready to go online. Judging from the results tonight, I'd say it works."

"You think our buddy General Clement is behind this, too?" Bolan asked.

"Unless you've got another suspect for us, my money would be on him."

"What are your plans for bringing him in?" Bolan asked.

"Our plans are to find him first. We'll worry about bringing him in after that."

CHAPTER TEN

Minneapolis, Minnesota

Isaac Madhoff slowed his vehicle and tried once again to contact Ze'ev Hazan on his cell phone but couldn't reach the man. Hazan had never failed to answer one of Madhoff's calls. The man was a paragon of reliability. The only possible reason that Madhoff could imagine for Hazan's failure to respond would be that his friend and comrade was either gravely wounded or dead. Arrest wasn't a possibility; Hazan would never allow himself to be taken alive.

If Hazan was dead, he had to have died at the hands of the tall American. Madhoff hadn't even entertained the possibility that Hazan's ambush of the American and the Israeli agent might fail. He'd given even less consideration to the almost infinitesimal chance that the pair being ambushed would turn the tide and get the best of one of the most experienced operatives the great nation of Israel had ever produced. If he had thought this even remotely possible, he might not have given the assignment to Hazan because of the cargo Hazan carried. The former Mossad agent was bringing Madhoff a memory stick containing updates from their various operations around the country. Included were the locations of the bombings planned for the following day.

Normally, Madhoff wouldn't have involved Hazan in a hazardous mission while carrying such sensitive cargo, but that night's mission had been both unplanned and absolutely necessary, and they'd literally had to plan the mission with less than a moment's notice. The detail of dealing with the memory stick had been overlooked in the frenzied premission planning. In hindsight, Madhoff now realized that had been a major detail to overlook.

But there simply hadn't been enough time to secure the memory stick. Madhoff needed someone he could trust, and someone he knew was capable of carrying out the mission. Of the few people available to him at that moment, only Hazan fit that profile. As such, the former Israeli agent was the only logical choice. In hindsight he probably should have gotten the memory stick from Hazan prior to beginning the mission, but since he considered his role as sniper to be the most dangerous, by a huge margin, it seemed to make more sense to leave the information with Hazan. Besides, the information Hazan carried was protected by virtually impenetrable encryption. It seemed inconceivable that anyone could crack it.

Madhoff drove to his safe house on Irving Avenue. He had a dozen of Omar's top men guarding the place; it was his most secure location in the Minneapolis area, and right now he felt the need for security. Hopefully the men wouldn't have heard about what happened to Omar. These were all hard men, real soldiers, but the

death of their leader would upset them. There was no
telling how they would react. Of course if they had
any inkling that it had been Madhoff himself who shot
Omar, then all bets were off, but they had no way of
knowing that, and they weren't the type of men to sit
around pondering abstractions such as who did what.
Still, to be safe he was going to play dumb and act as if
he was just hearing the news for the first time if anyone
broke the news to him that Omar was no longer among
the living.

Madhoff turned down the alley leading to the safe
house. He hit the garage door opener before he even
saw the garage, and when he turned onto the approach
the door was already fully opened. The Israeli parked
his Jeep inside and shut the garage door. He walked to
the backdoor of the house, careful to avoid the pressure
sensors in the grass, and unlocked the back door. Stepping inside, he didn't note anything unusual. Several of
Omar's men were playing video games and listening to
loud music in the basement recreation room. The men on
duty sat around in the parlor on the main floor, watching
television, their MP-5 machine pistols at the ready.

Madhoff almost stepped in a pile of feces on the
kitchen floor. The mess belonged to Robert's dog, a
foul-tempered pit bull that the man occasionally entered in dogfights. The dog was a menace, a stupid,
mean animal, but compared to his owner the dog was
a prince and an intellectual. Madhoff couldn't stand
Robert, but Robert was Omar's cousin and he came
with the property; the house was, in fact, registered in

Robert's name, even though Omar was the real owner. Or at least he had been up until the moment Madhoff put a bullet through the gangster's brain.

Carefully avoiding the pile of feces, Madhoff poured himself a glass of single-malt whisky. Not being able to contact Hazan had shaken the Israeli, and he needed something to calm his nerves. The liquor helped. If one was good, two had to be better, so he poured himself another shot to take up to his bedroom suite.

The men paid him no attention whatsoever as he passed through the parlor. Clearly the men had yet to hear about what happened to Omar. That was good, at least for the time being, but when they did hear about the death of the man who they practically worshipped as a god, the situation would undoubtedly turn very tense. Madhoff always slept with his Glock beneath his pillow; this night he would also have a couple of extra loaded magazines with it.

Thinking about tension caused Madhoff to return his thoughts to Hazan. He had to find out what happened. He had a police-band radio in his bedroom suite. He should be able to learn what had happened using that, since the police would have been called to the shooting site by now. This entire situation had Madhoff tied in knots. The whisky hadn't really helped, and Madhoff couldn't afford to drink any more since he needed to keep his head on his shoulders and be prepared for whatever that night might throw at him. He needed to be ready.

Harrisonburg, Virginia

GENERAL JOE CLEMENT COULDN'T tell if he was feeling
elated or agitated. It was probably equal parts of both,
he decided. The elation he felt was the result of the success of his men, his "tribe," as his religious guru, now
deceased, would have called them. But his tribe included
more than just the brave warriors out paving the way
for the Second Coming of Christ; it included all white
Christians everywhere.

His mentor wouldn't have approved of Clement's
partnership with the man he was trying to call. Isaac
Madhoff was a Jew, and his mentor believed that the
tribe of the white Christian was at war with the tribe of
the Jew, a racial war, a life-and-death struggle in which
only one race would be victorious. Clement shared that
belief with his guru, but sometimes war made for strange
bedfellows. Besides, the Christians needed the coop-
eration of the Jews if they were to lay the groundwork
for His glorious return. It said that right in the Bible.
Clement's certainty in the imminent Second Coming
of Christ was unshakable, but the Bible said that Christ
couldn't return until the Jews built a new temple on
the Temple Mount. If that meant that Clement and his
tribe would have to help the tribe of the Jews build that
temple, so be it.

Besides, the Lord helped those who helped themselves. In the last years of his life his mentor had ad-
monished his followers to take action, to accept their
obligations to their race and do what needed to be done.

And in his very soul Clement believed that what needed to be done was everything possible to pave the way for the return of Jesus. If that meant taking thousands of lives, then he'd take thousands of lives. If that meant taking millions of lives, then he'd take millions of lives, especially if those lives were the lives of godless heathens. That God-fearing white Christians were killed as collateral damage was unfortunate, but if they were true Christians they'd soon be with Jesus anyway, and that was the ultimate goal of this entire exercise.

His religious muse might not have approved of his alliance with the Jews, but the man had never come close to accomplishing what Clement was on the verge of accomplishing. In spite of devoting his entire life to making the world a decent place for white Christians, his mentor had been ineffectual, when all was said and done. If it took getting in bed with a Jew to bring back Jesus, then that's what Clement would do.

And as far as Jews went, Madhoff was all right. He was a real warrior, a fighter like Clement himself, perhaps even more so. And he'd been stone reliable. His planning and intelligence work had made this entire operation possible. Clement had done the recruiting, but Madhoff was the man with eyes and ears in all the world's intelligence operations. It was thanks to Madhoff's meticulous planning and careful monitoring of intelligence-gathering operations that the attacks by Clement's men had taken the country by surprise. Madhoff may have been a Jew, but the man was a rock.

Clement almost felt bad that Madhoff would be left behind in the Rapture with the rest of the Jews.

But if the bastard didn't answer his phone pretty soon, Clement decided he really wouldn't feel that bad about Madhoff's not being called home by the Savior. Earlier that day Madhoff had warned Clement that the Feds had a warrant for his arrest, allowing Clement to escape before agents came to serve the warrant. The warrant had nothing to do with the sniper attacks; it was for stealing weapons from the military. And Clement had been stealing weapons, but not to sell them in Mexico, as he was being accused of doing. Certainly he had sold a few odds and ends to the Mexican cartels to raise funds to carry out his plan, but for the most part he'd taken the weapons to equip his men. And he'd scored some amazing weaponry in the process.

As a result of decades of hard work, he'd gathered together what might have been the most potent private army ever assembled. Like many of his colleagues in the highest ranks of the military, Clement had studied Machiavelli, who defined a functioning state as an entity that maintained a monopoly on the use of violence. Whereas the others had taken Machiavelli's words as a warning to maintain a strong central government through military and police forces, Clement saw it as an avenue through which he could achieve his ultimate goal of setting the stage for the return of Christ.

While Clement wasn't a man given to contemplating the nuances of irony, he couldn't help but note that his devotion to Jesus had both contributed to his rapid rise in the military and his dedication to destroying the very government that the military served. Virtually all of Clement's colleagues professed to share his devotion to Christ, yet they continued to serve a corrupt government that only did the work of Satan. On the surface Clement seemed as devoted to furthering Satan's earthly empire as did everyone else whose checks came from the government, but privately he was putting his faith into action. He was the general in charge of the foot soldiers dedicated to saving white Christiandom.

Sometimes those foot soldiers came in seemingly incongruous packages. A lot of his men had questioned the general's partnership with the Satan's Slaves Motorcycle Club. But Clement had known their president Mel Schmidt since he'd been in the Air Force, and he knew that Schmidt's heart was true. Schmidt was as dedicated to making the world safe for white Christians as was Clement himself. Schmidt had strayed after leaving the military.

Clement blamed himself for that. If he'd started assembling his private army earlier, he would have made Schmidt a top lieutenant; the man had natural leadership abilities. But that was nearly thirty years earlier—Clement's master plan was still just the seed of an idea back then. It only made sense that Schmidt had gravitated toward the outlaw motorcycle club scene after leaving the service. One percenter clubs, as they called themselves, offered the same sort of rigid, disciplined structure that gave shape to the lives of military men. As a result, such clubs were filled with military veterans.

It also made sense that a man with Schmidt's leadership abilities would become a leader in such a club. In his own way, Schmidt had become a powerful man. In fact, it was Schmidt's motorcycle club that inspired Clement's idea for a private army. Like Clement's forces, outlaw motorcycle clubs threatened the state's monopoly on the use of violence because of their organization and discipline. This is why, Clement thought, they were hounded so relentlessly by law enforcement agencies.

To be sure many people in motorcycle clubs engaged in such illegal activities as prostitution, usury, narcotics trafficking and pretty much every other illegal activity one could imagine. But by and large these were the actions of individual members and not the policies of the clubs themselves. The members engaged in these nefarious activities simply used the club for connections and protection. But the government usually portrayed the clubs themselves as the criminal entities and attacked entire clubs rather than prosecuting the individual members who broke the law. That's because the very existence of these extremely organized paramilitary motorcycle clubs was much more of a threat to the government than was the illegal activities of individual members.

The mistake made by the clubs was that they existed publicly. From the very beginning Clement had taken great care to cover his tracks. He assembled a mighty white Christian army completely under the radar of any authority. Eventually, he even brought Schmidt back into the fold. The very name of Schmidt's organization—Satan's Slaves—had generated some grumbling among Clement's top lieutenants, but Clement had convinced them that the name was an advantage because it added another layer of confusion for anyone investigating the group's true purpose. Who would expect a secret army devoted to setting the stage for the Second Coming of Christ to work in conjunction with an outlaw motorcycle club called Satan's Slaves? No one. Besides, the discipline and loyalty of the club members—along with the code of silence that they rigidly followed—made them ideal partners for an operation in which complete secrecy was of utmost importance.

The one glitch in the plan had been the arrival of the Jew. Isaac Madhoff had been the only person shrewd enough to discover Clement's arms-stealing operation. An Israeli spy working in the U.S., Madhoff had uncovered Clement's operation in the course of snooping on U.S. weapons development. The Jew was a smart one, no doubt. When he'd confronted Clement, the general was certain that he'd failed in his mission. Madhoff couldn't directly reveal Clement's crimes without revealing his own spying activities, but he certainly could have exposed Clement through alternative channels.

Instead, once Madhoff grasped Clement's true goal of rebuilding the temple on the Temple Mount, he'd proposed an alliance. Madhoff saw the potential in Clement's organization and saw how it could be used to Israel's advantage. And he convinced Clement that those advantages would be mutual. Clement's original plan had been to conquer Israel as well as the Muslim world and rebuild the temple himself, but with Madhoff's help the Jews would rebuild the temple themselves, once the Muslim world had been laid to waste. Although Clement considered the tribes of Judah to be his mortal enemies, per the teachings of his religious guru, it ultimately didn't matter if the Jews weren't annihilated along with the followers of Islam. Once the temple was rebuilt Christ would return and the Rapture would begin. The white Christians would then ascend to heaven, leaving the cursed Jews and dark-skinned peoples to fight for scraps amid the chaos of the Apocalypse.

Once Madhoff came on board, everything moved ahead much more quickly. Clement had to admit that the man was a tactical genius, even if he only admitted that to himself. Madhoff brought his own shadow organization to the table, the Irgun, a group of radical Jews that was even more well-organized and more clandestine than Clement's white Christian soldiers. Madhoff's involvement turned out to be the key to finally taking action and putting the plan into motion.

Other than having the operation discovered by Madhoff, which turned out to be a fortuitous mistake, everything had gone off without a hitch, at least up until that day. Sure, they'd lost a couple of teams in the initial sniper attacks, but that had always been expected. That's why they had contingencies for cleansing any scene in which any team members might have been compromised. But that day it seemed as though the wheels were starting to come off the operation.

It started with the warrant for his arrest. He'd known

that federal agents were investigating his activities, which was to be expected. Once they set the operation into motion he'd had to ramp up his weapons appropriation program. That had entailed increasing his exposure to risk, but it meant little or nothing at that point. When he'd pushed the button on the sniper operations, it was no longer a matter of degree of risk, but rather it had become all or nothing. He hadn't expected the Feds to act so quickly, however. According to the master plan, the government would be too busy investigating the sniper attacks to pursue the investigation. Only a phone call from Madhoff had prevented Clement's arrest. Now he was hiding out in western Virginia in a compound they'd used for sniper training prior to the beginning of operations.

They'd equipped the compound to serve as an operations center just in case Clement had to go to ground, so the arrest warrants weren't a major impediment to the operation. The general had set up camp and before the last of that day's sniper attacks had occurred in Hawaii he'd been directing his troops from his new digs.

But after that day's sniper attacks, things had really started to go south. It started out with the disappearance of Pete Tressel, the biker in charge of the Minneapolis Slaves' operation. He'd always considered Tressel a weak link because he questioned the man's commitment to Jesus Christ as his personal Lord and Savior. Tressel professed to be every bit as much a true believer as Clement and Schmidt, but Clement suspected his real motive was earthly power. Clement figured he'd know for certain where Tressel stood on the day of the Rapture. He suspected that Tressel would be one of the cursed ones left behind, in spite of the lip service he paid to the Lord.

That afternoon the Slaves' clubhouse in Minneapolis had gone dark. One minute everything was fine, and the next it appeared no one was home. During a brief phone call with Madhoff earlier in the evening, the Israeli claimed that a lone gunman had stormed the clubhouse and abducted Tressel, but that hardly seemed possible to Clement. The clubhouse was a virtual fortress. There was no way an intruder would survive, much less abscond with the queen bee of the hive. Madhoff claimed he had the situation under control, that he had a crew going to neutralize Tressel.

Clement knew what kind of crew Madhoff would be using: blacks. The general worked with the Israelis, but he drew the line at working with blacks. Madhoff had no such qualms. When it came to his own personal Christian army, white was the only color Clement allowed.

Since then the general had heard nothing from Madhoff. Clement had called Schmidt after his conversation with the Israeli, but Schmidt knew little more than what Madhoff had already told Clement. Madhoff had called Schmidt and told him to expect trouble, and that was the last the biker had heard from the man. Now Schmidt no longer answered his cell phone, which meant that the trouble the Israeli had warned about had to have arrived.

To make matters worse, he'd just tried to call Eric von Holt to get an update on the Southern California operation and found von Holt's phone as quiet as Schmidt's, Tressel's and Madhoff's phones. For the first time, Clement was starting to panic. All the other operations had checked in and reported everything was going according to plan, but the fact that three key operations centers had gone dark was a bad sign. Clement was about to dial Madhoff's number one more time when his phone rang.

Minneapolis, Minnesota

THE SERIOUS, WELL-DRESSED woman who emerged from the north Minneapolis house barely resembled the tarted-up stripper who'd brought Bolan to the house earlier. Even more amazing was the fact that she'd made the transformation in less than ten minutes. The soldier's respect for Westerberg increase by the moment.

"So how are we going to crash the police investigation? Especially with you dressed like some sort of cross between a ballet dancer and a cat burglar?"

Before Bolan could answer two cars pulled up to the front of the house. Westerberg had her gun drawn and was prepared to do battle the instant the cars appeared in the closed-circuit television monitors mounted above a workbench in the garage. "Aren't you going to help out?" Westerberg said.

"No need. They're on our side." Bolan went outside and met the two men driving the cars. They gave the

soldier a package, then left together in one of the pair
of matching Crown Vics, leaving the second behind.
He returned to the garage, presented Westerberg with
authorized papers identifying her as a federal agent,
complete with badge, and began to change into the suit
the men had brought him.

"I still am not sure what you mean by 'our side,'" she
said, "but you seem to have access to some impressive
resources." Bolan didn't answer, but in truth he was
impressed himself. He hadn't expected Kurtzman to
come through for at least an hour. Bolan adjusted his
shoulder rig, made sure his Beretta was secure and put
his suit jacket over his weapon load.

"You clean up rather nicely," Westerberg said.

"I was thinking the same about you," Bolan replied,
"but let's save the compliments until later. We have work
to do." The two got in the big Ford sedan and headed
back toward the ambush site. Brognola had issued orders
to the investigators on the scene that federal agents Matt
Cooper and Rachel Silverman would be in charge of the
operation. This would undoubtedly ruffle the feathers
of the local investigators, but Bolan needed answers fast
and didn't have time for political niceties. He drove the
big black Crown Vic like a two-ton land missile, using
the emergency vehicle traffic light preemption equipment to ensure all traffic lights worked in his favor,
hitting the siren and flashing lights through every in-
tersection just in case some preoccupied driver wasn't
paying attention. They made it to the crash scene in less
than seven minutes.

Once at the scene, Bolan introduced himself in the terse, arrogant fashion that the local investigators would expect from a federal agent and went straight to the pickup that still protruded from the glass storefront. Investigators were still photographing the scene and hadn't yet touched anything. Bolan and Westerberg went to the body lying in the box of the pickup.

"That's Hazan," Westerberg said.

Bolan could tell that the sight of the man had shaken his partner. "How well did you know him?"

"Very well. Intimately, you might say. I was just starting my career. He was the superstar of the agency. I think you get the picture."

"How did it end?"

"That's a rather personal question, don't you think?"

"I apologize," Bolan said, "but I need to know everything you know if we're going to stop these attacks."

"He frightened me. The more I got to know him, the more I became convinced that the man was unhinged. I wasn't the only one who felt this way. Hazan was a hero in Mossad. He'd sacrificed a great deal for our nation and he was held in the highest regard, at least officially. Secretly, I don't think there was a single person who wasn't relieved when he retired. I believe my opinion of his mental state was held by most of my superiors, if not all of them."

"Why were you following him?" Bolan asked.

"I began to suspect his activities when we were together. I began to believe that his behavior was motivated by something other than his workaholic tendencies and his eccentricity. I suspected that some of his outside associations might border on criminal, perhaps even traitorous. I began to suspect that he might be involved in some sort of resurrection of the Irgun."

"Do you know who all was involved in this?"

"No. Hazan was smart. I stumbled on this information through pure luck. I've spent the past several years investigating this, but the only name I've been able to get was 'Amos.' I have no idea who Amos really is."

By this time Bolan and Westerberg had donned latex gloves and were examining Hazan's body. The local police were busy collecting shell casings and other evidence from the scene. Bolan let them go about their business, even though he knew that half the casings came from the guns he and Westerberg carried. The rest had most likely been appropriated by General Clement. There was little to be learned from the effluent from their earlier battle, but it kept the locals busy and allowed Bolan and Westerberg to examine Hazan's body undisturbed.

Bolan produced a cell phone from one of Hazan's jacket pockets. He popped off the back, removed the SIM card and popped it into a slot on his handheld computer. Within moments the information on the card was winging its way to Kurtzman at Stony Man Farm. They continued searching the body, but other than the cell phone, they were finding few clues from Hazan's remains, at least until Westerberg removed a Montblanc ink pen from Hazan's pocket.

"Nice bit of kit," Bolan said.

"I gave him this for our six-month anniversary."
Bolan could see that discovering the pen had upset the
Israeli agent. He watched as Westerberg took apart the
pen while Bolan continued to search the body.

"What's this?" She removed a memory stick from
the inside of the pen. "Typical Hazan move," she said.
"Think about it—if your average street cop discovered
a pen this valuable, what are the odds that he or she
wouldn't just pocket the pen without reporting it as evidence? Clever—hiding something in such a valuable
object that it's more likely to be stolen than it is to be
examined. He always was a smart one."

By this time Bolan was already on his cell phone
talking to Kurtzman. "Get ready for a download," he
stated. "We pulled some data off Hazan's corpse." He
took the memory stick from Westerberg and plugged it
into his handheld computer. "I'm sending the data right
now."

Minneapolis, Minnesota

ISAAC MADHOFF STILL COULDN'T grasp the fact that the
American and the Israeli woman had not only survived
Hazan's ambush, but had counterattacked and success-
fully took out Madhoff's right-hand man. But that was
exactly what happened, according to the reports coming
in over Madhoff's police scanner. Who was this American? And how could an organization capable of fielding such a super agent even exist without Madhoff's
knowledge? This question was beginning to become an

obsession with the Israeli, though he hardly considered it an irrational obsession, given the havoc the man had wreaked in Madhoff's operation over the past twelve hours.

This man pursuing him had a reach that extended far beyond Minneapolis. In addition to wiping out one of the most capable agents the Mossad had ever produced with seeming ease, this interloper had used whatever information he'd gathered from Tressel to wipe out the Satan's Slaves' headquarters in Texas in a matter of hours. No lone wolf operating on his own could ever be that effective. He'd warned Schmidt to be prepared for some sort of action when Tressel had been abducted, but he never expected anything on this scale.

Had Schmidt been taken alive, most likely that would have been the end of the operation. Schmidt knew far too much about Clement, and Clement knew far too much about Madhoff. Clement was the only person other than a few trusted former Mossad agents to know Madhoff's real identity. He regretted the necessity of sharing that information with Clement, but it was the only way he could gain the general's trust. Now the general had become Madhoff's greatest liability.

He'd known that the general's falling apart under pressure was a likely outcome from the beginning. In Madhoff's mind, there were two types of thought— dogmatic and pragmatic—and the two forms were at odds with each other. Ever the pragmatist, Madhoff considered dogmatic thought a form of mental illness. Once a person made his logic subservient to his dogma, that person's intellect was no longer functioning at full capacity. Hence, the person was mentally impaired. It didn't matter if the dogma was political, religious or even focused on a type of vehicle or some other fetish object. Once a person identified himself with any sort of dogmatic belief system, the person would invariably function on a lower mental level.

Clement was a slave to dogmatic thought. A born-again Christian, every action the general made was governed by his tenacious belief that Jesus was about to come back to Earth, this in spite of the fact that there existed no empirical evidence that the man had ever been here the first time around.

Madhoff suspected that Clement bought into other darker dogmas, too. Not that it mattered. As an Israeli spy, he was used to working with all sorts of lunatics and sociopaths. Since he didn't ascribe to any dogma, he was free to be pragmatic, and the alliance with General Clement was the most pragmatic one yet. The general might be motivated by childish superstition and asinine prejudices, but the end result was that the man had the infrastructure to carry out Irgun's goal of wiping out the Muslim world in a single stroke. This goal wasn't motivated by any sort of abstract dogmatic concept like "patriotism"; rather, it was motivated by the ultimate pragmatic motivator: the will to survive. The Muslim world made it clear that it wouldn't rest until the state of Israel had been wiped off the face of the Earth. The pragmatic solution to that was to beat them to the punch and wipe out the Muslim world.

In this task General Clement would be a willing and able partner. Of course this alliance would be temporary. Madhoff would keep his end of the bargain. Once the Muslim world had been reduced to rubble, he would personally oversee the rebuilding of the temple on the Temple Mount. For a while this would placate the fundamentalist Christians and keep them occupied waiting for Jesus, but when their Savior failed to float down from wherever he was hiding himself, they'd start to get restless. They'd probably just fight among themselves, for the most part, but the crushing disappointment of not getting called up in the Rapture would be so great for some of them that they'd snap and become dangerous. Madhoff pegged the general as a candidate for that latter group—that was, if the general hadn't snapped already. His behavior was becoming increasingly erratic.

The general had his uses, though. He certainly provided the best military toys available. The Reaper drone had proved extremely useful, as had the skilled operator the general had provided. After Tressel had been nabbed, Madhoff had ordered the drone to circle above San Leon and monitor the Satan's Slaves' Texas compound. The vehicle was amazing, providing the operator with real-time aerial footage of the siege along with a means of cleansing the scene once all hope was lost. The operator had been able to destroy the compound while operating the drone from an installation half a continent away from the theater of action.

He'd deliberately kept General Clement out of the loop regarding the use of the drone to cleanse the Texas compound, however. The general had a dangerous sentimental attachment to his men, a typically unpragmatic attitude. Madhoff supposed the general's childish attachment represented was what the Americans called a "man crush," or to use the current parlance, a "bromance." This was especially true regarding his relationship with the filthy biker Schmidt. Madhoff worried that this emotional connection might prevent the general from doing what needed to be done regarding eliminating the threat that a captured Schmidt would have posed to the operation.

As the plan progressed, the general had become increasingly unstable. As a result, Madhoff was becoming increasingly frugal with how much information he shared with the man. As Clement spun further and further out of control, it became easier to keep facts from him. Now that he was safely squirreled away in the Virginia compound, his erratic behavior was even less of a problem. But now, as much as Madhoff dreaded it, he was going to have to call Clement with a litany of bad news. He hoped it wouldn't be enough to make the general go completely off the deep end. He dialed the number.

"What the fuck is going on?" Clement demanded. Unlike most American military men, Clement didn't curse like a drunken frat boy; to hear this sort of language meant that the man was genuinely upset.

"I'm afraid I have some bad news, General. We failed to kill the American."

"What? How could you fail? Why didn't you have Hazan take care of it?"

"I assigned that task to Hazan."

"And he failed? I'll have him horsewhipped!"

"Hazan is dead," Madhoff told the general.

"What? How?"

"I don't know the details. Hazan was to ambush the American. I led him into a trap that he should not have had one chance in a million of surviving. Somehow he did. Not only that, but he counterattacked and killed Hazan."

"How is that even possible?"

"That's all the details I have right now. I won't know more until the morning, when I can access the police reports. But I do know one thing—this man is the most highly skilled adversary I've ever encountered."

"Did he get any information off Hazan?" Clement asked.

"Perhaps. Hazan was carrying electronic files that showed the location of tomorrow's planned bombings, among other things."

"Are you fucking kidding me?" Clement was apoplectic. "Why in the name of almighty Jesus would you send a man on a mission when he was carrying such sensitive documents?"

"He was already on a mission to deliver those documents to me when the ambush was added to his duties. We had only moments to prepare the ambush. There wasn't time to secure the files. But don't worry. The encryption on the files is impenetrable."

"I'll worry if I damned well feel like worrying," Clement said, "and right now I feel like worrying. I should think you'd feel the same. Don't you think a man who can single-handedly break into the Satan's Slaves' clubhouse and kidnap their leader right out from under their noses is capable of penetrating documents that are supposedly impenetrable? Don't you think someone who could turn the tables and kill a man like Hazan is capable of just about anything?"

Secretly, Madhoff worried that Clement was correct, but he felt it was in the general's best interest to lie to him at that moment.

"Don't worry, General. Even if they can defeat our security measures, they won't be able to do so until after the bombs have gone off. At that point our man inside will have convinced the President to declare martial law. By this time tomorrow we will be in complete control of the United States' nuclear stockpile."

This appeared to at least partially placate the general. "What's going on in San Leon?" he asked. "I haven't been able to contact Schmidt all night."

"I'm afraid I've got some more bad news," Madhoff told the general. "The compound is gone, along with everyone inside of it."

"What? What do you mean 'gone'?"

"We had to destroy it, General. Federal agents had captured Schmidt. He knew too much and would have talked."

"How did you do it?"

"AGM-114s, General, a pair of them fired from the MQ-9."

"He wouldn't have talked," the general said, but with less vigor than he'd shown earlier in the conversation. Clement knew full well that Schmidt would sing like a bird when the Feds put the screws to him. "What's going on in California? I can't get hold of anyone in Long Beach."

"Same story, General. The compound was raided by federal agents. That von Holt kid detonated the fifteen-ton GBU-57A/B explosive device according to our pre-determined contingency plan."

"Ah, no," the General moaned. "Did he really have to do that?"

"There was no choice, General. The Feds had raided the facility and killed everyone inside but von Holt. Had they discovered our explosives production facility, they would have known what to expect from future attacks. We would have lost the element of surprise and neutral-ized tomorrow's mission."

This explanation appeared to placate the general a bit but he still seemed dangerously upset, so Mad-hoff changed the subject. "Did you hear from our man inside?"

"Yes," the general replied. "He believes that once the bombs go off, the President will have no options other than declaring martial law."

"He's got the situation under control?" Madhoff asked. "Now that you're out of the Joint Chiefs, we're completely depending on him to coax the President to do our biding."

"I have complete confidence in him," Clement said. "Besides, the national security adviser and the rest of the Joint Chiefs have come around and now support declaring martial law as soon as possible. And that's before tomorrow's wave of bombings. Afterward, the President won't have a choice."

CHAPTER ELEVEN

Bolan's phone vibrated in his pocket. He didn't bother looking at the screen since it could only be one of three people: Barbara Price, Hal Brognola or most likely Aaron Kurtzman. "I hope you're calling to tell me that you've broken the encryption on those files I sent you," he said to whichever of the three he was speaking with.

"Not yet," Kurtzman replied. "This is some of the most sophisticated encryption we've ever encountered. But we're working on it and we'll get it."

"Let's just hope we get it before any more innocent people have to die," Bolan said.

"I do have some good news, though," Kurtzman said. "I think we have a location for that Jeep you were chasing. Not an exact address, but I've been studying real-time satellite images and I've got it nailed down to the right block. It's somewhere on the 9700 block of Irving Avenue North. You're going to have to do a little breaking and entering to figure out exactly which house it's at, though."

"Anything you can give me to help me narrow it down?"

"Yeah," Kurtzman said. "Only a few of the houses in that neighborhood have garages. I'd focus on those."

"Is Hal there?"

"He's flown back to D.C.," Kurtzman said. "He's been called to a meeting with the President, his security advisers and the Joint Chiefs. I think it's going to be a showdown to get the man to declare martial law."

"Is Hal going to tell them about Clement's involvement in this?"

"He's going to play it by ear."

Bolan didn't envy Brognola. The soldier found the world of political maneuvering and backstabbing intolerable. He much preferred to operate out in the world, where he usually knew what the threats were and he always knew how to deal with them. When he hung up, he flipped on the flashing lights and once again made record time across north Minneapolis.

"Where are we going?" Westerberg asked.

"We've got a line on your friend Amos."

As they got nearer to the neighborhood, Bolan turned off the flashing lights and slowed the car. He identified the three houses that were likely candidates on the first pass. All three were on the west side of the street. He circled the block and drove through the alley behind the houses. Light came from the windows of only one of the houses. Given that it was 3:00 a.m. on a weeknight, Bolan figured that was as good a place as any to start searching.

He got out of the car in the alley and let Westerberg drive away. She would keep circling the block until he had either determined that Amos wasn't there or he needed backup. North Minneapolis was a rough neighborhood, and no one would question an unmarked police car cruising around in the middle of the night. The two exchanged cell phone numbers.

"I'll call you when I need you to pick me up," Bolan said.

The three houses with garages were all next to each other. The reason that more houses didn't have garages was in part because the alley was too narrow to allow approaches to garages. The three houses had circumvented this by sharing a single approach to all three garages. The center garage was set back from the alley, with its door facing the alley. The other two were on either side of the approach, with their doors facing each other across the approach. The two garages on either side were in poor repair. Both had older hand-operated doors with windows that allowed the soldier to look in and determine that the Jeep wasn't inside either building. The middle garage, the one with the door facing the alley, looked about as old and dilapidated as the other two, but it had a fairly new door, one with an automatic door opener, and no windows. That garage belonged to the house with the light shining out through the windows. Bolan, who had changed back into his blacksuit, removed his listening device and determined that there was no one inside the garage.

He removed a remote-control device from a pouch on his utility belt, plugged it into his handheld computer and began to run a program that Kurtzman had installed. The program went through the entire range of radio frequencies that might possibly activate a garage-door opener. When the program sent the correct frequency through the remote device, the garage door began to rise. Once the program detected that the signal was working, it remained on that frequency.

When the garage door was up about eighteen inches, the soldier hit another button on the device and the door stopped rising. He rolled under the door into the garage, where he found himself beneath the rear bumper of the Jeep Grand Cherokee SRT8 he'd chased earlier. He placed a global-positioning transmitter deep inside the bumper mount of the vehicle, where it would be virtually impossible to find, then rolled back out into the driveway and pressed a button on the remote to shut the door.

Bolan crept up to the house, watching for trip wires, pressure detectors or lasers that might be linked to an alarm system. He found two of the three. Regularly spaced patches of fresh-looking grass on the otherwise dying lawn turned out to be artificial turf, which most likely disguised pressure detectors. Had the lawn been greener he wouldn't have been able to make out the detectors, but apparently watering the lawn hadn't been as high on the priority list of the caretakers as it should have been. Once he got near the house he detected laser beams around the foundation and around each of the windowsills. That meant that he most likely had the right place, but it also meant that getting in undetected was going to be difficult.

Instead of curtains or blinds, the basement windows were covered with terry cloth bath towels. Bolan couldn't see anything through the towels except shadows moving around in the basement. He counted at least five distinct forms. He crept around the house, looking for a window he could use to get inside, but all of them had lasers placed so that it would be impossible to even open the windows without tripping the lasers, much less pass through them.

The soldier placed a two-sided mirror in one of the laser beams to break the beam without tripping an alarm and was about to place a second mirror that would create a gap in which he could work when he heard a dog start to bark inside the house. He heard a voice yell, "Shut up!" at the dog, but it kept barking. After the dog barked for a few moments the back door opened and a man let the dog out. "Goddamn it, you're a pain in the ass," a voice said, but the dog, a large Rottweiler, had torn around the house and was coming at Bolan before the man could say the word "ass."

Bolan drew his suppressed Beretta and fired a shot at the dog just as it leaped for his throat. He stepped aside as the dog thumped to the ground beside him. The gun was fairly quiet, but it still let out a powerful *whump*, followed by the even louder thump of the dog's body hitting the ground. The man on the porch had to have heard something because he asked, "Are you all right, boy?"

The Executioner froze as the man on the back steps came trotting around the side of the house. The man, who was wearing the traditional red colors of the Rollin' 30s Bloods froze when he saw Bolan. The tall African-American man raised the large-caliber revolver that he

carried in his right hand, but before he could squeeze off
a shot the soldier fired three rounds, two into the man's
chest, one into his head. The man fell dead beside the
body of his dog.

Bolan paused to see if anyone inside the house noticed anything, but the loud, thumping music coming
from the basement had to have prevented anyone from
hearing anything. Bolan went around to the back door,
which was still open, and stepped carefully inside. He
found himself in a darkened kitchen. A door opened
off the room and led to the basement. Off to one side
was what once had been a living room or family room.
Standing back in the shadows so he couldn't be seen,
Bolan glanced through the door and saw several gangbangers sitting around on couches, each armed with
HK MP-5s. Full-auto machine pistols like that were not
typical gangbanger fare; these young men had some sort
of weapons pipeline with military connections. Bolan
was certain that that pipeline could be traced back to one
General Joe Clement. He had come to the right house.

Bolan counted the men in the room. There were four
of them, but two of them were sleeping, and the other
two looked like they were fighting hard to stay awake.
If he was going to get any farther in the house he'd have
to take them out quickly, before any of them got off a
shot from their unsupressed HKs. The soldier planned
his attack—one bullet from the suppressed Beretta into
the head of each of the men who were starting to nod
off, followed by a bullet to the head of each of the men
who were sleeping. He'd have to be quick if this was

going to work. Bolan aimed at the man farthest from him and squeezed the trigger. The Beretta coughed once and the man's head erupted in a geyser of blood, brains, bone and hair.

The other man looked at his friend's head exploding. Before he could register the threat a bullet cleaved the top third of his head in two. Bolan shifted his position and fired directly into the face of one of the men who had been sleeping on the couch, but who had started to awaken because of the commotion. A small crater appeared between the man's eyes, and a much larger crater erupted from the back of his head. The fourth man never woke up at all.

Bolan had just squeezed off a round into the fourth man's head when he heard a voice behind him say, "What the fuck?" The soldier turned to see a large African-American man wearing a baggy gym suit standing in the doorway that led to the basement. The soldier whirled and put three rounds through the man's heart. He fell face-first to the floor.

He was a big man, over three hundred pounds, and when he hit the floor the whole house shook.

"What the fuck's going on up there?" a voice shouted from the basement.

When no answer came, Bolan heard heavy footsteps thudding their way up the stairs. He holstered his Beretta, pulled his bowie knife from its sheath and hid behind the door. When the man emerged from the basement, the Executioner grabbed him from behind, wrapped his arm around the man's mouth to keep him from screaming and sliced his throat from ear to ear. When he was done, only a thin ribbon of skin and flesh held the decapitated head to the neck. Bolan carefully set the man down on top of his fallen comrade and crept into the living room.

Several rooms occupied the main floor, an office and a few bedrooms, but they were empty. Bolan didn't know much about the mysterious Amos, but he figured it was a safe bet that the man wasn't downstairs listening to hip-hop and playing video games with a bunch of gangbangers. Upstairs seemed like a more promising direction in which to search for his quarry.

Bolan crept up the steps and stopped to listen at the top of the stairs. He could hear the sounds of someone having sex behind a door at the end of the hall. There appeared to be just one other bedroom on the top floor, which was empty.

Bolan walked toward the door at the end of the hall as quietly as humanly possible. Judging from the sounds, there was some serious sex going on behind it. He waited until all was quiet, then kicked the door open, revealing a large, muscular Caucasian man and a young black woman. The man looked like he was at least the same age as Bolan, but the young woman looked to be in her late teens.

"Freeze!" he said.

The man rolled over on the bed with such speed that the soldier didn't have an opportunity to get off a shot without jeopardizing the young woman. The man held her in front of him as he spun around, using her as a human shield. From behind his back he pulled a gun, laid it over the teen's bare shoulder and fired, hitting the soldier square in the chest. Bolan's body armor held, but the blast was from a powerful gun and it knocked him back out of the room, cracking some ribs in the process.

Before Bolan could regain his footing and go back inside the room, he heard footsteps running up the stairs. It sounded like at least five separate pairs of feet were heading his way. Instead of getting up, the Executioner aimed his Desert Eagle at the top of the steps. One man appeared on the landing, followed by a second. The two were so close they were touching. Both men had MP-5s in the ready position, but they were expecting to see someone upright, not lying on the floor. Before they could adjust their aim Bolan fired. The powerful .50-caliber bullet penetrated the chest cavities of both men, sending them back down the stairs.

Before the attackers had a chance to regroup, Bolan pulled the pin on an M-67 fragmentation grenade and lobbed the bomb down the stairs. The grenade exploded just as it hit the bottom of the steps and decimated the men coming after Bolan. He got up and moved to the top of the stairs, looking down for survivors. Blood, guts and gore covered the entire area. Most of the gunners had been reduced to random body parts, but one man still lived, though with his left arm, shoulder and half his face missing, *living* was a strong word for his condition. Bolan put a .50-caliber bullet through what was left of the man's head, ending his suffering.

The soldier went back to the bedroom and found the teenager still in the bed, clutching a sheet to her nude body. The Caucasian man was gone, apparently having escaped out an open window. Bolan looked out the window but saw no signs of movement. Then he heard the Jeep tearing out of the garage.

Washington, D.C.

HAL BROGNOLA LOOKED AROUND the room, wondering if any of the people present were involved with General Joe Clement in the sniper attacks. Clement was just about as high up the ladder as possible; his position in the Joint Chiefs was J-4, which meant that he was in charge of logistics, a position that had provided him with access to the entire U.S. arsenal. If Clement was involved in this, any of the Joint Chiefs could be involved. Even the national security adviser was suspect, though Brognola didn't believe she was involved. He'd known Lt. General Ellen Kuznia for decades. The big Fed's advice had in part led the President to select her as his assistant for national security affairs, though with her stellar service record it hadn't been a hard sell.

There were a couple of members of the Joint Chiefs who Brognola also considered beyond suspicion, too. Both the army chief of staff and the Marine Corps commandant had long histories working with Brognola. He'd known both since they were all young men. His gut told him that these men weren't involved, and his common sense backed his gut.

The only other person in the room absolutely beyond Brognola's suspicion was the President. Like most presidents, the current one was neither good nor evil. He was, like all of his predecessors before him, a politician, no more, no less.

Other than the President, no one was really completely above suspicion, but Brognola didn't have the luxury of methodically investigating each and every possible subject. Every second that they dillydallied could mean the difference between life and death for hundreds, perhaps thousands of people. He had to use his common sense and focus his efforts on investigating the people that his gut and logic both dictated should be investigated.

Brognola couldn't shake the feeling that he was rapidly running out of time. They still hadn't uncovered the purpose of these attacks, but whatever it was, it had to be huge. He knew that the very first day, when no credible source claimed credit for the attacks. Of course crackpots up the old wazoo had stepped forward and claimed credit, but these people ranged from schizophrenic Arabs living in flea-bitten flophouses in Hamburg, Germany to drug-addled Nazi skinheads in Orange County, California. Every single claim so far had been dismissed as the ravings of lunatics.

When Brognola learned of Joe Clement's involvement, he wasn't completely surprised. He'd always questioned the man's sanity. The Justice man didn't begrudge a person his or her spiritual beliefs, but when a grown man wore his religion on his sleeve the way Clement did, the big Fed questioned both his maturity and his sanity. It didn't matter what the religion. Whenever a grown man began or ended the majority of his sentences with some variation of the phrase "God willing," that person had some misfiring synapses.

Clement might have been a nutcase, but he was smart and he was capable. Brognola couldn't imagine the man going to all the trouble of organizing such meticulous attacks if the end goal had simply been to create general chaos. He figured Clement and his as-yet undiscovered coconspirators had to have a much grander master plan. The sniper attacks were most likely just phase one. Brognola had no idea what the subsequent phases might be, but judging by the horror of phase one he hoped the world would never find out.

The one thing he was certain of was that part of the goal of the attacks was to get the President to declare martial law. He'd suspected that from day one, but once he learned of Clement's involvement he became even more certain of that fact. Each of the Joint Chiefs had urged the President to declare martial law, and even General Kuznia had come to share that position as the sniper attacks wore on, but Clement had been the first to suggest it and had been one of the most adamant members of the martial-law camp from the very first day of the attacks.

The other member of the Joint Chiefs who had been strident in his support of martial law was Admiral Leroy Scarborough, chief of naval operations and also chairman of the Joint Chiefs. Scarborough was something of a mystery to Brognola. His service record was stellar, as was Clement's, but unlike Clement, he didn't appear to feel some sort of personal mission to ensure that everyone on Earth shared religious beliefs that were identical to his own. He did attend the same church as Clement, though that didn't mean much because many top-ranking military personnel attended that church, as did a great number of lower-ranking officers and enlisted personnel.

The church attended by both Clement and the chairman of the Joint Chiefs was one of the new breed of nondenominational evangelical mega-churches.

Their services took place in a giant modern auditorium with a state-of-the-art sound system and JumboTron television screens on every wall. The church seated tens of thousands of people, and their carefully choreographed services made an awards show ceremony appear thrown together by comparison.

Their services were broadcast on cable television from coast to coast and attracted the highest ratings of any such broadcast. It only made sense that anyone attracted to this sort of spectacle would go to this church. Scarborough and Clement both attended services there, but so did approximately 100,000 other people during the course of any given week. Millions more watched it on television.

Still, Scarborough bore watching, and Brognola kept one eye on him as he delivered his message to the assembled group.

"Gentlemen, madam," the big Fed said, "I apologize

for calling you together at this ungodly hour of the morning, but I have some critical information that I need to share with you. I have nothing to report on the sniper attacks, except that we are investigating some promising leads. I do, however, have some bad news about one of your colleagues. You may have noticed that General Clement is absent. I'm afraid he's become a fugitive."

Brognola watched Scarborough's reaction as he delivered this news. While the rest of the room let out an involuntary and collective gasp, Scarborough simply looked worried.

"We attempted to arrest the general earlier this evening on weapons-dealing charges, but he had fled. His whereabouts are currently unknown." By this time Scarborough had begun acting as incredulous as the other assembled members of the President's security team, but his initial reaction had increased Brognola's suspicions.

Minneapolis, Minnesota

ISAAC MADHOFF HAD JUST ROLLED away from the teen-aged prostitute when the bedroom door burst open. Knowing that none of Omar's men would intrude on his personal space, Madhoff knew he was under attack and reacted instantly. He rolled off the bed, carrying the young woman with him, placing her between himself and the intruder's line of fire. As he'd expected, it was the American.

With the prostitute's body shielding his vital organs,

Madhoff grabbed the Glock 21 he kept beneath his pillow, leveled it over her shoulder and squeezed off a round. The bullet caught the American right in his center of mass and sent him flying back through the doorway. It was a good shot, but judging from the lack of blood, the intruder was wearing some sort of body armor, so Madhoff had only bought himself a few seconds of time. The footsteps he heard pounding through the first floor of the house told him that reinforcements were coming; Madhoff hoped the gangbangers downstairs could hold off the big American long enough for him to escape through the window.

The first shot from the hallway told Madhoff that the intruder would be busy, at least for a short time. He grabbed his pants, shirt and shoes and climbed through the window, which opened out to the roof of an addition that had been built onto the house at some point in its history. From there it was about a nine foot jump to the ground. Madhoff felt slightly ridiculous running across the lawn in the buff, but if he took the time to get dressed he would be a dead man.

He ran to the garage, fishing the key to the walk-in door on the side of the garage from his pants pocket as he ran. He fumbled with the lock for just a second because he was distracted by the sound of the explosion coming from the house. The intruder had to have used a grenade because Madhoff hadn't trusted the untrained and undisciplined members of the Rollin' 30s Bloods enough to equip them with explosive ordnance. By the time the shock wave of the explosion had subsided he was inside the Jeep and punching the start button. He threw the vehicle in Reverse before the garage door had even finished rising and when he backed out of the structure the top of his vehicle cleared the door by mere millimeters. Not that he would have cared if he'd scraped the roof of the Jeep—at that moment his priority was staying alive, not preserving the appearance of his vehicle.

Nor was he concerned with babying its transmission; he backed into the alley with all four tires squealing. He kept the accelerator floored and barely touched the brakes when he slammed the shift lever into Drive. The powerful engine reduced the protesting tires to smoking rubber doughnuts as he rocketed down the alley. He exited onto the street in a four-wheeled drift, keeping the accelerator pinned to the floor.

When he'd put enough distance between himself and the American to feel comfortable, he slowed a bit and tried to get dressed while still driving. He managed to put on his pants and shirt, but was unable to tie his shoes. Then he reviewed the events of the past couple of hours in his head. How had the American found his safe house? There could only be two possible answers.

The first was that the American had access to satellite surveillance, which was altogether possible. The big stranger seemed to have virtually unlimited resources, and the man clearly knew a lot more about Madhoff's operation than Madhoff knew about the stranger, which amounted to virtually nothing.

The second possibility was that the man had retrieved

the information from the memory stick that Hazan carried when he'd been killed, but this seemed highly unlikely. The encryption on the files could be cracked—no security measure was foolproof—but there was no possible way that the information would have been accessed so quickly. Besides, Madhoff didn't even know if the memory stick had been found.

Then there was always the third possibility: that this stranger was some sort of golem, an inhuman vengeful monstrosity created to punish Madhoff for his sins, which were numerous. Once again his sexual appetites had put him in a compromising position. The American had literally caught the Israeli with his pants down. Only his lightning-fast reflexes had saved Madhoff from being captured by the American. He shouldn't have been dallying with the prostitute; he should have been expecting trouble and preparing for an attack on the safe house.

But he also knew this sort of thinking bordered on the childish superstitious beliefs that people called religion, and represented the sort of behavior he most despised. The big American wasn't a supernatural creature. Madhoff had seen for himself that the man was as vulnerable to a .45-caliber bullet as was any other flesh-and-blood mortal. The possibility of his being some sort of golem was the function of Madhoff's agitated state of mind and lack of sleep.

The second possibility—that the Americans had captured and accessed the information Hazan carried—while improbable, was at least statistically possible. One of the files on the memory stick contained the locations of all their safe houses, including the location of the sniper-bomber teams as well as the compound in which the general was holed up. Because of that slim statistical possibility, Madhoff decided against going to another safe house. Madhoff would have to find somewhere else to go.

If the most likely scenario—that the Americans had tracked him using real-time satellite imagery—was the case, Madhoff wasn't terribly concerned. That would be an easy problem to solve. The only reason it had been possible to track him to the safe house was because there was virtually no other traffic on the road at that time of night. It would be child's play to confuse a satellite camera by getting into freeway traffic and taking a circuitous route around the city. Vehicles such as his were commonplace in a northern city, where residents had to deal with snow and ice several months each year. Most of the Jeep Grand Cherokees on the road weren't hot rod SRT8 versions like the one he drove, but they all looked the same from above.

Madhoff got on Interstate 94 and began following a route that led him to all four corners of the metro area, taking last-minute turns onto exits, then doubling back on clover-leaf intersections. It took him nearly ninety minutes to drive a distance that would have normally taken him twenty minutes, but by the time he arrived at the nondescript building on a seedy part of West Seventh Street in neighboring St. Paul, Minnesota, he was absolutely certain he had shaken any eye in the sky that might be watching him.

Madhoff went to the side door of the building and knocked four times, slowly. A panel slid open in the door. The man peering through the opening recognized him and let him in. Once inside, the Israeli accustomed himself to the loud music, dim lights and smoky air. Minnesota had long since outlawed smoking in public places, but this establishment operated outside the constraints of the law. Madhoff pulled out a chair at the base of the stage and started watching the girls dancing in front of him.

They weren't really dancing or even pretending to dance. One girl made a half-hearted attempt to swing around the pole in the center of the stage, but the girls weren't up there to dance; they were up there to advertise their wares. He recognized a few of the girls and they seemed to recognize him, because none of them came to the area on the stage in front of his chair. Madhoff had earned a reputation here as something of a rough customer. Finally, one of the girls parked herself in front of him and started to perform a lap dance. She wasn't his type. She was heavier than he preferred, and older. She had to be at least twenty-five, but she did have certain charms.

"You like that, sugar?" she asked.

"It's all right."

"You want a private dance in a back room?"

"How much?"

"Are you a cop, sugar?"

"Not even close. How much for a private dance?" Madhoff asked.

"If you want a mouth dance, $100 for an hour. If you want more, $250 and up."

"Let's go."

She took him by the hand and led him to one of the small bedroom cubicles in the back of the building. Madhoff knew he was something of a hypocrite, since he knew this is exactly what had just about led to his near capture earlier, but he couldn't help himself when faced with this kind of temptation. Besides, he needed to do something to kill the time.

CHAPTER TWELVE

Bolan picked up the robe lying on the floor and covered the weeping woman in the bed. "Come on," he said. "Let's get you out of here."

"They won't let me leave," she said. "They'll kill us both."

"I don't think there's anyone left to kill either of us," he told her. "Let's go. I'll make sure nothing else happens to you."

At least I'll make sure nothing else happens to you tonight, Bolan thought, but didn't say anything. He had no idea what this young woman's story was, but he knew that whatever it was, it involved a lot of pain. He'd take care of her for, at least for tonight, get her to a woman's shelter where she'd be safe for a while, but that safety was only temporary. Soon she'd return to what passed for her normal life, to the exact people and circumstances that had led her to this situation.

It pained Bolan to see people in situations like this, but he knew that there was nothing he could do to help them. Only they could help themselves. The fact that an impoverished community such as the one living in north Minneapolis even existed spoke volumes about the problems facing the entire country.

At least Bolan would be able to help the woman this night; as far as the rest of her life went, he'd just have to hope she'd beat the odds and break out of the cycle of poverty that had led her into the slavery of prostitution. He picked her up and carried her out of the now-destroyed house.

When Bolan reached the alley, Westerberg had already brought the car around. "I heard the gunfire and explosion," she said. "Did you capture Amos? And who's this?"

"He got away, and I have no idea who this is. She was in Amos's bedroom."

"My name's Shaniqua," the young woman said. Bolan set her down in the backseat of the Crown Vic and got in the passenger's seat.

"And his name's Isaac," the girl continued, "but I'm the only one who knows that. Everyone but me calls him 'Amos.' That, or just 'the Jew.'"

Westerberg drove out of the alley and asked, "Where are we taking her?"

Bolan had already pulled up a list of battered women's shelters on his handheld computer. "There's a highly rated shelter twelve blocks straight south on Irving," he said, and read her the address.

Westerberg looked over her shoulder at Shaniqua and asked, "How do you know his name?"

"He liked me to use his name when we had sex."

"What exactly did he say?" Westerberg asked.

"He liked it when I said, 'Please, Isaac, don't hurt me,' while he fucked me. Not that it mattered. He hurt me no matter what I said. He just hurt me less when I said his name, so I said it. He said if I ever told anyone his name, he'd kill me for real. Sometimes I hoped he would."

"What did he look like?" Westerberg asked.

Shaniqua didn't reply, so Bolan said, "Big guy, but muscular, not fat. He had a little salt in his black beard and hair. He had a V-shaped scar under his left eye, and he appeared to have some sort of birthmark on his lower right buttock."

"You got a good look at his buttocks?"

"I caught them in the act," Bolan said.

"The birthmark looks like an apple," Shaniqua said.

"Are you sure?" Westerberg asked.

"I'd know. I had my face buried in it often enough. The motherfucker liked to make me toss his salad."

"I think I know who 'Amos' is," Westerberg said. "His name is Isaac Madhoff."

"How did you know that? You've found yourself face-to-face with that birthmark?"

Westerberg glared at Bolan. "Don't be a pig. Unfortunately, I have seen that birthmark on a man who looks just as you described. Isaac Madoff is—" she corrected herself "—*was* a close friend of Ze'ev's. He's something of an enigma. He was in the Knesset for many years, but I'm not sure what he does now. I used to see him at state dinners, and once he was at a resort where Ze'ev and I spent a weekend. Like too many Israelis, Madhoff likes to parade around in skimpy swimwear at the beach.

That's where I saw the birthmark. Combine that with the scar and I think there's little doubt that he is our man."

When they got to the women's shelter Westerberg took Shaniqua in and got her settled.

As soon as she left, Bolan called Kurtzman. "Bear, I have a name you need to check out immediately. Isaac Madhoff."

"Ah, Mr. Madhoff."

"You know who he is?" Bolan asked.

"We think we do," Kurtzman said. "We think he's an Israeli spy. We can't prove it, but we've had our eye on him for a few months."

"Why haven't you acted on this?" Bolan asked.

"To be honest, he doesn't appear to be a very good spy. We've got our own eyes and ears in the Mossad, and so far Madhoff has yet to deliver a single piece of intelligence of any value. Combine our lack of hard legitimate evidence with the fact that he doesn't appear to be a particularly effective spy, and he became a low priority. He certainly wasn't worth the risk of upsetting our relationship with Israel."

"I think you need to move him to the very top of your priority list," Bolan said. "He's one of the people behind the rebirth of the Irgun. He's our Amos. Find out everything you can about him, and about anyone connected to him in any way. Pay close attention to anyone jointly connected to Madhoff and Hazan. See if any of the names from the SIM card I pulled from

Hazan's phone are also connected to Madhoff. Those two seem to be key players in this whole mess."

"Any idea where he is now?" Kurtzman asked.

"I know exactly where he is," Bolan said. "I'm tracking his vehicle with a GPS transmitter right now." The soldier looked down at the display on his handheld computer. "He just turned off of U.S. 169 onto eastbound Minnesota 62."

"I might have something to help you," Kurtzman said. "We've broken the encryption on one of the files. It's a list of hundreds of addresses around the country, mostly residential houses, but some commercial property. We already recognize one of the addresses as the site we raided in Long Beach. Another belongs to the house that you just hit. We suspect that the rest are safe houses, too. One of them probably houses our buddy General Clement. We've narrowed down the general's location to just a few possible options. As for the rest of the addresses, we've got teams going to as many of them as we can, but it's going to take a while—there are nearly one thousand addresses on the list. I'm sending you all the addresses in the Minneapolis metro area right now. Check your in-box."

"Any luck breaking open the other files?"

"Not yet," Kurtzman said. "This is incredibly sophisticated stuff. Each individual file uses its own unique form of encryption. It's probably going to take all night."

"Let me know as soon as you learn anything," Bolan said.

Westerberg returned to the car in a matter of minutes

and found Bolan staring at his computer screen, watching a blinking light circle around on a map of the Minneapolis area freeway system. "Playing video games?" she asked.

"No. I'm tracking Madhoff. Head out to the freeway. Take 94 south to 35W."

Harrisonburg, Virginia

GENERAL JOE CLEMENT KNEW he shouldn't call Admiral Leroy Scarborough. The plan had been for all communications between the admiral and the general to go through Madhoff, but Madhoff's increasing inaccessibility was starting to unnerve the general. He'd tried to pray as a means to calm his jangled nerves, and that had worked for a while, but after being cooped up by himself in the safe house all day he was starting go stir-crazy. Even though it was nearly dawn, he knew the admiral would be up. Most likely he would have just finished meeting with the President and his security team, if the pattern of recent days held true.

He'd been able to communicate with the admiral at least to a degree when he'd been attending those meetings himself, but in the past twenty-four hours everything had changed and he'd been tossed out of the loop. The news of the warrant issued for him had to have hit the Joint Chiefs like a bomb. They lived in a culture where, once you reached a certain level, you were beyond reproach. That culture of not questioning one's peers was what had made it possible for Clement and Scarborough to initiate this plan in the first place.

Although he kept his own council when it came to religion, Scarborough was every bit the devoted believer that Clement himself was, and he was as passionate about bringing about the Rapture as was the general. The two of them had risked everything for their love of Jesus, and they believed that if they failed, they would be martyrs, like the saints and the apostles.

The two men differed in one key area—their belief in the racial makeup of what constituted a Christian. Unlike the general, the admiral wasn't a devotee of any religious leader. The admiral held the childish belief that everyone was the same in Christ, that even a Jew could be saved if he or she accepted the Lord Jesus Christ as his or her personal savior. In all the years that they'd worked together—and plotted together—Clement had been careful to keep his racial views from the admiral. Had the admiral suspected that Clement held such views, he likely would never have become involved in the master plan.

It wasn't as hard to keep his views hidden from the admiral as a casual observer might think. Clement had a lot of practice. Had it become known that he was a follower of a radical Christian guru, the general's military career would have been over. Since it was that career that put him in a position to bring about the return of Jesus, the general was very careful about discussing racial matters. In this Clement wasn't alone. Generally speaking, some of the leaders of all branches of the military were no less racist than some of the general public, but they were forced to pretend otherwise to protect their careers because racial tolerance was official military policy and had been for generations. Bigotry was not tolerated.

Scarborough might have had a soft spot for those cursed with dark skin, Clement thought, but he did share the general's contempt for the Jewish race, at least for those Jews who refused to convert to Christianity. His hatred of the Jews was based on economics, though, and not theology. Scarborough had a doctoral degree in economics and he blamed the Jews for destroying the world's economies. He firmly believed that those of the Jewish faith ran the banking industry.

Although Scarborough was fanatically devoted to Christ, Clement wasn't one hundred percent certain that the admiral would carry through with the plan until the banking crisis of 2008. The way the bailout of the financial industry was handled was what really pushed the admiral over the brink. It was an incredible scam, Clement had to admit. The Federal Reserve nearly bankrupted the country printing money that it loaned to the banks interest-free. The idea was that the banks would in turn lend out this money and jump start the economy.

Instead of pumping that money back into the economy, the Jews running the banks—Scarborough believed—had turned around and loaned it back to the taxpayers for higher interest rates. Instead of writing loans, the banks used that money to buy government bonds and treasury notes at three-to-four percent interest. In other words, the taxpayers borrowed the bankers' money interest free, and the Jewish bankers turned around and loaned that money back to other bankers at three percent interest. Given that the total amount of money exceeded three trillion dollars, three percent interest was substantial and further hastened the inevitable bankruptcy of the country.

Clement himself didn't care about any of that; none of it would matter one whit when Jesus returned. That was Mammon's business—Clement wanted to serve only God. The main reason he paid attention to the situation was because it provided Scarborough with motivation to finally act against the satanically controlled government.

Although he knew doing so was against the agreement Clement had made with Scarborough and Madhoff, the general had to know how things went at that morning's meeting with the President. He knew that whatever was going on in Minneapolis would prevent Madhoff from carrying out his end of the agreement and keeping Clement's information current, so the general had no choice but to dial the admiral's number.

"Why are you calling me?" Scarborough demanded. "You were supposed to contact me through Amos." Even though they spoke through a scrambled, untraceable signal, the admiral used Madhoff's code name.

"Have you spoken with him tonight?" Clement asked.

"No," Scarborough responded. "I was expecting him to call."

"Don't hold your breath, Leroy. Things are going to

hell in a hand basket on his end. They killed Hazan and have the files."

"Are you joking? Who's 'they'?"

"I most certainly am not joking," Clement said, "and I don't have a clue who 'they' are. All I know is that they seem to be onto Madhoff."

"Can they trace us from those files?"

"If they can crack them open. Madhoff assured me that would be impossible, but then he also told me it would be impossible for anyone to trace him to Minneapolis, and the last I heard from him he was running like the hounds of hell were on his trail."

"This is a problem." Scarborough had always been a master of understatement.

"It might not be as bad as it seems on the surface," Clement said. "Almost all the bombs for both waves of tomorrow's attacks have been placed. There's no possible way to stop the attacks now."

"What do you mean 'almost'?"

"Apparently there was a disruption in the Long Beach operation. There was a raid by federal officers. They had to use the GBU-57A/B bunker buster to cleanse the facility."

"Was von Holt at the site?"

"I assume so. He would have been the person who pulled the trigger on the bomb."

"Damn." Scarborough had been fond of the young marine, as Clement himself had been.

"Don't forget why we're doing this, Leroy. We're setting the stage for the Rapture. We'll be together again with Eric soon enough. We need to stay strong. The plan is in motion. There's no stopping it now. The only thing that could lead to failure would be if you were unable to convince the President to declare martial law tomorrow. Everything's in your hands now, Leroy. How did your meeting with the President go?"

"The news of the arrest warrant issued for you came as quite a shock, I must say."

"Do they suspect that I'm involved in the attacks?"

"I don't believe so. According to the arrest warrant, you've been stealing weapons and selling them to Mexican cartels."

"Who delivered the news? The President?"

"No, they brought in that clown from Justice, Hal Brognola."

"I can't believe that fool still has a job," Clement said. "What is it that he does again?"

"Mostly he seems to sit around chewing on unlit cigars and looking nervous," Scarborough said, and both men chuckled. "Why they keep a relic like him on staff is one of life's great mysteries, but we should be glad that the nation's top police officer is an ineffectual old chair warmer. It makes our job easier. I do think he's responsible for the President's refusal to declare martial law up until this point, though."

"Do you think you'll be able to convince the President otherwise?" Clement asked.

"I don't know how he can avoid declaring martial law after the bombs go off tomorrow. People will be so afraid that they'll be begging the government to deprive them of their Constitutional freedoms. Even the national security adviser has changed her position and now supports declaring martial law. I'd say that martial law could be considered fait accompli, at least as long as the bombings take place tomorrow as planned."

"I don't see any possible way they could be stopped at this point," Clement said.

AFTER SPEAKING WITH SCARBOROUGH, Clement felt more at ease. He'd become too used to everything going exactly as planned. He should have expected that there would be some glitches in the process. It was childish to become so distraught when the inevitable occurred. Ultimately, the loss of Madhoff wouldn't be that much of an impediment at this stage.

Still, Clement hoped the man would survive. It wasn't because of any personal attachment to him, though if Clement could see past his hatred of the Jews as a group he would have seen that he'd grown to genuinely like Madhoff as an individual—he was a smart, pragmatic and resourceful individual in spite of his faith. But even if he could admit such a thing to himself, such petty emotions wouldn't have mattered when the salvation of the white Christian race was at stake.

The real reason Clement hoped that Madhoff would survive was because after the nuclear attacks on the Muslim world, his job was to oversee a military coup in Israel, one that would overthrow the Knesset and install the Irgun as the ultimate political authority. Madhoff had the network in place to make that happen, awaiting his order to begin the coup. Clement couldn't have cared less about who or what ran Israel, as long as whoever it was remained committed to rebuilding the temple on the Temple Mount.

Oh, well, Clement thought, Madhoff doesn't make it, we'll figure out another way to get the temple built.

Now that he'd finally relaxed, he felt overwhelmingly tired. He'd barely slept in days, and now his eyelids felt unbearably heavy. He'd been sitting in the main control room, watching a bank of monitors connected to the closed-circuit cameras that covered every corner of the property, but now he thought it was time for a short nap so he went into the adjoining lounge and lay down on one of the couches. He'd just drifted off when the alarms started going off in the control room.

St. Paul, Minnesota

BOLAN AND WESTERBERG TAILED Madhoff as he circled the freeway system in his Jeep. Westerberg drove while Bolan monitored Madhoff's progress on his handheld computer. The woman was as smart as she was beautiful, and maintained a distance of approximately a kilometer to avoid being detected. There was no need to keep a visual lock on their quarry since they had the GPS system.

When the Israeli spy finally got off the freeway in downtown St. Paul, he headed southwest down West Seventh Street, turning into a parking lot after about a mile and a half. Bolan noted the address of the building next to the parking lot, which didn't correspond to any of the safe house addresses Kurtzman had given him. He sent the address to the computer expert and a few moments later his phone began to vibrate.

"You're going to love this, Striker," Kurtzman said. "Madhoff went to a place called the Playboi Club, but there's no signage on the building identifying it as such. That's because it's not a club. It's a whorehouse."

"Can you get me something on the layout of the building?" Bolan asked.

"Sorry, Striker, but I can't help you. The only blue-prints on record are old, from when the place used to be a supper club decades ago. My guess is that whatever modifications they've made since then aren't exactly up to code."

"What's the story on the place?"

"Typical whorehouse story," Kurtzman said. "Techni-cally it's a bottle club, where members bring their own booze, so they don't have to deal with the bureaucracy of getting a liquor license. Not that that stops them from selling booze, drugs or flesh, for that matter. It looks like the sort of operation that stays in business by giving freebies to big shots in the police department, sheriff's department and members of the city council. It's the oldest story in the book."

"What's your assessment of the security situation?"

"My guess is it's pretty tight. And you can't just shoot your way into this one, Striker. The place is filled with innocent people. Well, innocent's probably a stretch—I doubt anyone who sets foot in there stays innocent for very long—but you know what I mean. The only person we can be sure is a bad guy is Madhoff."

"Have you gotten any more information from the files I sent you?"

"No," Kurtzman said, "but the team thinks we're close to breaking the encryption on a second set of files."

"How about the SIM card from Hazan's phone? Have you gotten any names of people who might be linked to both Madhoff and Hazan?"

"A bunch, including your new friend Ms. Westerberg. They traveled in the same circles, as do many other people. But Hazan sent calls to and received calls from several individuals who are of particular interest. See if Ms. Westerberg thinks any of them are worth investigating."

Kurtzman read a list of names of possible Irgun conspirators and Westerberg identified a half dozen of them as people who might have both the political beliefs and temperament to become involved in the radical movements.

"I've been investigating their connection to Hazan," she said. "I have files on all six of them."

"Where are the files?" Bolan asked.

"Here," the Israeli agent said, producing a key chain from her purse. The fob on the key chain was a cheap-looking pink memory stick. "Ze'ev hid his files in an expensive pen. I hide mine in plain sight. The files are encrypted, but I'll pull over and open them so you can send them to your friend Mr. Bear."

They were about a block away from the place where

Madhoff was holing up when she pulled the Crown Vic up to the curb and parked. While Westerberg opened the files on the soldier's handheld computer, Bolan formulated a plan for getting into the building and capturing Madhoff. She finished opening the files and handed the computer back to Bolan, who sent them straight to Kurtzman and his cyberteam at Stony Man.

"Got them," Kurtzman said. "Have you figured out how you're going to get into the club?"

"I believe I'm going to look for a woman."

"That sounds like a plan," Kurtzman said. "What do you need from me?"

"I need the names of the dirty cops who are covering up for the brothel, at least a few of them."

Kurtzman was a genius at hacking computer systems and mining information. He could get into the systems of the world's top intelligence agencies with ease, so hacking into the St. Paul Police Department system and getting names of cops who were in positions to look the other way and let the brothel operate was child's play for him. He had names for the soldier in a matter of seconds. "Try Jacob Nelson, Jeffrey Falla or Kurt Scalleta. All three of them appear to be heavy users of the cop freebies offered by the Playboi Club."

"Let's go with Nelson," Bolan said. "Have a couple of agents pay him a visit ASAP, like in the next fifteen minutes. Have the agents explain how Nelson's going to get a call from the Playboi Club manager and that he's going to vouch for us. His only other option is to be indicted on federal corruption and racketeering charges. My guess is that he's going to vouch for us."

"You're not exactly dressed for whoring," Westerberg said after Bolan had finished talking to Kurtzman, "and this cop-mobile is not exactly the best vehicle to bring to the parking lot of a club like that if you want to disguise yourself as a john."

"Unless I'm not a john," Bolan said. "If I'm a detective looking for a freebie, then I think I'm right in character."

"What about me?"

"My dyke partner looking for a good time."

"You're a pig."

"You have a better idea?" Westerberg remained silent. "If you do," Bolan said, "I'm all ears. But we have to get inside the place somehow and this is the best I've got right now."

"So how are we going to pass as St. Paul police detectives?" Westerberg asked. "Last time I checked, those IDs you got us said we're federal agents."

"You think they're going to look that closely at our badges? We're dressed like cops. We're driving a cop car. We're going to act like cops. Drunken cops. They're going to expect us to be cops, and they're not going to take the time to check out the details on our identification badges. They're just going to want to make us happy and hope we don't stay long."

"When we don't go straight to the back rooms with girls, they're going to get suspicious."

"Not if we have a few drinks up by the stage first.

Especially if we throw a lot of money around. Ever had a lap dance?"

"No." Westerberg's reply was as icy as her blue eyes. "It's not something I've ever felt the need to experience."

"Well, start feeling the need, because we're going to get at least a couple of them apiece."

"I still think they're going to be suspicious."

"Probably. Being suspicious goes with their line of work. But if we act drunk they'll be less suspicious."

"You don't look drunk."

The soldier loosened his necktie, ruffled his hair and rumpled his jacket and slacks. Then he pulled his zipper halfway down and untied one of his shoes, retying it sloppily. "Is this better?"

Westerberg studied him. "Better," she said, "but what about me?"

Bolan took her face in his hand, licked his finger and smeared her mascara just a bit. He ruffled her hair, took off her suit jacket and unbuttoned her blouse one button past sexy. He leaned back and studied his work. Now she looked like she'd been partying, but something still wasn't quite right, so he leaned forward and kissed her hard on the lips. At first she responded, their tongues playing on each other's lips, but then she came to her senses and slapped Bolan across the face, leaving a red hand-shaped mark on his cheek. That would add to the effect he was trying to achieve.

"What are you doing?" Westerberg shouted. "What makes you think I wanted to kiss you?"

"That wasn't the point," Bolan said. He studied her face. Now, with her lipstick slightly smeared, she looked the part of a horny lady detective with a buzz on. "Look in the mirror," he commanded.

"I look like I've been out drinking all night," she said.

"Now let's go," the soldier said.

Harrisonburg, Virginia

GENERAL JOE CLEMENT LIKED to pass himself off as a warrior, but in reality the only fighting he ever did was fighting off the boredom of being a desk jockey, and he had the soft, white belly to prove it. Oh, he was a warrior for Jesus, and he'd sent plenty of people to their deaths in his quest to bring Jesus back, but when it came to actual fighting, deep down he knew he really lacked the stones for the task. Now he was going to have to find those stones and find them fast.

He ran through the possible ways in which federal agents could have discovered the location of this compound. Even though his panicked mind wasn't thinking as clearly as it should have been, the only possible way this location could have been discovered was if the Feds had cracked the electronic files Hazan had been carrying. If they had cracked one file, how long would it be until they cracked the rest? Clement only hoped it would be long enough to allow that day's bombing campaign to take place.

When he saw the officers approaching the compound on the closed-circuit television monitors, he had to fight to retain control of his bladder. He'd always thought a person wetting himself when afraid was a theatrical device. When he almost did exactly that, he understood it was a very real phenomenon.

The compound was equipped with enough weaponry to arm an entire platoon, but Clement had never been particularly adept with firearms. That wasn't unusual for Air Force personnel, and over the course of his entire career he'd never felt pressured to become a better marksman. In fact, it had been years since he'd actually held a firearm.

Not that he'd have much of a chance fighting off this attack even if he had been skilled in the use of firearms. There had to have been a dozen agents storming the compound. He wouldn't have a chance against that many people, regardless of how handy he was with a gun. He figured he stood a much better chance if he tried hiding. The safe house had been designed for just such activity anyway. Clement went into the tiny storage room behind the wall of monitors and felt along under a shelf holding some cleaning supplies. He found what appeared to be a brace for the shelf, but was in reality a handle for opening a panel in the wall.

The walls in the closet were made of unfinished plasterboard; the panels in the sheetrock hadn't even been taped over. The reason for that was so that the gaps on the panel that opened to the hidden exit would look exactly like all the other panels on the wall. The one that was connected to springs taken from the hood of a car popped open like a hatch cover. Clement crawled into the space behind it and pulled the panel back down until it clicked back into place.

They'd built the main building in the compound into the side of a hill, and this panel opened into a natural cave that they had purposely left unsealed. Instead, they had opened the cave and made it possible for a person to pass through it, eventually ending up in the hills above the compound. The general wasn't exactly at his physical peak anymore and it took him quite a while to work his way through the maze of the cave. A couple of times he took wrong turns and nearly found himself stuck in one of the offshoot passages of the cave that led nowhere. By the time he came to the opening above the compound he could barely catch his breath.

The opening above had been closed off with large rocks to keep spelunkers from discovering the escape route, and also to keep large animals from living in the cave, but the rocks had been strategically placed, and they'd left a large pry bar on the inside of the cave, behind the rocks. It took a little work, but the general pried away the top three rocks and squeezed himself through the opening into the light. When his eyes adjusted to the brightness, he found himself staring down the barrels of M-4s, being held by three federal agents.

CHAPTER THIRTEEN

St. Paul, Minnesota

"Open up!" Bolan shouted drunkenly, banging on the door to the brothel. "This is the police!" He clumsily waved his badge at the man behind the opening in the door.

"Do you have a warrant?" the man asked through an intercom.

"Hell, no, I don't got no warrant," Bolan said, staggering a bit as he spoke. "What I got is a big old boner." He pointed at his crotch.

"What do you want?" the man asked.

"Pussy!" Bolan bellowed.

"Go away. You're drunk."

"Goddamned right I'm drunk, but I still want some pussy. Jake Nelson told me this was the place to get it."

"Who's your friend?" the man asked.

"She's no friend, she's my partner. She likes a bit of pussy herself."

"You sure Nelson sent you?"

"Did I mumble, pal?" Bolan asked. "How do you think we found out about this place?"

"Wait here a second," the man said. He was gone

for a moment. When he returned he said, "Okay. Nelson vouched for you. You can come in, but behave yourselves."

The place was seedier than Bolan had expected, smelling of body oil and booze and cigarette smoke, with an underlying scent of old sour sweat and body odor. An acrid cloud of smoke hung in the air, part tobacco, part marijuana, and at least a hint of rock cocaine and methamphetamine.

If the scene was pathetic, then the supposed dancers on stage were even more so. Still, Bolan and Westerberg needed to stay in character, so they went to the bar and demanded drinks. "This is a bottle club," the bartender said. "You have to bring your own alcohol. We only sell soda for mixes."

"That's not what Jake Nelson told me," Bolan said just a bit too loudly. "He said you knew how to take care of the po-po. Do you know how to take care of the po-po?"

The bartender looked at the manager, who nodded and mouthed the words, "On the house."

The bartender nodded back and asked Bolan what he wanted. "Scotch. Johnnie Walker. Blue Label."

"We don't got no Blue Label. We got Black or Red."

"You holding out on us?" Bolan asked. "'Cause I don't like it when some shit bird holds out on me."

The bartender shot another look at the manager, who nodded again. "I've got some Gold Label behind the counter. Will that do?"

"I suppose. And get the lady whatever she wants."

"I'm easy," Westerberg said. "Captain and Coke."

The bartender handed a tumbler of Scotch to Bolan, who downed it in one gulp. "Another!" he shouted. The bartender grumbled to himself and poured another tumbler half full of the expensive Scotch.

Bolan and Westerberg took their drinks to the chairs that lined the stage and sat down to watch the dancers. Most of them looked too drugged out to actually dance, even if they'd known how. The woman at the pole appeared to be using it more for support than for any sort of performance. At first the girls kept a little distance between Bolan and Westerberg, giving them a moment to talk.

"See anything?" Bolan asked.

"I caught a glimpse of the hallway through the back," Westerberg said. "It was lined with doors. It must be where the hookers take the johns. Most of the doors were open and the rooms looked dark. Only a couple of doors were shut."

"Slow," Bolan said, "but what would you expect this time of the morning? You think our boy is in one of the rooms?"

"I'd bet money on it. What do we do now?"

"Now we wait for him to come out. And I was serious about those lap dances. It's the only way we're going to be able to stay without each taking a girl in the back." Bolan put a five-dollar bill on the stage and a girl came over and began dancing, or rather, wriggling in front of him. She lay down on the stage face-first and thrust her ample bottom in the soldier's face. Bolan glanced over at Westerberg and gave a quick nod toward the stage. Westerberg took the hint and put down her own bill. Soon she too had a personal show.

The more money the pair put down on the stage, the bawdier the show became. When Bolan laid down a twenty, he asked the woman, "Lap dance?"

"No problem, sugar," she said. Like the other women, this one would never have gotten a job in a real strip club. The women here were real working girls, hard-edged pros with dull, soulless eyes. Though they were mostly on the skinny side, it was an unhealthy skinny, not like the lean, muscular athletic types found at real strip clubs. There were fake breasts in abundance, as at a real strip club, but the cellulite that dimpled the women's buttocks and thighs was all too real. These "dancers" wouldn't even get through the door at a high-end strip club. Still, they had everything that a patron of the Playboi Club could possibly want.

The woman prostrating herself in front of Bolan took the twenty, got off the stage and straddled Bolan's lap. "No, honey," Bolan said, using his drunken slur voice. "Reverse cowgirl." The lap dancer complied and turned so that her back was facing the soldier. Bolan requested this position because it allowed him to keep an eye on the doorway to the back rooms from which Madhoff would emerge when it was time for him to leave.

The young woman on Westerberg's lap was actually fairly cute. She looked to be in her late teens, which meant she probably hadn't been working here long—places like this tended to age girls fast. The woman gyrating on the soldier's lap looked to be in her early thirties, but in reality Bolan would have been surprised if she was a day over twenty-two. Very few women could survive in this line of work until they were in their thirties. If they did it long enough, they more often than not died of disease, overdoses or violent johns. The vast majority of those who survived retired by the time they were twenty-five or so, at which time they usually looked much older and weren't in terribly high demand anyway.

More than anything, what gave away the newbie status of the young woman gyrating on Westerberg's lap was the gleam that still sparkled in her eye. This was a person who hadn't yet learned to hate life. She was having fun, and in particular she was having fun fooling around with Westerberg. Westerberg didn't seem to be having too bad a time herself.

But enjoying herself or not, Westerberg kept one eye peeled on the doorway to the bedroom cubicles, as did the soldier. They'd gone through three complete lap dances before anything happened, and Bolan was putting increasing amounts of money on the table to keep his lap dancer from putting the hard sell on him and trying to talk him into going to a room in back. If that happened and he refused, they'd both likely be thrown out before Madhoff emerged.

Finally, some sort of commotion began, but it wasn't Madhoff emerging. Rather, a large black man came running out from the hallway and whispered something to the manager. Bolan supposed the man from the back rooms was the bouncer and served as the girls' bodyguard. Johns could get rough with working girls, so there was usually somebody around to keep things from getting too far out of hand. But these people were skilled at dealing with unruly johns and seldom had to seek assistance from the manager of the establishment. Something big had to be going on in the back rooms, because after the bouncer spoke to the manager, both of them ran back to the rooms.

Westerberg caught the activity, too, and shot Bolan a glance. He mouthed the words, "Be ready," to her. A moment later they heard the first shot come from the back room.

Stony Man Farm, Virginia

CLEMENT TRIED TO TAKE HIS arrest like a man. He tried to remain strong. It's how he told his men to act should they find themselves in a situation like this. He kept telling them that nothing in this earthly life mattered; the only thing that mattered was accepting the Lord Jesus Christ as their personal Savior, which they all had most certainly done. Soon their work would be complete, the temple would be rebuilt and Jesus would come down for the Rapture and take them all away to heaven. If he had to spend the remaining time between now and then in prison, it would be a small price to pay to have paved the way for His return. And if they executed Clement, then he would just be with Jesus that much sooner.

But when they placed the hood over his head, Clement

lost all his resolve. At that moment he also finally lost control of his bladder. He felt a warm stream of liquid rolling down his legs as the officers put the dark, heavy hood over his head and led him to a running helicopter. Since he couldn't see where he was going, the officers helped him into the helicopter and strapped him into a hard seat. There was a time when Clement could have identified the helicopter by the sound of its engine, but all he could tell was that this one was powered by a single turbine. It was probably something like a Bell JetRanger.

Whatever it was, it was loud and uncomfortable as hell for a man wearing a pair of wet pants. Clement kept thinking about the helicopter because it was something he could comprehend. Having a hood thrown over his head and being flown to some undisclosed location was also probably within his comprehension, had the general chosen to comprehend it, but he preferred to not think about it and focus on the helicopter instead. Imprisonment he could face. Even death was something he was mentally and emotionally prepared for. But the only reason he could think of for this treatment was that he was going to be tortured, and he was fairly certain that was not something he could handle.

Clement was devoted to the cause of bringing back Jesus. He knew he wouldn't betray that cause—or the people helping him achieve it—through any normal interrogation methods used by official law-enforcement agencies. But he never imagined that he would be hogtied, blindfolded and hauled away to some hidden place to be tortured. There had been some outsourcing of interrogations to other countries where torture was accepted during the Iraq war—extraordinary rendition, they'd called it—but Clement had never dreamed they would use that on a U.S. citizen. The thought of it brought him to the brink of losing control of his bladder once again, so he went back to meditating on the type of helicopter in which he might be riding.

The general had always liked to fly. That's why he'd joined the air force in the first place. He'd become a proficient helicopter pilot, but he excelled at flying jets. He'd even logged some combat time during Operation Desert Storm, knocking down a couple of Iraqi jet fighters. He would have loved to have kept flying fighters, but a major promotion had landed him in an administrative position. His career had been put on the fast track. And now he was in chains and likely heading somewhere to be tortured.

He was willing to suffer for his faith. He had always known that was a possibility, and in some ways he expected to suffer. Part of him even welcomed martyrdom, but only when that had been an abstract concept. Now that the possibility of it had entered the realm of the concrete, he felt more afraid than he'd ever thought possible. He tried praying to calm his nerves—after all, hadn't the saints found solace in Christ at the moment of their martyrdom? But try as he might, he found no comfort in prayer at that moment. For years he'd felt total and complete confidence in the righteousness of the course of action he'd chosen, but now he felt something that had previously been completely foreign to him: doubt. He wanted nothing more than to be strong at that moment, but try as he might, he was unable to keep himself from weeping. At that moment he was grateful for the hood that covered his head.

The flight took much less time than Clement expected, which gave the general some hope. At least he wasn't in Guantanamo. Yet. His captors led him from the helicopter into a building and sat him down. When they removed his hood he saw that he was in a holding cell.

The general was starting to get extremely uncomfortable from sitting in urine-soaked pants. He couldn't believe his life had come to this. Sitting in a concrete cell in a pair of cold, wet pants wasn't the way he imagined martyrdom would be. But the reality of martyrdom was probably much closer to this than to the way it was often portrayed, now that the general thought about it. Most of the saints probably soiled themselves in their final moments on Earth.

That thought comforted Clement some, but he still couldn't shake the feeling of doubt that clouded his thoughts. Once again he prayed for strength. By the time his first interrogator entered the room, he had begun to find just a bit of that commodity.

He couldn't believe his eyes when he saw who came into the room: Hal Brognola, the boring codger from the Department of Justice. The old fool even had an unlit cigar clamped between his teeth. Clement felt his strength returning. "No one's read me my rights," he said. "I want my lawyer."

"No one's read you your rights because you're not under arrest," Brognola said.

"Then I demand to be released."

"I'm afraid I can't release you. You see, officially we don't know where you are. You're still a fugitive from justice. We didn't find you at the Virginia compound. We have no idea where you are, so how can we release you?"

"What are you talking about?" The reality of the situation started to sink in. He really was in Guantanamo, or at a place where, like Guantanamo, rights didn't exist. "Are you going to torture me?"

"I won't lie to you, General. I honestly don't know what's going to happen to you. I don't want to know. Plausible deniability and all that. But you can save us all a lot of trouble if you would just talk to us."

"Talk to you? Why? You're just a tool, one of Satan's minions. Don't you get it? Let me ask you a question— have you accepted the Lord Jesus Christ as your personal Savior?"

"My religious beliefs are my own business," Brognola said, "but why do you ask?"

"Because the time for equivocation is rapidly coming to an end! We are on the verge of the Rapture, when Jesus will call his flock home. Woe unto those who are left behind."

Brognola was starting to understand—the general was utterly and completely mad. Logic and reason wouldn't get him far in dealing with a madman. He'd need to try another approach. "How can you possibly know this? Isn't such knowledge the dominion of God alone?"

"God works through His emissaries on Earth," the general said. "He always has and He always will."

"And God has chosen you as His emissary?"

"God has chosen us all as His emissaries. Some of us just have the courage to act on His will."

"And it was His will to kill hundreds of innocent people? How was that God's will?"

"It was God's will that the Jews kill His only begotten son Jesus Christ the Lord! And it's God's will that His only begotten son Jesus Christ the Lord shall come back to Earth and bring all of His white followers home in a glorious rapture!" Clement chastised himself for letting the "white" slip into his speech. After years of keeping that part of his gospel from even his closest associates, he was starting to get sloppy. He blamed it on the pressure of the situation he now found himself in.

Not that it mattered at this point; soon enough all of Christ's white followers would rise up to heaven and the dark cursed ones could debate such finer points in a lake of fire. Still, it was hard to shake a lifetime of hiding his true views, and he watched Brognola to see how he reacted to the slip, but if the man was surprised, his reaction gave nothing away. The old fool probably didn't even catch the slip.

"I understand that," Brognola said, "but I still don't

see how you could possibly know that the time of the Rapture was near."

"How can you not understand that? Look around you! Look at the degraded morality of our young people! As they associate more and more freely with the dark-skinned cursed ones, they fall further and further into the grips of Satan! Now we have a world where teenage girls equate sex with a handshake! We have a government completely controlled by Jewish bankers! The money changers have retaken the temple and it's time white Christians took it back!" As he became more agitated, the general threw caution to the wind. It felt good to finally speak the truth.

"Again," Brognola said, appearing to be genuinely interested in the general's sermon, "I understand all that. But I can't understand how killing innocent people will help you take back the temple."

"You will," the general said. "Soon enough it will be completely clear."

"Could you please tell me what you mean?" Brognola asked, but the general only smiled at him, looking remarkably serene for a man in chains and urine-soaked pants.

St. Paul, Minnesota

WHEN THE FIRST SHOT RANG out from the back rooms of the Playboi Club, both Bolan and Westerberg jumped up from their chairs, guns drawn, knocking their respective prostitutes to the floor.

"Stay down," Bolan ordered the woman who'd been gyrating on his lap. "Everybody, stay down!"

Another shot rang out from the bedroom cubicle area. The doorman had drawn a gun from an inside-the-waistband holster and the bartender had pulled a short-barreled pump shotgun from under the bar.

"Is there a way out through the back?" Bolan asked the doorman.

"Yeah, but if anyone leaves that way they'll trip the alarm."

Bolan and Westerberg moved toward the doorway leading back to the cubicles. When they got closer, they saw the manager's prone body lying in the open doorway to one of the cubicles. Bolan and Westerberg crept along opposite walls toward the open door. When they got closer, Bolan mouthed the words, "Now." The two sprung into the doorway, ready to shoot anything that moved, but there was no one alive left in the room. The bouncer was dead on the floor a couple of feet from the manager, and a hooker lay dead on the bed. Both the bouncer and the manager had been shot, but there was no evidence of bullet wounds on the prostitute's nude body. The lack of evident trauma except for the blood trickling from her mouth, nose and ears indicated that she'd probably had her neck snapped.

"Madhoff has a reputation for liking rough sex," Westerberg said. "Where did he go?"

"Careful," Bolan said. "He could be hiding in one of these other cubicles." By this time the bartender and the doorman had come back to see what was happening.

The soldier turned to the doorman, who appeared to be the sharper of the two, and said, "Where does the door at the back of the hallway lead?"

"To the offices. There's an employee lounge that we use for private parties back there, too, and behind that there's a storeroom. The only door leading out the back is through the storeroom, and that's wired to an alarm, so we'll know if someone leaves through that."

"So he's still in here?" Bolan asked.

"He must be." Before the words finished leaving the doorman's lips, a shot rang out and a cavity opened up in the man's chest. The bartender whipped around and fired his shotgun at a figure that had burst from one of the other bedroom cubicles and was fleeing down the hallway toward the stage area. People thought of shotguns as having wide patterns that took out anything in the general direction in which they were fired, especially a short-barreled shotgun, but Bolan knew that the reality was that at short distances the pattern was only a few inches across at best, and it was easy for an untrained shooter like the bartender to miss, which is exactly what happened.

Bolan and Westerberg raced after the fleeing figure, but they couldn't get a clean shot at him because he was directly in line with the hookers cowering behind the now-empty stage. The man grabbed one of the hookers—the young, fresh one who had been giving the heartfelt lap dance to Westerberg—and used her as a human shield. When Westerberg dared to sneak a glance around the door frame, she was rewarded with a shot that hit the frame, missing her head by less than an inch. Splinters of shattered wood pierced the side of her face.

"Are you all right?" Bolan asked.

"A few slivers. I'll live. It's definitely Madhoff."

Bolan looked at the bartender and asked, "Is there another way to get to the bar area?"

"Yeah, through the offices. They're locked, though."

"Do you have a key?"

"Yeah."

"You're going to take me there. Sarah, you talk to Madhoff. Distract him."

After Bolan and the bartender headed back to the office area, Westerberg said, "Isaac, why are you doing this?"

"Sarah? I thought that was you. I can't believe you killed Ze'ev."

"He was trying to kill us."

"He didn't know it was you," Madhoff said.

"Do you think it would have made a difference to him?"

Madhoff chuckled. "Probably not."

"How is all this going to end, Isaac?"

"One way or another, it's going to end with me getting out of here alive. I'm afraid I don't see you or your American friend having such a happy ending. Who is he, anyway?"

"I have no idea." Westerberg told the truth. "All I know is that I wouldn't want to piss him off."

"From what I've seen so far, that seems like sound advice."

"Why are you doing this, Isaac? Why would you try to revive the Irgun?"

Madhoff was surprised to hear Westerberg mention the Irgun. He knew she was investigating Hazan, but they'd been meticulous about maintaining the utmost secrecy about their ultimate goals. As far as Madhoff knew, only four people on Earth knew about the Irgun, and one of them had been killed earlier that night, effectively diminishing their ranks by twenty-five percent. Westerberg knowing about the Irgun changed everything. Madhoff had planned to use his hostage to facilitate his escape as quickly as possible, but now he had to cleanse the scene completely; he had to kill everyone in the building. Including Westerberg. He decided to use his hostages to draw his targets out where he could shoot them.

"Sarah, I need you and your friends to drop your weapons and come out with your hands up. That includes the bartender and the angry American agent."

"We can't do that, Isaac. You know that."

"Then I can do this." Madhoff selected one of the women cowering on the floor and aimed his Glock at the back of her head. With the exception of the lovely young African-American woman he used as a human shield, all the women there had a few extra pounds on them, but the one in the sights of his handgun was the only woman who could be described as truly fat.

"Can you see this woman on the floor, Sarah?" he shouted. "Can you see this fat cow?"

"I can see her."

"If you don't come out right this instant, I'm going to kill her."

The woman began shrieking so loudly that he could barely hear Westerberg when she said, "I'm sorry, Isaac, but you know we can't do that."

"Then I can do this." He squeezed off a shot and a .45-caliber bullet entered the woman's head at the exact point where her spine met her skull. She flopped to the floor face-first into a pool of her own tissue and fluids with a wet splat. "If you don't come out unarmed, I'll keep this up until I kill each and every one of these women."

"Then I'm afraid those women are doomed," Westerberg said, "because we can't come out." She had to shout at the top of her lungs to be heard over the wailing and screaming of the women cowering on the floor in front of Madhoff.

"That's really how you feel? Suit yourself. Which woman should I kill next?"

"Is that really necessary, Isaac?"

"You tell me. Are you ready to come out?"

"That's not possible."

"Then it's necessary." Madhoff selected another of the women. "How about this one, Sarah? Can you see the woman I've selected?"

"I can see her."

"Can you tell her that she has to die because you and your friend refuse to surrender?"

"She doesn't have to die, Isaac. You don't have to kill her."

"But I do, Sarah, because you refuse to come out of your rat hole." He squeezed the trigger of his Glock and shot the unfortunate woman in the side of the head. She flopped to the floor.

"Isaac, you can shoot all of those women, but you know that won't change our position."

Madhoff considered shooting another of the women for emphasis, but they were the only tools he had to draw out his adversaries and he didn't want to use them up all at once. "Well, Sarah, it looks like we have what the Americans call a Mexican standoff."

"I don't think very many Americans actually call it that anymore." Westerberg wanted to keep Madhoff talking to give Agent Cooper time to flank him from the rear. Hopefully Cooper would act soon, before Madhoff killed another woman.

THE BARTENDER LED BOLAN down a hallway that ran parallel to the bar-stage area. The hallway took a ninety-degree turn and ended at a doorway that opened into an office suite. The offices were surprisingly clean and sterile-looking for being part of such a seedy establishment. The administrators of the operation were apparently much more concerned with hygiene than were the worker bees out front. The suite consisted of several cubicles and two enclosed offices along the far wall. A door opened back toward the bar area. The bartender unlocked that door, and let Bolan into a room that served as a sort of pantry for the bar area.

"Does that open out to the bar itself?" Bolan asked.

"Yeah. That will let you out right behind the bar."

Just then they heard a shot from the bar. Bolan knew he was running out of time. "Do you have a key to disable the alarm at the back door?" Bolan asked.

The bartender didn't say anything, but nodded in the affirmative.

"Let yourself out and run as fast as you can. Do you have a cell phone?"

Again the bartender nodded yes.

"When you're a block away, call 911 and get help. But make sure you're safe, first. You won't do us any good if you get yourself killed." The bartender took off just as the second shot rang out from the stage area. Bolan hoped Westerberg was all right.

The Executioner pressed his ear to the door and heard the shrieks and screams of the women by the stage. He acted fast, using their noise as cover. He eased the door open just enough to slip through and crawled out behind the bar. Rather than looking over the top of the bar, where Madhoff might be expecting him to appear if he suspected that the soldier was trying to flank him, he crept to the edge of the bar and peered out from its base, keeping as low as possible.

Madhoff still held the young hooker close to him. Two of the other prostitutes lay dead on the ground. The others cowered and wailed, most likely driven to the verge of madness with fear. Bolan mentally ran through his options. Ideally, he'd like to take Madhoff alive, but the odds of that didn't seem very good. But the odds of shooting him from behind weren't much better; because of the way that Madhoff held the woman, Bolan couldn't get a decent shot at the man without risking overpenetration that could very likely kill an innocent woman. The soldier's best option appeared to be sneaking up on the man and taking him out with his bowie knife.

Because of the moaning and weeping of the women on the floor, the soldier knew he could sneak up on Madhoff without being heard, at least as long as Westerberg kept the man busy talking, and so far she was doing an excellent job of engaging the man. She was a real pro, and obviously had experience in dealing with hostage situations. The biggest danger was that one of the hostages would see him coming and give him away, but that was a chance he was going to have to take.

Bolan waited until Westerberg and Madhoff were engaged in a particularly intense exchange regarding their mutual friend Hazan and crept out from behind the counter. As quietly as he could, he covered half the approximately fifty-foot distance between himself and Madhoff. Westerberg saw him, of course, but she was careful not to look directly at him. Instead, she focused on Madhoff and his hostage.

When Bolan was within twenty feet of Madhoff, he prepared to lunge at the man. At that distance he stood a good chance of reaching the Israeli before he could draw a bead on the soldier and get a shot off. He coiled his body, ready to put all the energy he had into sprinting the remaining distance, but just as he was about to uncoil and rush the man his greatest fear was realized— one of the prostitutes on the floor saw him. Her eyes went wide and she let out an involuntary yelp.

Madhoff spun, still holding the young woman in front of him for a shield, and leveled his gun in the direction the hooker on the floor had looked. His front sight landing dead center on Bolan's face. He tensed his finger, preparing to send a bullet where the soldier's body armor would be of little use, and the soldier heard the report of a gun. He prepared to finally meet his end, but instead of being hit in the face with a .45-caliber bullet, he watched as the top of Madhoff's head separated from his skull. The Israeli's eyes registered surprise and then their lights went out as all his brain functions ceased. He fell to the floor, revealing Westerberg standing in the doorway, her Glock still pointed at the spot where Madhoff's head had been just milliseconds earlier.

Bolan and Westerberg walked toward Madhoff's body. He looked at the corpse and said, "A couple of centimeters higher and you would have missed him."

"I shot high," Westerberg replied. "I didn't want to risk hitting the girl." She paused a moment. "Or you."

"Good thinking." The soldier began searching Madhoff's body. He pulled out a thick wad of cash from his pants pocket, at least $10,000 worth, it looked like, mostly in fifty- and hundred-dollar bills. He handed the roll of money to the terrified woman who'd been held hostage.

"You girls split that up among yourselves," he said. "Consider it a tip. But make sure it's out of sight before the cops get here or they'll confiscate it as evidence." The only other item of note that Bolan found was a cell phone. Again, Bolan removed the SIM card and transmitted its data back to Stony Man Farm.

By the time he was finished they could hear sirens in the distance. "Let's get out of here," Bolan said, "or we're going to waste the rest of the night in a police station, trying not to answer questions we can't answer and filling out redundant forms."

The two left through the front door and were two blocks away from the parking lot when the first squad car arrived on the scene.

"Those girls are going to have a tough time explaining what just happened," Westerberg said.

"That's because they have no idea what just happened," Bolan replied, "but they're tough. They know enough to say as little as possible. That was some impressive work back there. Thank you for saving my life."

"What? You're not going to criticize me again for shooting too high?"

"I apologize if that sounded like criticism. It was just an observation on an extremely good shot. I honestly uttered that remark because I was impressed with your aim and I apologize if you took it as anything other than a compliment."

"Apology accepted. And I apologize for being such a prude about going into the brothel. I must admit I was surprised by how much I enjoyed myself in there. I don't think I'll switch teams anytime soon, but I have to say, that lap dance was rather nice." She smiled at Bolan, then said, "Don't you think it's time to call home? Your parents might be starting to worry."

Bolan agreed and dialed Kurtzman's number. "We didn't take Madhoff alive," Bolan told the man, "but we got him. We got the SIM card from his cell phone, too. Cross reference all calls between Madhoff's phone and Hazan's phone, both incoming and outgoing."

"Will do, Striker. In the meantime I've got some news for you—we brought in General Joe Clement."

"Where are you holding him?" Bolan asked.

"Here."

"At the Farm?"

"Yeah. We brought him in with a hood over his head. When the blacksuits put the hood on him, he got so scared his bladder let go. He's still wearing his soaking-wet pants."

"Has anyone interrogated him yet?"

"Just Hal. We'd like to have you take a crack at it, though. That means you have to get back here as soon as possible. Jack's got the jet fueled up and ready to go at the St. Paul downtown airport."

"Is Hal done with the interrogation?" Bolan asked.

"Yes. And he wants to speak with you. I'll put him on."

"Striker, I need you here twenty minutes ago. You'll have to have a word with General Clement, see if you can get something besides apocalyptic drivel out of the man," Brognola said.

"I'll do what I can. How did the meeting with the President go?"

"He didn't declare martial law, if that's what you're asking, but if these attacks continue, or, God forbid, ramp up, I'm afraid we've lost this one."

"Any idea who Clement was working with?" Bolan asked. "You know he wasn't working alone."

"I have a suspect in mind," Brognola said. "Admiral Scarborough."

"Leroy Scarborough? The chairman of the Joint Chiefs of Staff?"

"I wouldn't bet my life on it," Brognola said, "but right now he's my best guess. I've got Bear and his team looking into any connection between Clement and Scarborough, and we're keeping a close eye on the man. So I need you here pronto."

CHAPTER FOURTEEN

Bethesda, Maryland

Admiral Leroy Scarborough prided himself on keeping a cool head in any situation. Prior to his assignment to the Joint Chiefs of Staff, he'd been a united combatant commander and had overseen operations in both Iraq and Afghanistan. During that time he'd been unflappable. Now he was starting to experience something he had never before encountered: panic. He was, he supposed, becoming flappable. He would have found his own witty wordplay somewhat amusing in less stressful circumstances, but given the current situation he wasn't amused.

The master plan had gone remarkably well up until the past twenty-four hours, but since then it seemed nothing had gone right. It had started the previous night, when he hadn't received his regular update from Madhoff. He'd been monitoring the news reports in the Minneapolis–St. Paul area and the region appeared to have devolved into a war zone. It started with a bloodbath at the clubhouse of the Satan's Slaves Motorcycle Club. The police had been slow to respond to this event, and all subsequent events, for that matter. That didn't

surprise the admiral. Police forces around the country
had been stretched beyond the breaking point trying to
combat the sniper attacks. They had very few resources
remaining with which to deal with even ordinary crime.
They certainly weren't equipped to deal with a large
metro area erupting in what appeared to be an all-out
war.

If the definition of *war* was in part dependent on how
high the body count went, then calling the events that
occurred in the Minneapolis–St. Paul area over the past
twenty-four hours "war" wasn't hyperbole. The carnage
had been horrific. The final tally of the attack on the
Slaves' clubhouse had been twenty-five dead and the
number continued to rise as the police found gunned-
down bikers in the river and storm drain beneath the
clubhouse. At first the police assumed that this was
some sort of interclub warfare, but further investigation revealed no evidence that any other club had been
involved.

After that the fighting moved to north Minneapolis,
and that battle had been much fiercer. This time the
fighting involved members of the Rollin' 30s Bloods
street gang, and the police didn't appear to have the
slightest clue who was on the other side, but they were
certain it had to have been a fairly large gang, judging
by the vast number of Bloods who had been killed in
the fighting. But they knew literally nothing about the
opposing forces, because the only bodies found at the
scene of the battle were members of the Bloods, just as

the only victims of the attack on the biker clubhouse were members of the Slaves.

That was, the only bodies found at the scene of the north Minneapolis battle had been members of the Rollin' 30s Bloods with one exception; the police had found the body of Pete Tressel, the president of the Minneapolis chapter of the Slaves, hanging nude in a garage at the scene of the Bloods massacre. Apparently, he was being tortured at the time the battle broke out. Scarborough had been monitoring reports coming out of the Minneapolis Police Department, but they hadn't been terribly informative. The presence of the president of the Slaves at the scene of the battle told the police that the carnage at the Slaves' headquarters and the carnage in north Minneapolis were related, but that fact just confused investigators even more.

Scarborough knew that the Bloods and the Slaves had a connection that the police couldn't possibly have known about—both worked for Madhoff. And both organizations had been virtually wiped out in a single night. The attacks continued until nearly the next morning. Seven people had been murdered at some disgusting establishment called the Bald Kitty Klub, a strip club that was a favored hangout for members of the Rollin' 30s Bloods, and moments later a full-fledged battle had erupted several blocks away, one that included heavy machine guns. That battle had claimed the life of an Israeli national whose name was being withheld by the police, though the admiral knew it was Hazan.

Soon after that, a north Minneapolis house owned

by a known member of the Bloods had been the site of yet another massacre. The police had yet to determine a body count at that attack, since explosives had been used and forensic investigators had yet to piece together all the remains found at the scene. This was the house from which Madhoff had issued his last communication to Clement and could possibly have been Madhoff's waterloo, but Scarborough didn't think that was the case. That honor most likely belonged to yet another battle that had broken out earlier that morning, this one taking place at a brothel in St. Paul called the Playboi Club. The body count had been lower there, but unlike the other violent incidents that had occurred that night, most of the victims had been identified as civilians, innocent bystanders. There was one important exception—the body of yet another unidentified Israeli national had been found at the scene. Scarborough believed that body was most likely Isaac Madhoff.

Scarborough had never been comfortable about their partnership with the Israelis, but Clement had convinced him that this was the best way to accomplish their goal of rebuilding the Jewish temple. He'd made a persuasive argument and the admiral had grudgingly bought into the alliance, but he'd never completely trusted Madhoff and Hazan, or any other Jew, for that matter. Still, the Israelis had proved to be intelligent and resourceful partners. Because of their involvement the master plan had gone from just being a lot of talk interspersed with intermittent training exercises that really didn't amount to much more than Clement and his disgruntled veterans playing army out in the woods.

Once the Israelis came on board, everything changed. Things started to really happen, and the time frame of the master plan sped up dramatically. The Israelis weren't the kind of men who were content to sit around and complain about the state of the world and fantasize about the Rapture. These were men of action, and once they became part of the plan, they acted. Before the Israeli's arrival, Scarborough and Clement had been working according to a vague five-year plan that kept getting pushed out five years into the future. Within a year of Madhoff's arrival, they were ready to send the sniper teams underground. Six months after that the attacks began.

If the admiral were to be completely honest with himself, he would have to admit that he would probably have been content had the entire operation never left the realm of hot-air paramilitary fantasy. He was as guilty of engaging in fantasy as was Clement and the others, and he truly did desire the Rapture with every fiber of his being, but at the same time he was comfortable with his earthly life. More than comfortable, in fact; he'd long ago figured out how to profit financially from his position, through legal means and not-so-legal means, and he'd squirreled away a vast sum of money in a Cayman Islands bank account. He had genuinely believed that the plan would always be set for some vague time five years in the future, and would keep moving ahead at the same rate that time passed. By the time Madhoff got the ball rolling in earnest, it was too late for the admiral to back out. He was in too deep. He would have been a dead man. Even his millions in the Cayman Islands wouldn't have saved him from the retribution of the Jews if he'd backed out at that point.

Now they were dead, or at least the two he'd been working with were dead. He knew they had partners back in Israel who would oversee the rebuilding of the temple once the Muslims had been wiped out, but Scarborough had no idea who they were or how to contact them. The only Israelis they had worked with directly were Madhoff and Hazan, and Clement had been the primary contact with both of them.

Speaking of the general, the admiral had no idea what had become of Clement. After the general's frantic phone call a few hours earlier, he'd heard nothing from the man. Given Clement's panicked state of mind during the earlier call, Scarborough had expected to receive a steady stream of calls from the man—the admiral had been dreading those calls, in fact—but all he had heard since that initial contact was silence. Scarborough had used his official connections to try to find out if the general had been arrested or killed, but there appeared to be no official record of the man having been brought in.

That left one of two possibilities, one bad one and another that was even worse. The first possibility was that some sort of domestic black-ops team had gone in and assassinated the general. Though the official stance was that the U.S. government operated no organizations of this type, everyone with any kind of clue whatsoever knew that the government unofficially operated many such organizations around the world, domestically as well as internationally.

The government denied operating such organizations, especially within the borders of the United States, officially and unofficially. It denied international black-ops programs to placate U.S. allies, and it denied domestic black-ops programs, because such programs were expressly prohibited by the *Posse Comitatus Act* of 1878. The admiral had no evidence that such organizations existed, but he also knew that every country in the world operated such organizations domestically, and he saw no reason to believe the United States should be any different. This would have been the sort of organization that went after Clement. This would have been the sort of operation that had assassinated the general, if the first option was indeed what had happened.

The second option was that such a team had captured the general. This would be extremely bad for the admiral, but it was also the most likely option. Scarborough had known Clement since they were both fairly young men. He knew the general's strengths as well as his weaknesses. His primary strength was his unshakable belief in Jesus Christ as his personal Savior. His primary weakness was that in his heart of hearts, Clement was a coward. The man would not go down fighting. Rather, when confronted with force, Scarborough knew that Clement's response would be to roll over and show his soft underbelly in a display of submission.

Either way, Scarborough knew that it would be only a matter of time before the same black operators came after him. If he stayed in Washington, D.C., and tried to carry out his mission, he would either end up being captured or killed. And at that point in time, the odds of finishing the mission had started to look impossibly slim. With Hazan and Madhoff out of the picture, the wheels had come off the master plan. Clearly, it was time to get out of Dodge. The admiral kept a yacht at Hilton Head Island in South Carolina. It was his escape hatch: fully stocked, fueled and ready to reunite him with his stolen millions in the Cayman Islands at a moment's notice. The admiral believed the time had come to exercise that option. The sun would soon be up, and the new day promised nothing but disaster for the admiral. He dialed the number of his personal secretary. "Have my helicopter fueled up and ready to go within the hour," he ordered.

St. Paul, Minnesota

WESTERBERG LOOKED AT THE sleek jet awaiting them at the small airport on the shores of the Mississippi River just across from downtown St. Paul. She knew she shouldn't have been surprised that Cooper would have access to an aircraft like this, but still, she was. She'd worked her way to the very top of Israel's intelligence agency, yet when she flew somewhere, she still flew commercial. She had no idea who Matt Cooper was, and who he worked for was an even bigger mystery, but whoever he was, she could tell he carried some serious weight.

The Israeli agent made herself comfortable in the expansive rear seat of the cabin and as soon as the jet was airborne, she stretched out, closed her eyes, and tried to get some much-needed sleep. She was still for about ten minutes, hoping sleep would come, but try as she might, she found it impossible to drift off. She couldn't get her mind to stop racing, reliving the events of the previous twenty-four hours. That was unusual for her. She'd led an extremely exciting life and had been involved in all sorts of action during her career with Mossad. She'd put her life on the line many, many times, and in the course of her duties she had been forced to take a few lives in return, but nothing could compare to the events that had occurred since she first laid eyes on Cooper. It had started with her tailing Hazan to the Slaves' clubhouse. That was where she'd first witnessed the tall stranger who had appeared moments after Hazan left.

Hazan had instigated the kidnapping of Trembley. Once the Slaves had brought Trembley to the club house, Hazan had left. She'd stuck around to see what the Slaves had in store for Trembley. When she'd seen that the Slaves intended to beat the man to death, she'd considered intervening and rescuing the man, but before she could act, Cooper had appeared on the scene. She'd known he was trouble when she saw him rescue the unfortunate Hellion from being beaten to death by the Slaves. The ease with which he'd dispatched the Slaves told her that this was no ordinary man. She knew she was dealing with a well-trained professional from the start. Who he worked for had been and still was a mystery.

The appearance of a highly skilled American operative on the scene had been a major development, so rather than continuing her surveillance of Hazan, she'd decided to tail this newcomer and see if she could learn more about him. She assumed that the American was investigating the recent wave of sniper attacks that had been occurring across the United States, and she suspected Hazan was involved in those attacks in some peripheral way, too. Since her investigation into Hazan was turning out to be a dead end, she decided she might learn more by tailing the American for a while. In the process she'd learned more than she'd ever bargained for.

Westerberg had been appalled when she witnessed what she thought was the torture of the Slaves' leader. Not that she felt any pity for the man; she'd been watching Tressel for weeks and knew he was a beastly creature. She firmly believed the world was a better place without him, but the torture had appeared to be particularly brutal; worse, even, than some of the things Hazan had been suspected of doing when he was in the Mossad. It was Hazan's brutality that had turned Westerberg against her former lover, brutality she had witnessed firsthand; judging from the apparent torture of Tressel, this stranger appeared to be even more of an animal than Hazan.

When Cooper had explained his ruse to trick Tressel

into cooperating, she'd admired his cleverness. At first she hadn't been completely convinced by his explanation, but everything she'd seen in the intervening hours told her that she could believe this man and trust him implicitly. Cooper had shown remarkable gentleness toward the young woman he rescued from the gangster house. He'd even taken time from his extremely critical mission to ensure that she was cared for, even though no one would have blamed him if he'd just left her to the wolves. No one would have even known the difference; the young woman, Shaniqua, was invisible, as far as the authorities were concerned, a nonentity, completely disposable. If she had been among the victims at the safe house where Cooper found her, Westerberg doubted anyone would have even claimed her remains. Yet he had gone out of his way.

Likewise he'd shown remarkable kindness toward the prostitutes at the brothel. Rather than look down on and judge those unfortunate women, Cooper had done everything in his power to save their lives. The experience at the brothel would be one that Westerberg would remember for the rest of her life.

At first she'd thought Stone's plan to infiltrate the brothel idiotic, but it had, in fact, turned out to be a stroke of brilliance. Pretending to be corrupt cops had been the easiest way to gain access to the brothel, and it had put the noncombatants involved in the least amount of danger. Certainly the mission hadn't been completed without some collateral damage, but if they hadn't been present to put Madhoff down, the body count would have likely been much higher. Had Madhoff not met resistance, he most likely would have killed everyone on the premises to cover his tracks.

Westerberg had no qualms about killing Madhoff. The man was a mad dog, and like a mad dog, he needed to be put down. Ideally they would have brought him in for questioning, but Madhoff was a hard man and Westerberg doubted that they would have retrieved any useful information from him even if they had resorted to actual torture. It was just as well that she had killed the very dangerous man.

She could just as easily have killed Cooper when he kissed her in the car. At the time she'd thought him a disgusting pig. In the intervening hours her opinion of the man had shifted one hundred and eighty degrees. Now she wished the man would kiss her again. If the opportunity presented itself, she'd do more than that...

Stony Man Farm, Virginia

BOLAN WOKE WESTERBERG as the plane neared Stony Man Farm and said, "We'll be landing soon. I don't think you're going to be happy about this next part," Bolan said. "I'm genuinely sorry to make you do this, but I'm afraid you're going to have to put this on before we can land." Bolan handed Westerberg a black hood.

Westerberg couldn't believe her eyes. "Are you insane?"

"Sarah, I'm truly sorry about this, but I'm bringing a known foreign agent into a top-secret U.S. facility.

I'm breaking a lot of protocols. You don't know how many hoops I had to jump through to get the people running the place to allow me to bring you there." Bolan didn't mention that he was one of those people running the place, but he was telling the truth about having to do some fast talking to get Brognola, Price and Kurtzman to agree to let him bring an Israeli agent to the installation.

But at this point he considered her a critical part in the investigation; her involvement would be key in nailing the remaining Irgun conspirators in Israel. "I was only able to get approval because we need you on the inside to help us capture the remaining members of the Irgun, but that approval required a compromise on our part. That compromise involves me blindfolding you before we arrive at the facility."

Westerberg had grown to trust this man. They'd only known each other half a day, but she felt a connection with him. She decided to swallow her pride and wear the hood.

Once the hood was in place, they flew on for another five minutes, then she felt the plane plummet down to the ground and land on what appeared to be a very short runway. Cooper led her off the plane, across a tarmac runway and into a vehicle of some sort, most likely a large SUV, based on the roominess of the seats inside. The vehicle traveled for what Westerberg estimated was about seven minutes and stopped. Cooper led her from the vehicle into some sort of a building. Once inside the structure, he led her on a circuitous path that involved an elevator ride. He only removed the hood after they were deep inside the bowels of the structure. What Westerberg didn't know—couldn't have known—was that she was inside the War Room at Stony Man Farm.

Brognola had returned to D.C. to meet with the President, and also because he didn't want Westerberg to see him at the facility, which he wasn't supposed to even know about officially, so only Price and Kurtzman were on hand to meet the pair. "Barb, Bear, this is Sarah."

"Pleased to meet you," Kurtzman said, wheeling his chair up to the comely Israeli agent. "As you might imagine, we don't get a lot of visitors here. Especially not lovely ladies such as you." Westerberg extended her hand and Kurtzman gave it a gentlemanly kiss.

"And I'm Barbara," Price said, extending her hand.

Price knew that there hadn't been any other options to bringing Westerberg to the site; Kurtzman needed to debrief with Westerberg and Bolan needed to interrogate Clement. While Kurtzman could have conceivably met Westerberg somewhere else, there hadn't been time to set up an off-site meeting in a location where Bolan could interrogate Clement. They couldn't just waltz into a Denny's and interrogate a captive member of the Joint Chiefs of Staff, nor could they do the deed in a local police station with a man supposedly missing from the face of the Earth. Even if such things had been options, there just wasn't time; they were only hours away from another likely wave of attacks.

"Ms. Westerberg," Kurtzman said, "I've cross-referenced the numbers on the SIM cards from the phones of Hazan and Madhoff. Thanks to the files that you provided us, I've narrowed the possible Irgun conspirators down to just three names. I'd like to discuss them with you."

"It would be my pleasure." Westerberg found the wheelchair-bound American to be surprisingly charming for a man named Bear. "Will Mr. Cooper be joining us?"

"I need to pay a visit to General Clement," Bolan said. "I'll see you after we're finished."

Kurtzman took Westerberg to a conference room to review his findings. When the door shut, Price turned to Bolan and said, "She's beautiful."

Bolan looked Price in the eye and said, "Yes. She is. She's smart and extremely capable, too." If Price had asked any more personal questions, the soldier wouldn't have lied to her, but she would never ask such questions and he knew it. Instead of discussing the matter any further, she turned and went back to work.

The Executioner went to a small room next to the holding cell where Clement was being detained and observed the general through a two-way mirror. The man appeared to be in a fair amount of distress, alternating between fidgeting uncomfortably and bowing his head, his lips moving in what appeared to be silent prayer. Bolan watched him go through this cycle several times. He never seemed to finish a prayer before becoming agitated again. The soldier realized he was watching a man who was on the brink of descending into complete madness and decided to get the interrogation over with while the general still had the faculties to answer questions in any sort of a coherent manner. Based on the man's behavior, Bolan feared it might already be too late.

Bolan entered the room and said, "Hello, General Clement. I need to ask you a few questions."

"Questions?" Clement said. "All the answers you'll ever need are in the Good Book."

"Perhaps," Bolan said, "but I'm going to ask anyway, sir. What were you trying to accomplish by these attacks?"

"Daniel had a dream," Clement said, "in which he saw four great beasts arise from the sea. The first was like a lion with eagle's wings. The second to rise up was like a bear, and behold, it had three ribs in its mouth. The next was like a leopard with four wings and four heads, and dominion was given to it. The last, dreadful and terrible, had great iron teeth, and it had ten horns. In these beasts Daniel saw the collision of kingdoms."

"I don't follow you," Bolan said.

"Are you blind?" Clement asked. "Can you not see? These prophetic symbols represent the different races. They rose up from the winds of the great sea. The bear is the Asiatic race, the oriental. The lion is the European race, the white man. The leopard is the African race, the Nigra, the cursed dark-skinned peoples. The dreadful and terrible beast with ten horns is the race of the cursed Jew, the murderer of our Lord and Savior Jesus Christ! The winds that blow upon the great sea are the conflicts between the races."

"I can see how you might come to that conclusion," Bolan said, doing his best not to appear condescending to the raving madman in front of him, "but I still don't understand how that is an answer to my question."

"Behold," the general said, "a goat came from the west on the face of the whole Earth and touched not the ground. Are you stupid, man? That goat is Satan."

"I apologize for my ignorance, sir," Bolan said, "but I still don't follow you." Bolan lied; he was indeed starting to follow the general's train of thought, insane though it may be. The man might be a raving lunatic, but Bolan was starting to see a pattern in his madness.

"I've answered your question," Clement said. "We are at war. We're at war with Satan. Satan is rising up on the winds of the great sea and spreading across all the Earth. He's working through the Jews and the cursed dark-skinned ones. His goal is nothing less than the enslavement of white Christians. Man is powerless to stop him because most men are working with him. The only one powerful enough to stop him is our Lord and Savior Jesus Christ! He has to come back before we can have the Rapture, and we white Christians must do everything in our power to make His Second Coming possible!"

Now things were starting to make sense to Bolan. The general's quoting of the book of Daniel had been the key to the soldier's understanding of the situation. Bolan knew that there existed a train of thought among fundamentalist Christians who believed in only the most literal interpretations of the Bible. Such people believed that the rebuilding of the Temple of Jerusalem on the Temple Mount was a prerequisite for the Second Coming of Jesus. They came to this conclusion based on what Bolan considered a misinterpretation of the Book of Daniel, but in certain circles the belief held powerful sway.

"So you plan to rebuild the temple," Bolan said. "Don't you think the fact that the Temple Mount is in the Palestinian-controlled portion of the West Bank might pose some challenges for rebuilding a Jewish temple at that site?"

"Are you a simpleton?" Clement asked. "Am I speaking to a child? Do you think such trivial details would pose a challenge for the Almighty? God has told us himself that the final battle will begin when the Antichrist— the abomination of desolation—stands in the Temple of Jerusalem. Why would He tell us this if there was to be no temple in which the Antichrist could set up shop? The rebuilding of the temple will happen, and it will happen soon. This generation shall not pass until all these things be fulfilled."

Bolan decided against pointing out the fact that Daniel had been wrong when he'd told his followers that the Messiah would come during their lifetimes. The fact that Daniel had been incorrect in his prediction of the Messiah's imminent appearance didn't seem to keep people from quoting the man's unfulfilled prophecy time and time again. Each and every time someone claimed that the then-current generation would be the generation that witnessed the coming of the Messiah, the person making the prediction had been wrong, but the zero-percent batting average of these supposed prophets didn't seem to deter the true believers. In the case of the general and his cohorts, they had believed in such an improbable prophecy strongly enough to kill hundreds of people, or perhaps even more than that.

Now that Bolan had the general talking, he prodded him to keep him going. "I still don't understand how you plan to get the Palestinians to allow you to rebuild a Jewish temple in the West Bank," he said.

"He has divided mankind into three parts," Clement replied. "The Christians, the Mohammedans and the Jews. We will rebuild the temple, even if it means slaying a third."

"You mean you plan to kill all the Muslims?" Bolan asked. "How do you intend to do that?"

"We have the means at our disposal," Clement said.

"Who are 'we'?"

"We are the white Christians. We are the Lord's holy warriors."

"I see," Bolan said. "Admiral Scarborough is part of this plot, too." This last statement seemed to shock some of the crazy right out of General Clement and he quit talking, but the soldier had already heard all he needed to hear. The general had confirmed Brognola's suspicions about the admiral when he said "white Christians." Clement and Scarborough were the only Caucasians on the Joint Chiefs of Staff. The Army Chief of Staff was an African American and the Marine Corps Commandant was Hispanic. "Thank you, General.

You've been very helpful." The general remained silent.
Somewhere deep inside his brain, some obscure corner
of gray matter that hadn't gone completely mad realized
that he'd said far too much.

CHAPTER FIFTEEN

Westerberg and Kurtzman reviewed the files of the three probable suspects that Kurtzman had pulled from the cell phone SIM cards. All three held powerful positions in the Israeli government. Between Westerberg's files and the information Kurtzman was able to dig up on the men, they were able to eliminate one suspect— Justice Minister Yuli Katz. Although Westerberg's investigations pointed to the fact that Katz was almost certainly corrupt, his corruption appeared to be aimed at achieving material rather than political gains. The contacts between Katz, Hazan and Madhoff seemed to have been efforts by the two Irgun plotters to grease political wheels with bribes and other payoffs to the justice minister.

The other two names that popped up—Ayoob Gamliel and Silvan Pinyan—were just as certainly coconspirators with Hazan and Madhoff. Both were high-ranking members of the Knesset. Gamliel currently served as Speaker of the Knesset and Pinyan was Israel's Minister of Defense. Both were among the most militantly anti-Palestinian members of the Likud party. Both men advocated radical military action against the entire Muslim world. Stony Man suspected that the two men had been behind a thwarted attempt to prompt the United States to attack Iran during the height of the Iraq war, but hadn't been able to prove the connection. If they'd had the information Westerberg now provided, they would have been able to do so. If Stony Man had been able to prove the connection, the original plan called for sending in a wet-work team to neutralize both men.

It looked like now was as good a time as any to revive that plan. Kurtzman didn't share that information with Westerberg—the U.S. needed to maintain plausible deniability in the assassinations of the two high-ranking Israeli officials—but the woman knew what was at stake, and she knew what needed to be done. She also knew that she really didn't want to know anything about what was about to take place. She would simply act surprised the next day when her superiors informed her that the two men had both been assassinated, and when she told them she didn't know anything about what had happened to them, she would be telling the truth. Her direct commander was aware that she was investigating the two men, but just as in every intelligence operation around the globe, in the Mossad operatives shared as little information as possible with one another for fear that the targets of investigation might have their channels in the agency. That most certainly would have been the case when it came to the Irgun conspirators.

Kurtzman and Westerberg had just finished reviewing the Israeli agents' files when a slender redheaded woman knocked on the door of the conference room. Kurtzman left the room to confer with Carmen Delahunt, one of the computer geniuses on his cyberteam. "What is it, Carmen?"

"We've cracked open another file, and this one's a doozy," Delahunt said. "It outlines the plans for today's attacks."

"Does it list the locations of today's sniper hides?" Kurtzman asked.

"There will be no more sniper attacks," Delahunt replied. "Today they plan to start a bombing campaign."

"What?"

"Today, at 3:00 p.m. eastern time, a series of bombings are set to take place at exactly the same time. Precisely three hours later a second series of bombings will occur. We've identified one hundred separate locations for the first wave of attacks and another one hundred for the second wave of attacks. According to the plan outlined in the document, the bombs should have already been put in place by now."

"Any word on the location of the sniper teams?" Kurtzman asked.

"We're still trying to open the remaining files," Delahunt replied, "but we're cross-referencing the bombing locations with all the safe house locations we identified earlier. We're having our teams focus on the safe houses that are located in a position that are central to the bombing sites."

"That should help us hit at least a few of the right safe house locations," Kurtzman said. Up until that time they'd been taking a scattershot approach, randomly selecting safe houses identified in the file they'd opened earlier in the night. With the exception of bagging General Clement, so far the only thing they'd accomplished was identifying safe houses that weren't currently being used.

"Teams of federal agents are going to hit ten of the most probable locations within the hour," Delahunt said.

"Good work, Carmen," Kurtzman said. "Get this information to Barbara. Tell her to get bomb squads to those locations immediately."

Bolan entered from the interrogation room moments after Delahunt left to go speak with Price. "Get Hal on the phone," he told Kurtzman. "Tell him that Scarborough is our man."

"Are you certain?"

"It can't be anyone else," Bolan said.

Kurtzman dialed Brognola's number.

"Tell me you've got some good news for me, Bear," the big Fed said. "It's been a long night and I need some cheering up."

"I've got some terrific news," Kurtzman said. "The sniper attacks are over. The terrorists are about to quit the sniper attacks and begin a series of bombing attacks."

"How is that good news?" Brognola asked.

"Because we've identified the location of the bombs and we're sending bomb squads out to neutralize them as we speak."

"Bear, I don't care how ugly you are," Brognola said, "if I was there right now, I'd kiss you."

"We should both be glad you're not here then. I've got more news, though."

"What's that?"

"I don't know how good you'll find this news, Hal, but after Striker interviewed Clement, he's convinced that Scarborough is our guy."

"That's right, Hal," Bolan broke in. "Your hunch was correct."

Just then, Price stuck her head in the room. "Scarborough's getting his helicopter ready for takeoff," she said.

"Tell Jack to fire up the Apache," Brognola said over the speaker phone.

Hilton Head Island, South Carolina

I'M GOING TO MISS flying this rig, Admiral Leroy Scarborough thought as he neared the heliport at the marina where he kept a slip for his yacht. Most likely this was the last time he'd ever fly, at least in a mechanical machine. He still hoped to live long enough to see the Rapture, even though he'd given up all hope of helping to bring that glorious event to fruition. Even if the bombings went off as planned, he was no longer in a position to seize power after the President declared martial law. Still, he would monitor the situation closely after the bombings occurred and if the circumstances devolved into complete chaos, he would be ready to pounce upon any opportunity that might arise.

He regretted that all the hard work he and General

Clement had put into this enterprise had resulted in failure, but he was happy to be escaping with his life. While he shared Clement's longing for the Rapture, the admiral didn't share the general's willingness to make himself a martyr for the cause. The admiral's preservation instinct was much stronger than the general's, and he'd always had a contingency plan should the entire master plan go south. Now he was almost home free; he was within fifteen minutes of the heliport. Another half hour and he'd be casting off and on his way to the Cayman Islands. He had fifteen more minutes to enjoy the incredible feeling of freedom that flying his helicopter provided him. There was nothing on Earth that could compare. Sure, he had his boat and he had his motorcycle. While the admiral enjoyed these toys, the excitement they offered was a pale shadow compared to the thrill of flying.

Scarborough was a wealthy man with more than enough money to live the rest of his life in comfort, but he still didn't have enough money to throw around on helicopters and jets. He had socked away millions of dollars, but that now had to last him the rest of his life. He could live for years on the money he'd spend on a decent helicopter or even a small airplane. The admiral was a frugal man by nature, and such extravagance didn't come naturally to him. He hadn't been born a little moneyed. He'd gone to the Naval Academy primarily because they'd offered him the best scholarship; he'd never felt a tremendous urge to be in the military and he still didn't feel any particularly patriotic urges.

Sometimes his urges were quite the opposite, in fact. Sometimes he was ashamed of his country. The way the international Jewish banking conspiracy had subverted what had once been a God-fearing Christian country disgusted him beyond measure.

Scarborough despised the Jewish financial oligarchs who ran the country, even though he had become quite wealthy as a result of them. He'd invested well over the years and had earned a small fortune in the bond markets. He'd earned enough to buy a nice boat. It was nothing too ostentatious—a forty-six-foot Sea Ray Sundancer. Although technically classified as a yacht, that was a generous description. It was comfortable, as comfortable as a two-bedroom, two-bath lake cabin, though most cabins had bedrooms that were more spacious than the two on his Sea Ray. Because the boat had been seven years old when he bought it, it had only cost about as much as a two-bedroom, two-bath lake cabin. It was on the small end of boats classified as yachts, but it was his, and it was paid for.

He would have bought a much nicer boat, except that doing so would have attracted the attention of the authorities, who in turn would have uncovered his appropriation of naval funds. The admiral had more than enough illicitly obtained money squirreled away to buy several sixty-foot Hatteras, with enough left over to purchase the Bell TH-57 Sea Ranger helicopter that the navy provided for his personal use, but such a purchase would have definitely given away his extracurricular activities. Besides, he wasn't the type of person to blow all of his money on toys. He was satisfied with his boat, and purchasing the helicopter would have put a serious dent in his savings. He'd have to learn to live without the helicopter. It was a damned shame; he was really going to miss this bird. It was an oldie but a goodie.

The way he saw it, he was trading the helicopter for his life. Another life wouldn't be easy to obtain regardless of how much money he had, and he had the feeling that he was escaping with the life he already had by the skin of his teeth. He knew he'd abandoned the plan, which required him to remain at his post until the very end. Convincing the President to declare martial law had been one of his two primary responsibilities. The President still may well declare martial law, but because Scarborough had abandoned his post he wouldn't be able to carry out the second part of his duties—staging the coup that would put him in charge of America's nuclear arsenal. Without the admiral in position to do that, the rest of the plan fell completely to pieces.

He regretted failing to fulfill his duties. He regretted even more all those who had devoted their lives to the cause, the people he was betraying by fleeing his post. The frontline warriors were, of course, the sniper teams who had been out in the field for months preparing for the attacks and who had done an admirable job in completing their missions. As far as the admiral knew, that day's bombings would still take place as scheduled because of the dedication of those brave Christian warriors.

But he'd betrayed more people than just the sniper

teams in the field; he and General Clement had in place
a second line of attack, key people placed at U.S. military installations around the world, people who would be
waiting for Scarborough to seize power from the President and give word that they were to do likewise at their
own bases. The bombings that would take place that
afternoon were to act as a signal to be ready. Beginning
that afternoon there would be top officers and enlisted
personnel from one end of the planet to the other ready
to spring into action as soon as Scarborough gave the
word. Now that word would never come and all those
good men would be left with their asses hanging out.
The military trained its warriors to never leave another
man behind; the admiral was leaving hundreds of good
men behind.

Admiral Scarborough could see the heliport in the
distance, then noticed the fast-moving blip coming
his way on the radar. He looked in the direction of
the blip and couldn't quite believe his eyes—an unmarked Apache attack helicopter was coming straight
toward him.

"GET READY, SARGE," Grimaldi said. "We've got a
narrow window to take that bird down before it gets
over a populated area."

Bolan sat behind Grimaldi in the cockpit of the
AH-64 Apache attack helicopter, manning the potent
war machine's weapon systems. Bolan and Grimaldi
had no intention of trying to capture the admiral.
Brognola had no intention of putting the man on trial.

Scarborough's fate had been decided. There would be no judge or jury for the man; rather, there would only be the executioner, Mack Bolan, the man riding shotgun in the Apache. Bolan set the sights of the 30 mm M-230 chain gun on the Bell TH-57 Sea Ranger and said, "On your three, Jack."

"One..." Grimaldi said, "two...three."

Bolan pulled the trigger and in a matter of seconds hundreds of 1.2-inch bullets chewed the little helicopter in the Executioner's sights to shreds. Scarborough's helicopter—or what was left of it—erupted in a ball of flame. When it hit the empty, swampy ground surrounding the heliport, the largest pieces remaining would fit inside a knapsack.

"Nice shooting, Sarge," Grimaldi said. "Now let's go home." He swung the chopper around and headed back toward Stony Man Farm.

"WE SAW THE ADMIRAL'S helicopter go down on radar, Striker," Kurtzman's voice said over the radio headsets a moment later. "Good work."

"Thanks, Bear. Any luck cracking open the rest of those files?"

"We've busted into all of them," Kurtzman said. "We have the names and locations of every sniper team, and we're sending teams of agents to each site right now. We're expecting heavy resistance, but this time we're not concerned about taking anyone alive so we can hit them with everything we've got."

"What about the Reaper operators?" Bolan asked. "We've still got a potent bird in the air to deal with."

"That was the first crew we went after," Kurtzman said. "We've already caught the two men who operated the plane, or at least the one that survived the raid. The Reaper was being operated by two National Guardsmen from a remote compound in Alabama, south of Montgomery. The two men had officially been killed in action in Afghanistan last year, according to our records, but according to the documents we found, their deaths had been faked. We're trying to identify the two men who died in the IED attack that supposedly took the lives of the two operators. Odds are they were Afghan captives who had been forced to wear the uniforms of the supposedly deceased soldiers. We know that this was a tactic the conspirators used to help disguise the identities of some of the other snipers involved in the attack."

"Did you get much resistance when you went after them?"

"Not much. They had four guards on the premises, but since the men involved weren't out in the field they weren't heavily armed. We knew exactly what we were dealing with because of the information in the files. We killed three of the guards and one of the drone operators. We didn't lose any men."

"Good," Bolan said. "Did those files list any other conspirators besides Clement and Scarborough?"

"Sure did," Kurtzman said. "They had inside people at every major U.S. military installation on the planet.

This thing is huge. It looks like they were planning nothing short of a complete military coup once the President declared martial law. Hang on a second." Bolan could hear Kurtzman talking to Price offline, but because of the noise in the helicopter cockpit he couldn't hear exactly what she was saying.

After Kurtzman finished speaking to Price, he said, "Barbara just told me that the initial raids on the safe houses went off without a hitch. Because of the information we have on the defenses of the locations, our men are reporting very few casualties. Things aren't going so well for the sniper teams, though. So far they seem determined to fight to the death, and we're doing everything we can to oblige them."

"How about the military men involved in the conspiracy?" Bolan asked.

"The arrests are taking place as we speak," Kurtzman said. "We've already brought most of them into custody. A few of the conspirators must have realized that something was wrong and they've gone AWOL, but we'll find them."

"That's great news, Bear," Bolan said. "I'll see you in about an hour."

"I'm afraid you can't come home just yet," Kurtzman said.

The soldier knew he could use some rest before being sent out on another mission, but he'd been at this long enough to know that rest was a luxury he could seldom afford. Maybe he'd have enough time to catch a nap while Grimaldi flew him to his next mission. "What have you got for me, Bear?"

"We've taken Ms. Westerberg to a hotel in D.C.," Kurtzman said. "She asked if you could meet her there. She said the two of you needed to debrief."

"I bet she did," Grimaldi said. The pilot started to say something else, but a sidelong glance from the soldier convinced him to leave it at that.

The Executioner®

Don Pendleton's

SHADOW HUNT

Organized crime threatens to take over the Big Easy....

When a U.S. Marshal goes missing in New Orleans, Mack Bolan sets out on a search-and-rescue mission and is thrown into an intricate web of corruption. It seems the Mafia is alive and well in the Big Easy and operating under the rule of a powerful new leader— making the entire city one massive death trap with the chances of escape dwindling by the minute!

Available July wherever books are sold.

GOLD EAGLE®

James Axler

Outlanders®

TRUTH ENGINE

An exiled God prince acts out his violent vengeance…

Cerberus Redoubt, the rebel base of operations, has fallen under attack. The enemy, Ullikummis, is at the gates and Kane and the others are his prisoners. The stone god demands Kane lead his advancing armies as he retakes Earth in the ultimate act of revenge. For he is determined to be the ultimate god of the machine, infinite and unstoppable.

Available August wherever books are sold.

AleX Archer
TEAR OF THE GODS

The early chapters of history contain dangerous secrets…secrets that Annja Creed is about to unlock….

A dream leads archaeologist Annja Creed to an astonishing find in England—the Tear of the Gods. But someone knows exactly what this unusual torc means, and he will do anything to get his hands on it…even leave Annja for dead. Now she is fleeing for her life, not knowing the terrifying truth about the relic she risks everything to protect.

Available July wherever books are sold.